"BEATRICE," HE SAID SLOWLY.

He stood close. Too close. Close enough for her to know the woodsy scent of his soap mingled perfectly with their surroundings.

"What am I doing here?" she whispered.

He tilted his head and the corner of his mouth lifted in a half smile. "Call it . . . *un coup de coeur.*"

A spontaneous attraction. She could hardly deny that.

His eyes went dark, but she couldn't drag her gaze away from that fathomless blue.

This was more than she had bargained for. Flirtation, yes, and the flattery of being the subject of his beautiful artwork. But never . . . *this.*

BOOK YOUR PLACE ON OUR WEBSITE AND MAKE THE READING CONNECTION!

We've created a customized website just for our very special readers, where you can get the inside scoop on everything that's going on with Zebra, Pinnacle and Kensington books.

When you come online, you'll have the exciting opportunity to:

- View covers of upcoming books
- Read sample chapters
- Learn about our future publishing schedule (listed by publication month *and author*)
- Find out when your favorite authors will be visiting a city near you
- Search for and order backlist books from our online catalog
- Check out author bios and background information
- Send e-mail to your favorite authors
- Meet the Kensington staff online
- Join us in weekly chats with authors, readers and other guests
- Get writing guidelines
- AND MUCH MORE!

Visit our website at
http://www.kensingtonbooks.com

Nothing But Deception

ALLEGRA GRAY

ZEBRA BOOKS
KENSINGTON PUBLISHING CORP.
http://www.kensingtonbooks.com

ZEBRA BOOKS are published by

Kensington Publishing Corp.
119 West 40th Street
New York, NY 10018

All Kensington titles, imprints, and distributed lines are available at special quantity discounts for bulk purchases for sales promotion, premiums, fund-raising, educational, or institutional use.

Special book excerpts or customized printings can also be created to fit specific needs. For details, write or phone the office of the Kensington Special Sales Manager: Attn.: Special Sales Department. Kensington Publishing Corp., 119 West 40th Street, New York, NY 10018. Phone: 1-800-221-2647.

Zebra and the Z logo Reg. U.S. Pat. & TM Off.

ISBN-13: 978-1-4201-0826-2
ISBN-10: 1-4201-0826-3

First Printing: August 2010
10 9 8 7 6 5 4 3 2 1

Printed in the United States of America

To my mom,
who indulged my love of
reading and books as a child and
always encouraged me to
work toward my dreams

ACKNOWLEDGMENTS

Thank you to my talented agent, Kevan Lyon, and to my enthusiastic editor, Megan Records. Also, thank you to the members of the Beau Monde chapter of the Romance Writers of America, who always point me in the right direction to find answers to all my questions about Regency-era England, no matter how obscure those questions seem.

Chapter 1

Paris
March 1815

"*Non, Maman.* I am French. Not an Englishman's son. You must not be thinking clearly."

Solange Durand's fingers fretted the sheets, but she looked her son in the eye. "Philippe. It is my body that has betrayed me, not my mind." It would not be long now, she thought, and yet shc'd left so much undone. So much unsaid.

Jean Philippe Durand shook his head. His blue eyes, so very like those belonging to the one she'd loved and lost, filled with pain and shock.

"Trust me, darling. Go to him, and you will see." Solange reached out a shaky hand to touch his cheek. Her boy. How had she done this to him? No, she reminded herself. She'd done it *for* him.

The sounds of the Paris streets filtered in through the open window, her only outlet to the greater world anymore. A pair of women laughed, a governess called to a child. Hoofs clipped along, then came to a stop. Solange sucked in a breath.

Was Richard home? Were they still safe? Rumor had it Napoleon was on the move again.

Richard had a way of landing on his feet, but it never came without a cost. How many lies, how many friends betrayed in the name of politics? Her husband's political intrigues ran deep. The constant uncertainty, spread across years, had depleted her.

Philippe scowled, drawing her attention once more. "If, as you say, I am the son of this Lord Owen, what use have I for him? He abandoned us both. Why should I go to him now?"

"Because, my son," she said softly, "you've spent your entire life trying to emulate him."

It was a lie. So many lies. Perhaps she was as bad as Richard. But this one she told without guilt, for it would serve him well. Solange's hand dropped to her side and her eyes slipped closed as the pain grew more intense. Her son needed to know. More importantly, he needed to leave France, lest he pay for her mistakes.

Philippe smoothed the sheets around her. His long fingers brushed her cheek, he assumed she slept. "Rest, *Maman*."

Summoning her strength, she squeezed his hand and whispered, "Lord Henry Owen is an Englishman, yes, but he is also Henri Gaudet, the elusive artiste you have for so long sought."

Philippe drew back. "No! That cannot be. Gaudet is *French*. Every brushstroke of every one of his works screams it."

Solange smiled inwardly, her face too exhausted to form the expression. Her son was not easily fooled.

"Please," she whispered, desperate to make him

understand what she'd sworn not to reveal. "Lord Owen. Go to him."

Richard Durand had worked too hard, too long, to give up now. He walked through the door to the Paris town house where his wife lay upstairs, dying. A shame, truly, but one he could not devote attention to—not with the latest news of the Emperor flooding the streets.

He'd met Napoleon Bonaparte when the future ruler was but a newly commissioned second lieutenant in the French army. Richard had outranked him at the time, but he'd sensed his fellow officer's potential even then. Bonaparte had fire, ambition.

Richard had ambition as well, but he lacked the vision to go with it, and he knew it. His main skill, as he liked to believe, lay in knowing the right sort of people. Building relationships and maintaining them—or, if necessary, destroying them.

He'd ridden his relationship with Napoleon all the way to his current level, though ever since Napoleon had abdicated last spring, Richard had professed to anyone who would listen that the Emperor had gotten out of hand, and that he no longer supported the zealous ex-ruler. Such political maneuvering had, once again, kept him on his feet—and kept him from being run out of Paris.

But times were changing once more. Richard punched a fist into the air, a silent celebration in the gloomy town house.

Napoleon had escaped his exile in Elba. Even now, reports said, he was on his way to Paris. If

Richard could position himself properly, there was tremendous potential here. But he had to be careful—the Emperor had angered too many people, too many nations. If he failed in his quest to return to power, Richard needed to ensure his name was not linked with that of his former boss. Self-preservation demanded it. Fortunately, Richard had a plan.

"Word from Vienna?" Richard eyed the messenger across the café table. Both men wore their hats pulled low, though it was unlikely either would be recognized in this part of town.

His companion nodded. "The Congress has committed—they say they can put 150,000 men in the field to defeat Napoleon."

"One hundred fifty thousand?" Richard Durand echoed. He'd spent the past four days pacing. Though the news he was hearing would soon spread throughout town, he'd paid extravagantly for the privilege of being the first to know.

"Each," the messenger added.

"Each?" The United Kingdom. The Prussians. The Austrians. The Russians. Richard did the mental calculation. It was too much.

"*Oui.*" The travel-worn messenger slouched in his chair.

"*C'est impossible.*"

"They are very determined, monsieur."

"Indeed."

"The French are gathering as well. Since the Fifth and Seventh Regiments returned their loyalty to Bonaparte, several thousand more have joined him, including Marshal Ney."

This, Richard already knew. The enthusiasm of the French army was encouraging. Their numbers were not.

"Merci," Richard said. "The information is timely, and useful. I cannot say when, or if, you will be contacted again. We will not meet here again." He slipped the man a purse, and watched him dissolve into the night.

Six hundred thousand men. Emperor Napoleon had no hope of countering a force so great. Even a fraction of that would prove difficult. How much support did he have within his own army? Would the remaining regiments join his cause, and how hard would they fight? They were battle-hardened, yes, but weary of political unrest. How far would they go for him?

Richard stood, pulled his hat brim even lower, and began walking. He'd exited his carriage several blocks away, then instructed his driver to wait. Though he did his best to hire loyal servants, it was prudent in some cases to prevent anyone from knowing exactly where, and with whom, he'd met.

Though the evening was brisk, he kept his pace measured, using the time to think.

Napoleon could do so much—had *already* done so much—for France. Far more than the weak-willed Bourbons.

If his army could not count on brute strength, they would need to gain an advantage by other means. Years of watching the self-appointed Emperor in military campaigns had taught Richard that the best advantage came from knowing your enemy.

An army of tens could defeat one of thousands, if the smaller force had the advantage of knowing where, when, and how the enemy planned to strike.

If Richard could provide that kind of information to the French—and if the French were successful in using it—then his own value to the Emperor would increase immeasurably. And his reward . . . ah, his reward, if nothing else, would be the knowledge that he, Richard, had made it happen. That he was valued, even priceless. The thought made him giddy.

Of course, it would not be easy. There was no time to slowly blend in, to cultivate new, trusting relationships that could be harvested for gain. He would have to use whoever was already in place.

He was not a spy by trade, preferring to leave the cloak-and-dagger operations to those who didn't mind risking discomfort, capture, and even their lives. But he'd spent years building a political network, one populated by men of questionable loyalties and even more questionable morals. No, Richard was not a spy. But he knew spies.

Chapter 2

England
April 1815

"This is the place, monsieur."

Philippe stared up at No. 6 Charles Street. "It looks abandoned." The home stood on an enviable lot on a street that was clearly home to some of England's nobility, but the windows were all darkened, with no discernable signs of life.

The hack driver scratched his head. "Lord Henry Owen, you said?"

"Yes."

"I been driving in this town for many a year, monsieur, and if I may venture to say, I don't believe Lord Owen spends a great deal of his time in London."

Philippe didn't know whether to feel angry or disappointed. After all, he hadn't written ahead to announce his visit. Given the way Lord Owen had dispatched his mother, along with any parental duties, he hadn't known whether his visit would be well received.

Truth be told, he wasn't entirely certain of anything about this mad scheme. It was unthinkable that he would ignore his mother's wish. But what had she hoped to accomplish by sending him here? For that matter, what sort of man was Lord Owen that he avoided London at the height of the Season?

"A recluse?" Philippe asked.

The driver shrugged uncomfortably. "Not my place to say, monsieur."

"Of course. My apologies." He shouldn't have been surprised. From the moment he'd first spied a Gaudet on display in the home of one of his mother's Parisian friends, he'd been enthralled. Tracking down the artist's other works had quickly become an obsession, but the artist himself had remained elusive. If Gaudet and Owen were indeed one and the same, the man clearly had an aversion to Society.

But stranger, and more painful, was the realization that if Owen were actually his father, then his *mother,* the person with whom Philippe had always been closest, with whom he'd shared everything . . . she had kept from him the nature of his very birth, let alone a past with a man she must once have loved—leaving Philippe to wonder if he'd ever really known her at all.

"Will ye be wantin' me to take ye elsewhere, now?"

The driver's question pulled Philippe back to the present.

"Yes." Philippe gave him the address of the hotel where he was staying, then climbed back into the coach. As long as he had to come to England, he'd planned to make the trip worthwhile, to build his artistic reputation here as he had at home and in Italy. Painting was his passion, and he thrived on the communities of fellow artists and patrons inspired by love of art. The work itself involved many solitary hours, but Philippe, unlike the artist who'd first inspired him, was far from a recluse.

Arriving at the hotel, Philippe paid the driver and went to his room to dress for dinner. A respectable establishment, the hotel afforded him greater privacy than staying with any of his London acquaintances. The only downside was the lighting and lack of space. Should he decide to begin a new painting, he'd be hard-pressed to set up a studio at the inn.

Ah, well. The point was moot.

As yet, nothing about dreary London had inspired him to pick up a brush.

Lady Beatrice Pullington smiled as her longtime friend, Elizabeth Bainbridge, entered the comfortable "family" salon of Bea's London town house. "You're looking exceptionally well. It's a wonder Alex doesn't insist on escorting you everywhere," she teased.

Elizabeth, the newly married Duchess of Beaufort, laughed. "He does. He only makes an exception for you." She settled herself further into the comfortable chaise.

"What a relief. Having him glower at me would certainly put a damper on our gossip sessions." Bea poured a cup of tea and passed it to Elizabeth.

"Come now," Elizabeth scoffed, a twitch of her lips betraying her merriment. "He hasn't glowered in months."

"Of course not. He's too enamored of you," Bea told her sincerely. She might be envious of her friend's newfound happiness, but that didn't mean she would see a single ounce of it stripped away, especially knowing all Elizabeth and Alex had endured before learning to love and trust one another. They hadn't had an easy time of it.

A happy flush spread over her friend's complexion. "Actually, Bea, I've come to ask a favor."

"Anything."

"You've heard of the painter, Jean Philippe Durand? There is to be a salon tonight held in his honor. The artiste himself is supposed to be present."

"Yes, I'd heard."

"I promised Charity I would act as her chaperone to the event. She has declared herself madly in love with the Frenchman."

It was Bea's turn to laugh. Charity was Elizabeth's younger sister, a beautiful blonde who, at eighteen, retained much of the impishness that had marked her childhood. In the midst of her first Season, she had suitors lined up for miles—not that any of them held her attention for long.

Honestly, the Medford sisters, though two of Bea's closest friends, always made her feel plain. Charity sparkled with golden beauty, while Elizabeth, less traditional but no less lovely, was a red-headed enchantress—just look how thoroughly she'd bewitched the Duke of Beaufort. In comparison, Bea was just . . . Bea.

"Would you attend in my stead, please? I'm

simply exhausted these days." Elizabeth's hand moved, almost unconsciously, to her lower abdomen.

Bea felt her eyes grow wide as a giddy rush pushed her to her feet. "E., never tell me you're expecting!"

Elizabeth smiled.

"Oh, how absolutely wonderful!" Bea skipped to the chaise to embrace her friend. "You and Alex must be beside yourselves with joy."

Elizabeth's smile grew into a grin.

"Of course, I'll attend the salon with Charity. You mustn't worry about a thing. You need your rest. And I don't mind the opportunity to lay eyes on Monsieur Durand, either. He has *quite* the reputation." It was true. Women across France and Italy had swooned before the popular artist, and now the females of England were lining up to do the same. Bea winked. "Honestly. Don't worry. I'll keep Charity out of trouble."

As Bea waved good-bye to Elizabeth later that afternoon, she couldn't help the pang of jealousy that made her momentarily pause and lean her head against the doorframe before wistfully closing it.

Marriage, and a baby. Well, Bea had experienced the first. At twenty-two, she'd already been a widow for over two years. For most of that time, she'd been grateful for her circumstance. Lord Pullington had never been cruel, but theirs was hardly a love match. When the old man had cocked up his toes a mere six months into their marriage, leaving her an independent woman, she'd felt nothing so much as relief. Only lately had she begun to wonder, especially watching her dearest friend Elizabeth, if life might hold more for her, too.

Between her mother, sisters, and Elizabeth and Charity, Bea never lacked for female companionship. Invitations to teas, soirees, even balls arrived with regularity. She danced when asked, and had been complimented on her conversational skills as a dinner partner. But none of that could erase the fact that Bea was—had always been, even during her brief marriage—alone.

When she'd first been widowed, her spinster cousin Ernesta had come to live with her for some months. The arrangement had been tolerable, though the two women had little in common. The presence of a companion allowed Bea to maintain the aura of propriety her parents and husband had drilled into her.

But last year, Ernesta had surprised them all by answering an advertisement for a teaching position in America. She'd heard that not only teachers, but women as a whole, were in short supply over there, so after thirty-five years of dull but respectable life in England, she'd decided to try her luck in the New World. Bea wished her the best.

When her mother had brought up the topic of a new companion, Bea had argued that the proximity of her parents, scarcely a block away, ought to be sufficient. It wasn't as though she was receiving callers of a questionable nature; not once since widowhood had she engaged in anything more questionable than offering her best friend, Elizabeth, a place to stay when she'd experienced some turmoil with her family. Which, come to think of it, was rather depressing.

She had her independence, but what good had it done her?

Of course, if she wanted to meet the right sort of man—the sort she could love and marry—she needed to attend the right sort of events, not the usual teas and musicales she was too polite to turn down.

Chaperoning Charity at Monsieur Durand's salon seemed like a good place to start. Still, years spent attending ton events left her skeptical. The only appropriate topics of conversation were meaningless—fashion, weather, and such. They left one with scarcely more than a surface-level acquaintance. This time, Bea wanted more. A second marriage to someone who didn't truly *know* her, and value her at that deeper level, might leave her feeling even emptier than she did now.

Chapter 3

The salon, hosted by Lord Robert and Lady Alicia Wilbourne, was a crush. Footmen scurried to gather pelisses and overcoats, while the butler worked double-time to account for the fact that many of the evening's guests had not been on the original invitation list. Thankfully, the Wilbournes were gracious enough to take this in stride, and their home large enough to accommodate Philippe Durand's many admirers.

Bea and Charity arrived just in time and melded into the receiving line to greet their hosts.

"Bea, lovely to see you again," Alicia Wilbourne said as they approached. "And Charity. The two of you make quite the lovely picture."

"Enjoy yourselves, ladies," Robert Wilbourne invited. "My Alicia here was beyond excited to learn Monsieur Durand was coming to England. He's never put in an appearance in our country before, you know, but we had the good fortune to meet him in Paris last year. So when we got the word, my lovely wife insisted we open our home to display his work." He winked. "If I didn't know how much she loves me, I daresay I'd be jealous of the man."

"Is Monsieur Durand present, then?" Charity asked eagerly.

Lord Wilbourne's genial smile widened. "Don't tell me you harbor a tendre for our artistic friend as well. The youth of London will be devastated. Yes, he's here, putting the finishing touches on part of the display. I'm sure he'll be out presently."

Bea and Charity thanked the host couple and moved into the small ballroom, where a number of paintings were already on display. Others remained draped in velvet, presumably to be unveiled later.

"Ooh, how exciting," Charity said. She clasped her hands, then anxiously smoothed her skirts. "Do I look presentable?"

"Absolutely." Bea studied her. Charity's golden hair and blue eyes were set to perfection by the ice-blue silk gown she wore. The design was simple, the color pale, befitting her status as a debutante, but each drape and fold was artfully designed to flatter.

"In fact, you are even more stunning than usual this eve, Charity." She smiled. "But I promised your sister I would not let you fall all over yourself before the Frenchman."

Charity's mouth dropped open in mock outrage. "Well, I never! Simply because I remarked once— all right, perhaps twice—that Monsieur Durand is known to be both handsome *and* charming, not to mention talented . . ."

Bea held up a hand, laughing. "Enough. I, too, am anxious to meet this paragon." And any other eligible gentlemen who happened to be present.

Charity moved closer to examine a painting of a

young girl peering through ferns, into a forest stream. "Amazing," she murmured. "The expression is so intent, you feel as though you are there."

Bea said nothing, drawn in as well. The lush strokes and colors of the work were so different, so much more alive, than the rigidly formal portraits of aristocrats that graced the homes of so many of her London counterparts. If only she could capture that same sense of life in words, in her own creative dabbling, perhaps she'd have the courage to pursue her love of poetry more openly.

Bea chuckled to herself and shook off the silly musing. Monsieur Durand was known as a flamboyant, flirtatious Frenchman. He painted in a style that disregarded current convention, then fearlessly opened his work to the public. Good fortune had smiled on him when the work caught on, but Bea couldn't envision baring her soul to the world like that—for baring the soul was what true art, in any form, did.

"Do you know," Charity remarked as they drifted toward another painting, "Monsieur Durand never accepts commissions. He insists on choosing his own subjects, whether they be peasants or nobility."

Lady Tanner, an aging but formidable member of the ton, poked her cane into their conversation. "I imagine the monsieur is successful enough to have earned that luxury."

"Now, yes," Charity told her politely, "but he has always done it thus."

"I declare, Charity, I've never known you to study a subject so avidly," Bea teased.

Charity had the grace to blush.

Lady Tanner looked pointedly around the room. "I

daresay half of London has a newfound appreciation for art. One can only hope it is caused by a desire for self-improvement."

Bea bit her lip to keep from laughing as Lady Tanner moved off, her cane clicking on the polished wood floor. The astute old lady obviously had surmised that many of the room's occupants had more interest in the artist than in his work.

"Well," Bea said brightly, "shall we continue our journey toward self-improvement?" She gestured to a large display across the room.

Charity grinned back. "Indeed."

She leaned toward Bea and whispered, "There's more . . . not only does he choose his own subjects, but there is rumor he shot a man."

"Shot?"

Charity nodded, relishing her news. "In a duel. The fiancé of one of his subjects claimed that though Monsieur Durand's portrayal of the young lady had her fully clothed, her expression, the painstaking detail with which he captured every nuance, could only have come from knowing her intimately. He denied it, of course, but the man demanded satisfaction." She sighed. "Have you ever heard of such a romantic figure?"

Bea rolled her eyes and redirected her enthusiastic charge toward the next painting. But the moment they stepped forward, a swell of murmurs filled the room.

Charity stopped, craning to look around a heavyset man in front of her. She sucked in a breath and grabbed Bea's arm. "There he is."

She pulled Bea to an open space as heads turned and bodies parted, revealing Lord Wilbourne.

Standing at his side was a tall man with golden, stylishly neglected hair and a gaze that seemed to not only see, but *absorb* his surroundings.

Bea was grateful for the steadying grip of Charity's hand as a sudden rush of awareness set her heart beating faster.

This was no ordinary salon, no everyday artist. She'd felt it when she'd glimpsed his work, but seeing him in person, the sensation hit her full force.

The man who'd created that living, magical art was a good ten paces away, but even at a distance he projected an aura—all indolent charm and undercurrents of passion. No wonder Charity was smitten. No young London fop would stand a chance against Jean Philippe Durand.

Lord Wilbourne held up a hand, and the murmuring crowd settled. "I'd like to thank you for attending tonight's salon, honoring the work of my good friend. It is my pleasure to introduce you to the creator of that work, Monsieur Jean Philippe Durand. Although he prefers to give no formal speech, save a brief welcome, please do not hesitate to approach him during the evening with any questions you may have, as he is happy to answer in an informal setting."

The Frenchman stepped forward. "*Messieurs* and *mademoiselles,* my lords and ladies, I am deeply honored and humbled by your presence tonight. This is the first opportunity I have had to experience England, and I must say I find it unexpectedly delightful." His English was accented but precise, his voice a resonant baritone.

He paused, one hand frozen in midair as he took

a deliberate gaze around the room. A smile spread across his features. Bea felt the jolt of it in her toes.

"Ah. The women of Paris mock their English counterparts, but now that I see for myself, I declare they speak out of jealousy," he said grandly. "Had I known London harbored such beauties, I would have come here years ago." He bowed. "Please, enjoy yourselves. I shall speak briefly about the remaining paintings as I unveil them, but there is no need for a formal audience, so let us mingle and enjoy the lovely home of my gracious hosts, Lord and Lady Wilbourne."

He flashed another smile, all polish and charm, and women's fans throughout the room fluttered vigorously.

Charity looked around. "Unbelievable."

"Oh, come now," Bea laughed. "Were you not the one who insisted we come? I thought you had a mad crush on Monsieur Durand."

"*Had.*" Charity tossed her head. "I don't like to be part of a crowd."

"You, darling, will always stand out from any crowd." Bea shook her head in amusement. Elizabeth's little sister was headstrong, but Bea had known Charity long enough to know she had a heart of gold and was steadfastly loyal to those she *truly* cared for. Apparently, Monsieur Jean Philippe Durand no longer rated in that category.

Charity's disillusionment, however, didn't diminish Bea's enthusiasm in the least. Though she'd heard of Durand, she'd never seen his work before tonight—and now she was captivated.

"Come." Bea nodded to where the first covered painting was being unveiled. "Let us see this new

work, and hear what the artiste has to say of it."
She led Charity to the edge of the crowd that had
gathered for the spectacle.

With a flourish, Monsieur Durand whisked away
the draping of amethyst velvet, revealing an or-
nately framed portrait of a woman. The subject
stood on the balcony of a Paris town house, gazing
pensively at the street below. She was lovely, yet to
Bea, she exuded the impression she longed for
escape.

The Frenchman cleared his throat. "This, friends,
is the last portrait of my mother." He spoke loudly
enough for everyone to hear, but without the showmanship used earlier. "She was taken by illness
earlier this year, but it is to her I owe my career, my
passion for art. She saw to my lessons from the time
I was young, and her connections afforded me the
exposure necessary for success."

Bea watched his features soften as he spoke.
Clearly, his mother had meant a great deal to him.
Never had she observed a man who seemed so willing, if not entirely at ease, about speaking of emotional matters before near strangers.

The artist paused in his speech. Those gathered
about remained respectfully quiet as well, seemingly content to admire the painting rather than
press questions.

"He's looking our way."

"Hmm?"

"He's looking our way," Charity repeated.

She was right. Bea glanced from Charity to the
Frenchman, who was most certainly gazing in their
direction, in spite of the fact that they stood on the
very fringes of the gathering.

"You see?" Bea said. "It is just as I proclaimed earlier—you stand out in a crowd. I predict you shall receive singular notice this eve. You look stunning, after all."

"Monsieur Durand?" A heavyset woman in a blue turban spoke up. "Is it true that you have studied in Venice, as well as France?"

The artist dismissed the out-of-place question with the merest shake of his head.

A low buzzing seemed to fill the air around Bea. Something extraordinary was happening. She turned to Charity, who seemed to sense it, too.

But when Jean Philippe Durand made his way through the crowd and came to a dead stop, it was not in front of Charity.

He lifted one hand, gesturing almost reverently toward Bea.

"*Belle.* You must be a transplanted rose, for in all of England, I have seen nothing so beautiful." He looked to Charity. "Please, permit me an introduction."

Charity appeared stunned, but recovered quickly, "Of course, monsieur. It is my pleasure to introduce to you Lady Beatrice Pullington, a dear friend."

"Lady Beatrice Pullington." He bowed lavishly, regaining some of his earlier showmanship. "A proper English name, indeed. Yet not so proper as to dispel the glow of beauty, of life, that enchants all about you."

Bea's cheeks grew hot, but she managed a coy tone to match his manner. "You have a charming way with words, monsieur."

He threw her a wicked grin. "Not nearly so charming as my way with paints. I am impulsive, *oui*, but I have learned to trust my instincts. They tell me now that you are the inspiration I have been seeking. A muse, gracing earth in human form. Please, let me paint you."

Everyone around them was staring.

Bea had long ago mastered the art of fitting in, mostly because she had rarely been singled out—at least never in such an overt manner. And yet the temptation to accept this sudden request . . . an offer most in the room would have paid dearly for, were payment an option . . .

"I know not if you are sincere, but if your request is made in earnest, then how could I refuse?" Bea murmured in response.

Triumph lit his features. "I am greatly relieved, yet hurt to think you question my sincerity. I assure you, I never issue such a request if I do not mean to follow through."

"He rarely issues such a request, period," Charity whispered. "Oh, do it, Bea. You simply *must*."

"I just said I would," she whispered back, loudly enough that Monsieur Durand laughed.

Heat suffused her face further.

"Oh, come now, *chérie*," the Frenchman pled. "I've no wish to embarrass you—only to have the honor of attempting to capture your spirit on canvas." He leaned in. "I shall leave you to the salon, for I see you are unused to such scrutiny, but I shall contact you through our hosts for the evening."

Bea could only nod.

"J'espère que nous aurons bientôt l'occasion de nous revoir," he said with another lavish bow. *I look forward*

to our next meeting. Smiling, he swept off to uncover the next of his still-draped works.

Bea was still in shock as Charity, face alight with excitement, whirled to face her. "Do you realize you have suddenly become the most envied woman in London?"

A familiar cane appeared. "The most envied, and, I predict, the most speculated about," Lady Tanner proclaimed. "You've always been a good girl, though. I'm sure your portrait will turn out lovely. Just keep your head about you."

Bea forced a smile at the unsolicited advice. Her head had deserted her the moment Jean Philippe Durand had entered the room. Lady Tanner had a point. She would do well to gather her scattered wits before spending any more time with the charismatic artist.

In spite of overhearing a few jealous comments to the effect of "I don't see why he found *her* so special," Bea was nearly floating by the time the salon ended. She and Charity bid their good-byes, then waited as footmen retrieved the outerwear they'd shed upon arrival.

A servant held out the rose-colored pelisse that matched Bea's gown. As she slipped her arm into the sleeve, she brushed against something stiff.

She paused, felt in the sleeve with her other hand. Yes, there it was. A small rectangle of paper, pinned to the lining of the garment.

Curiosity set her heart beating faster, but she gave the footman a bland smile as though nothing was out of the ordinary, and he moved off to assist the next departing guest. She glanced around her, but everyone seemed preoccupied with their own matters—no one was, at least that she could observe, paying her any special attention.

It was a note, she felt certain. And whoever put it there clearly hadn't wanted to make a public announcement of it. Who would wish to contact her in such a manner? She had no lover to slip her discreet little messages.

Monsieur Durand had said he would contact her through their hosts. This couldn't be what he had meant.

Belatedly, Bea realized Charity was a half dozen paces ahead, nearly out the door.

Bea hurriedly adjusted her gloves and followed, heaving a sigh as she resisted the urge to extract the missive and read it until she could do so as its sender clearly intended: in private.

Chapter 4

As soon as Charity exited the carriage, having been deposited safely at home, Bea tugged up the sleeve of her pelisse and unpinned the scrap of paper. She smoothed out the folds, then held it close to the vehicle's window.

The uneven light of the streetlamps afforded her limited visibility, though determination—and a good deal of squinting—allowed Bea to ascertain two things rather quickly: first, the note was written in French. Second, it was not addressed to her.

For that matter, it was not addressed to anyone.

How very vexing. She tapped her foot impatiently as the carriage traveled the remaining blocks to her home. Upon arrival, Bea hurriedly shrugged out of her pelisse and thrust it toward the butler, whose stoic, "Good evening, my lady," gave no indication that he noticed her unusual preoccupation.

She sped toward the little writing desk in the family salon and lit the lamp. There. She smoothed out the note, translating as she read.

*It is time for the planting of seeds. If properly
tended, they should flourish by May, perhaps June.
One cannot predict exactly, as the winds are subject to change. The best a gardener can do is plan
well, then monitor closely. To that effect . . .*

Huh?

The note merely described someone's intention
for planting their flower garden. How utterly odd.
Why would someone go to the trouble to pin such
a thing inside her sleeve? Perhaps it hadn't been intended for her after all, though that didn't answer
the question of why a gardening plan necessitated
such secrecy. There *had* to be something more.

She read a few sentences further, as the author
of the note went into detail regarding the proper
layout of a garden, factoring growth patterns,
which plants best complemented one another,
and such.

Wait. Bea frowned. Was her French that rusty?

She reread the sentence she'd stopped at. No,
that verb was conjugated improperly. And something about the author's choice of words struck her
as . . . off.

The author, perhaps, was a poor student of
French.

Or, Bea mused, perhaps not. She tapped a fingernail as she scanned the remaining few lines.

One phrase kept coming back to her . . . "Ten
clusters of night-blooming plants." Romance
often bloomed at night. Could the mysterious
note have another, hidden meaning? A lovers'
code of some sort?

Bea grew warm at the thought—either she had

interrupted the secret communications of an amorous duo, or she herself had an admirer who deemed her capable of interpreting such a message without any prior knowledge. The former scenario was more likely by far, which meant the polite thing was probably to burn the note and forget it ever existed.

But the temptation to uncover its meaning was simply too strong.

Years of reading and writing poetry had taught her to look for the meaning of a phrase beneath its surface. The "planting of seeds" in poems was often a euphemism for impregnating one's wife or lover.

Heavens. Bea suppressed the bubble of mirth rising in her. Was *that* what she'd intercepted? Evidence of an illicit pregnancy within London's elite?

Although—she returned to tapping her nail—the words of the note seemed to suggest the seeds in question were just now being planted. It was already April. If they were to flourish in May or June, that held more with an actual garden than a woman's time of expectancy, which lasted much longer. Unless by "flourish," the author meant only that the pregnancy would become evident—at least to the bearer, if not to everyone. But illicit lovers generally wished to avoid such consequences—yet the note referred to careful, *intentional* planning and monitoring.

Drat. It was impossible to discern the true meaning—let alone the author's intent in putting it to paper.

If the note was not meant for her, who *had* been the intended recipient? A woman, clearly. Bea's rose-colored pelisse was distinctive, but the salon had been well-attended, particularly by the fairer sex. She searched her memory. The women present that evening had displayed a veritable rainbow of gowns and accessories, but she could not recall with certainty any particular lady whose pelisse or cloak might be mistaken with hers. Without an addressee, the note offered up no further clue as to whom it had been meant for.

She yawned. The hour was late, her mind reeling from the evening's excitement—only a small part of which involved this note. Perhaps being asked to sit for the French painter wasn't quite what she'd had in mind when she'd pondered the dull routine her life had become, but fate had handed her an opportunity. And for once, she planned to take it without question.

Bea tucked the note into her desk drawer and turned down the lamp. She yawned again. Tonight she would dream of charming French artists and night-blooming jasmine. After a good night's sleep, she hoped, her mind would clear and the mystery of the note would reveal itself.

What was he to do without a studio?

Philippe paced the length of his hotel room. Ordinary furnishings, poor lighting—there was *nothing* here that could do the lady justice. And, of course, she was a *lady*. He could hardly expect her to visit the room of a strange man. After his very public request of her at last night's salon, the gossips had, understandably, been abuzz. He'd gleaned enough to know Lady Beatrice Pullington was a widow, and a respectable one.

He laughed. Had anyone in Paris told him he'd be fascinated, driven to use his artistic talent to portray a respectable English widow, he'd have laughed them out of his well-lit studio. But something about this particular widow spoke of life, of burgeoning but hidden passion.

So many of the English mademoiselles seemed to have inherited their looks directly from their country's landscape—pale and watery. Not Beatrice Pullington. *She* was a study in contrasts, her dark hair rich like French coffee, her complexion of the finest cream, tinted by delicate roses. He couldn't wait to study her further.

Unless—could he have been wrong? The excitement of the salon, a few glasses of wine. Had his mind played a trick on him, making the lady something more than she was?

He could simply finish his business in London, inquire as to Lord Owen's whereabouts, request a perfunctory meeting with the man, and return to France. Until twelve hours ago, that had been his plan.

But as he'd told Lady Pullington, his instincts were almost never wrong. And he never made an offer if he didn't intend to follow through.

Philippe realized that while his mind had wandered, his gaze had fixated on the brocade covering the chaise opposite him. An unremarkable piece, except that the fabric featured roses, entwined with gold thread. He'd compared her to a rose. An idea began to take form.

It was the beginning of the Season, with warmer weather just around the corner. He didn't need a studio. The lady didn't belong cooped up in an artificial, indoor setting. She belonged somewhere natural, somewhere primitive and just beginning to grow, to bloom. He would paint her as an enchantress, bestowing life and magic on an otherwise gray countryside.

The creative rush filled him, as it always did at the onset of a new project. It was what drove him, and was the reason he never accepted commissioned projects. He'd done so once, and the work had been bland and boring, so much that he'd hesitated to sign his name to the completed work. Never again.

Thankfully, he had no need of that now. The only thing he needed *now* was a plan to convince the respectable Lady Pullington to venture off into the wilderness with nothing but him and his paints.

Bea was having second thoughts. Elizabeth, her closest friend since their schoolroom days at Miss Fletcher's Academy for the Refinement of Ladies, did not seem to notice.

"I cannot believe I bowed out of attending the salon and missed the Season's most exciting moment!" Elizabeth lamented.

"The Season has hardly begun," Bea argued.

"A mere triviality."

Elizabeth had arrived as soon as the hour was decent, just before noon, forcing Bea to once more set aside her mysterious letter. It was a code, she was certain now, though she'd yet to puzzle out the full message.

The ladies were seated, as usual, in the family salon, sharing a light repast. Although, Bea noticed, she was the only one actually eating.

Elizabeth sipped plain tea, and had selected a bland biscuit over the delicate and creamy finger sandwiches on the tray.

"Are you still feeling unwell?" Bea asked.

"Not too badly." Elizabeth smiled. "It's to be expected, I believe."

The reminder of her friend's delicate condition brought Bea's thoughts back to her own dilemma. If she wanted to achieve the same state of marital and familial bliss as Elizabeth, she ought to be looking for eligible gentlemen—not playboy artists.

"How did you hear everything so quickly, anyway?" Bea asked.

"Charity, of course. I do believe she sent that poor messenger out before daylight in her determination to be the first to share the news."

"She wasn't put off by the turn of events?" Bea worried. "She said nothing last night while we were there, but after all, it was her interest in Monsieur Durand and his work that brought us there."

"Not at all," Elizabeth laughed. "Charity enjoys being the center of attention, to be sure, but I've never known her to be jealous. Besides, I doubt she could associate long with a man whose popularity might rival her own." The warmth in Elizabeth's voice made it clear she spoke with love and amusement over her sister's antics.

"Well, I shan't get too carried away. It may yet come to nothing." But the hair on Bea's neck prickled as she made that declaration. She stood, uneasy, and rifled through the day's correspondence— neatly arranged on a silver plate on her writing desk.

Bea sifted through the usual assortment of calling cards and notices, when one envelope drew her attention from the rest. The bold flourish of the handwriting was unfamiliar, but the moment she slid it open, she knew.

> *Lady Pullington,*
>   *As you can see by this missive, I am sincere in my hope that you will allow me to paint your likeness. After considering the matter, I believe an outdoor setting will best allow me to achieve the effect I envision. I am unfamiliar with England, and therefore beg of you to accompany me on an outing to the countryside so that we may discover an appropriate location. If you are amenable, I shall send a driver Wednesday afternoon at one o'clock.*

Veuillez agréer, Madame, l'assurance de mes sentiments distingués,

Jean Philippe Durand

"What's caught your attention?" Elizabeth leaned over her shoulder.

Bea handed her the note.

"Oh. My, he is bold. A bit improper, but then, he *is* French." She fluttered a hand over her heart and giggled. "'It may yet come to nothing?'" she teased, mocking Bea's words of moments before. "I think not. You, darling, are about to become the subject of Monsieur Durand's considerable talent."

Bea retrieved the card, reread it.

"You're going, aren't you?"

"Oh . . ." She set the card carefully back on the plate. "I, well, perhaps this isn't the best idea. As you said, it's improper."

Elizabeth cocked her head. "The most coveted

invitation in London, yet you are considering turning it down? Have you lost your mind?"

Bea searched for an excuse as her friend's eyes narrowed. "Ah. It's the attention," Elizabeth pronounced, as though she were a physician diagnosing an ailment. "It makes you uncomfortable. No. That's not quite it. *He* makes you uncomfortable."

Sometimes, best friends saw things too clearly.

How could she explain that she'd had the sense it hadn't been her polished self, her fashionable gown, that Philippe Durand had been looking at, but something else? Something internally, uniquely her. And Bea was afraid of whatever it was he might have seen.

Elizabeth had no such qualms. "You're going," she declared. "And I'm coming with you."

"I won't hear of it. You can't possibly traipse through the countryside in your condition."

"I most certainly can," Elizabeth argued. "I am nowhere near confinement yet, and I feel much better now that I've rested. A bit of fresh air will do me good."

Bea hesitated. A flutter, reminiscent of the excitement she'd felt at the salon, filled her. This was her chance to delve into the mind of the artist, to watch him at work, find out what drove him. For if she could figure out how he did it, she might understand whether she had it in herself to take those same risks with her poems—or whether she would dabble in secret forever.

Elizabeth sensed her capitulation. "It's settled, then. Write him back."

* * *

After Elizabeth left, Bea pulled out her mystery note once more, determined to decipher its code. The more she'd pondered it, the more she'd decided it unlikely the note was actually addressing the indelicate topic of pregnancy—poetic conventions about "seed planting" aside.

The author of the note advocated a planting and watering schedule based on days of the week. Presumably this made keeping track easier, but Bea found it oddly meticulous. Didn't most gardeners tend to their plants based on the plants' needs, and changes in the weather, rather than a preset timeline?

But if the author's insistence on establishing a timeline served another purpose . . .

The most likely reason—not that *any* reason was particularly likely—a woman might find a note tucked into her sleeve, Bea presumed, was to arrange a meeting she might not want others to know about. A lovers' rendezvous, perhaps, or payment of a private debt . . . even a bribe? Everyone had their secrets.

She returned to the note.

> . . . *the pleasure of a garden need not be limited to daylight. Last to be planted—on Saturday, for Sunday is a day of rest—are ten clusters of night-blooming plants.*

Saturday. Night. Perhaps ten o'clock? Where, where? Bea tapped a fingernail on her desk, and then it came to her. A pleasure garden. Vauxhall.

The salon had been Monday evening. Today was Tuesday. If Bea's interpretation was correct, then the secret meeting had not yet come to pass.

Bea was fairly certain *she* wasn't the one who'd been invited.

What if she were to attend anyway? She had nearly four days to decide.

Philippe strummed anxious fingers against his thigh as the unmarked carriage waited outside Lady Pullington's home. Her missive accepting this outing had come as a relief, even a bit of a surprise.

The door of the townhome opened and Lady Beatrice Pullington, dressed in a pale green gown with a light wrapper, descended the steps.

Philippe leaned forward.

Another figure, a woman with striking red hair and an emerald gown, followed behind her.

He sat back. A chaperone. Disappointing, but to be expected. The carriage door opened and the footman assisted both ladies up.

Philippe smiled broadly, falling back on the natural charm that had always come so easy to him. "Ladies. Welcome."

"Monsieur Durand. Permit me to introduce my companion this afternoon, the Duchess of Beaufort." Bea settled herself across from him, the redhead at her side.

Philippe gave a makeshift bow, as much as the tight space allowed. "Your Grace. It is truly an honor for a simple craftsman such as myself to spend the afternoon with not one, but two of Society's loveliest ladies."

The two women laughed and exchanged a glance. What was that about?

"A pleasure to make your acquaintance, Monsieur

Durand," the redhead said. "I was very sorry to have missed the salon, so accompanying my dear friend Bea is a welcome opportunity. May I ask our destination?"

Every inch of the young duchess bespoke polish and, Philippe sensed, a protectiveness of Lady Pullington. He paused and rubbed his thigh, weighing his answer. "*Je regrette* . . . I am unable to offer you a specific destination. As you may know, I am unfamiliar with England's countryside. I simply instructed our driver to take us a bit outside the city, and planned to explore until I found something that caught my eye."

The duchess arched a brow. "Am I to understand you intend to drag us into the wilderness without purpose or destination?"

Definitely protective. He gave her a smile designed to disarm. "Never without purpose. And your safety is my utmost priority, *vraiment*. It is only that I seek the very best setting to complement your friend's luxuriant beauty."

Beatrice Pullington was being remarkably silent, but he thought he detected a blush at his last statement.

"I see. What sort of scenery is it you envision?" the duchess asked.

He tilted his head. "Something natural, yet alive. To be honest, I hoped to observe Lady Pullington as she freely wanders. When it is right, I will know."

"Oh." Lady Pullington's eyes widened, and the spark of awareness that passed between them was nearly tangible.

He shifted back and cleared his throat. "Your

Grace, you are a native here. Perhaps you know of somewhere that will suit?"

The redhead smiled at his flattery, and Philippe silently praised Beatrice Pullington for her choice of companion. Had she shown up with an ancient harridan immune to charm, the outing would have been infinitely less pleasant.

"The gardens at Montgrave."

"An estate?" he asked.

"Yes, my husband's and my country seat. It is not terribly far—perhaps two hours, a little more."

"I see. The journey is manageable, though the return trip will limit our exploration. Are these formal gardens, then?" Philippe frowned.

"Not in the way of the sculpted gardens in France," Lady Bainbridge answered. "Montgrave does have some English gardens that are lovely, but if those do not suit, the grounds themselves are extensive and offer a great variety of natural scenery. If you find it to your liking, you might have access to it as long as you need."

It was a generous offer. Using the duke's grounds might make his subject more comfortable, as she would be under the implied protection of her powerful friends. He needed her relaxed. However Beatrice Pullington might fascinate him, and whatever his reputation with women, Philippe had always acted the part of a gentleman.

He smiled. "Montgrave it shall be."

Philippe watched as the duchess flicked another of those assessing glances first at Lady Pullington, then him. What was she planning?

More importantly, how did he get Beatrice Pullington to relax? She'd spoken barely two sentences the entire journey. Oh, she'd nodded, smiled, and murmured agreement as he and Lady Bainbridge tried valiantly to draw her into the conversation, but eventually they'd all lapsed into a desultory silence, lulled by the motion of the carriage.

The vehicle rolled through a set of stone and iron gates, signaling their arrival to the duke's estate.

Philippe turned his gaze from the perplexing women across from him to the small window. Outside, the grounds were manicured, with swans floating serenely on a pond. Too formal. A sprawling manor came into sight, and behind it on the left, a sun-dappled meadow framed by woods. He smiled. There was promise in those fields.

Their vehicle drew to a stop, and the three climbed out. The young duchess, moving slowly, was the last to emerge.

"We are not expected, but there is always a small staff in residence here if you would care for refreshments before starting," she offered.

"*Merci.* A kind offer, but if Lady Pullington is amenable, I prefer to take advantage of this fine afternoon and begin immediately." He shrugged a shoulder, indicating the satchel he carried. "As I did not know when we set out where we would end up, I did pack a light repast."

Lady Pullington opened her mouth to respond, but her companion cut her off. "Oh dear, I was afraid you'd say that."

"Pardon?"

The duchess passed a hand across her forehead in an expression of weariness. "I'm so very sorry, but

I believe the carriage ride has left my stomach unsettled. I think I shall go inside and have a lie-down while the two of you explore. Bea is familiar with the grounds, and you may, of course, wander freely."

"Oh, no, E.," Bea exclaimed, rushing to take her friend's hand. "I'll come with you."

"Don't be a goose," Lady Bainbridge chided. "We came all this way so you and Monsieur Durand could begin work. Why, 'twould be a crime to let the opportunity go to waste. Montgrave's staff is more than adequate to see to my needs."

Guilt twinged him. The carriage ride hadn't seemed taxing, but perhaps the lady was of delicate constitution. "I am terribly sorry to hear you are ailing. Are you certain we cannot be of assistance?"

"Quite certain. I'll be fine with a short rest, and then if the two of you are still in sight, I promise to join you. In the meantime, do not hesitate to ask the staff for anything." With an apologetic smile, she departed for the house, leaving him with the adorably flustered subject of his interest.

Philippe kept his expression neutral, hiding his amusement. He was no doctor, but Elizabeth Bainbridge appeared in fine color, and the spring in her step betrayed her claim of an unsettled stomach.

Damned if the duchess hadn't connived a way to leave him alone with the lovely Lady Pullington.

He'd have to thank her later.

Chapter 5

Well. So much for relying on one's friends. Bea watched as Elizabeth beat a hasty retreat. She had the sneaking suspicion that, though her friend *had* been queasy of late, that was not her only motive in seeking refuge in the house.

"Shall we, my lady?"

Bea whipped around. Monsieur Durand stood before her, offering his free arm, a gleam in his eye. The sun reflected on the deep gold of his hair, his chiseled profile.

Heavens. He was just as enigmatic as she'd remembered from the salon.

She threw one last glance toward the house. Propriety dictated she bring a companion, a maid at the very least. After all, that was why Elizabeth had accompanied them in the first place.

But Bea's status as a widow, and frustration with a lifetime of bowing to propriety, gave her the impetus to do whatever she damn well pleased.

Even if they were seen, Bea knew the duke employed only servants capable of great discretion.

She swallowed, summoning her courage. Never let it be said insecurity had gotten the best of her.

Bea gave him a brilliant smile and tucked her hand in the crook of his arm.

He flashed a matching smile, and they struck off across the grounds.

"Do you need no other equipment?" Bea asked, eyeing his satchel.

"Not today. I have my sketchbook. I usually do a few, ah, preliminary sketches, to get an idea of angles and such, before working on canvas."

"Oh."

"And then there is the matter of choosing the best light. A challenge of painting outdoors, for the light changes throughout the day."

"Oh." She would win no awards for witty conversation this day. Come now, Bea, she chided herself. *Oh?* Surely you can come up with something more scintillating than a one-word reply.

She tilted back her head to look up at him. "Would it be easier if we used an indoor setting?" she asked.

He met her eye. "Easier, yes. But less worthy."

Again, she had no response to that—except for the giddy rush of warmth at his assessment of her worthiness. Apparently, "dazzling conversationalist" was not among the criteria he used to judge. Thank goodness.

She turned her gaze forward, lest she trip, and they walked in silence for a while.

"I make you nervous."

Bea let out a breathless laugh at the blunt observation. "Yes."

"Porquoi?"

"Why?" she echoed. She swallowed, trying to pull her thoughts to the question at hand—and away from the long, lean-muscled artist beside her.

"You need not fear me." He slowed their pace enough to look her in the eye again. "It is an intimate thing, painting another person—at least it is if you hope to capture their true spirit. And I do hope to do so. You captivate me. But I would never attempt to harm you, to do anything you did not desire."

"Oh. Thank you for that."

His promise should have been reassuring. But Bea's fear lay not in what she did *not* desire, but in what she might very well desire. Her awareness had tripled at his open acknowledgement that they were embarking on an intimate venture. The world around them fell away, seeming immaterial to Bea, compared to the intense presence of the man beside her. She unconsciously gripped his arm more tightly.

Bea studied her footsteps as they continued toward the wood. Well she knew what Philippe meant—at least when it came to art. Writing a poem was, for her, a deeply intimate process—but a solitary one. Painting would be the same, she suspected, and when the subject was another person . . . Bea was suddenly, irrationally jealous of the other women Philippe Durand had painted.

Their wide, sun-dappled path led into the wood. The faint call of wilderness lured her feet along, as though in a few mere steps she could leave civilization behind. Though spring had fully reached the cultivated, open grounds of the estate, it came slower to the shaded depths of the woods.

Philippe released her arm gently. "Go on ahead, wander at will."

She nodded and moved off self-consciously as the artist fell back. She'd been in these woods before while visiting Elizabeth, but it had been winter then, and they had not wandered far. The trees were different now, the barest tips of green brightening the dreariness of winter. A week or two more, and the buds would be bursting with the new life of spring.

And with that thought, Bea knew exactly where her feet had subconsciously been leading her.

"Up ahead," she called, excitement filling her. Would he see it as she did? In winter, the little garden had been desolate, a place of forgotten dreams. But in spring?

She hurried along the path. Had it been this far?

Finally the trail opened into a small clearing, the site of a long-abandoned rose garden. Ivy and bramble competed with thorny branches, snaking over a chipped basin and curling around the feet of a small bench.

She stopped at the edge of the clearing. Philippe stopped just behind her, close enough that she could feel the heat of him. The air was still, the silence broken only by the occasional twitter of a bird or rustle of a squirrel.

Her heart beat faster. There was possibility here. She'd felt it before . . . the promise of poetry. Or, perhaps, art.

Softly, she quoted:

I heard a thousand blended notes,
While in a grove I sate reclined,

*In that sweet mood when pleasant thoughts
Bring sad thoughts to the mind.*

She paused, and the air around them held silent once more, save for the soft drip of water somewhere in the forest.

The French artist's expression was thoughtful. "I confess great ignorance of the English poets," he said, "but . . . Wordsworth?"

"Yes." She smiled, pleased—though somehow not surprised—that he'd recognized the piece.

"It is an appropriate sentiment." He smiled at her, then nudged her shoulder, indicating the garden. "I need to see you in it."

She nodded, self-conscious again. She stepped into the little clearing, ran her hand along the top of the bench, letting the mood of her surroundings seep into her, until she'd all but forgotten the enigmatic man observing her at the garden's edge. She picked her way across stones and ivy, careful not to disturb anything, until she reached the reflecting basin, now empty.

A broken robin's egg rested in the center. She touched it tentatively, then looked up, searching for the nest from which it must have fallen.

"Stop."

She froze, face lifted, breath held.

"Oui."

He moved to her, angling his head, pausing, considering. He gently repositioned her right hand on the stone basin. "Just so," he murmured.

Her body quivered at his touch, though she did her best to hide it. The tingling rush that always filled her at the beginning of a new poem was present now. The suspicion that he felt it too was confirmation of his earlier declaration—the process of painting someone, though they'd hardly begun, was an intimate one.

He stepped back, circled her slowly. "All right, relax a moment while I fetch my sketchbook." He went to rummage through the satchel.

Bea slowly released her breath

"You like this, then?" She gestured toward a wrought-iron arch, overgrown with the woody vines of roses gone wild.

"Very much. In a week, perhaps two, it will be perfect. A bit more hint at life, but not yet full bloom. We will have to hurry, if I am to have the canvas readied by then."

He fished out the sketchbook, a tin of charcoals, and settled himself against the trunk of a tree, taking in the abandoned garden. "Now, *chérie,* if you would resume the pose you held a moment ago . . ." He selected a thin charcoal stick and propped the sketchpad against his knee. His deft hands went to work, quick short strokes on the paper as Bea did her best to recreate the pose he liked.

She stood until her arms and neck ached, shifting only when Monsieur Durand would lift his head and gesture to her, indicating a minor adjustment to the pose. He spoke little, his entire concentration on the connection between her and the images he was creating on paper. His absorption in his work was a relief, for it spared her the necessity of inventing carefree banter when all she could think of was *him.*

Finally, his charcoal stilled and his intense focus

on her mellowed as he gestured toward the garden as a whole. "Whose was it?"

"I know not," Bea answered, sagging in relief as she allowed her arms to drop. Elizabeth hadn't known either, when they'd first discovered the place. "A past duchess, perhaps. It has been some time since it was tended."

"Ah, the misty veils that shroud the past. A forgotten place, though not a lonely one. It is perfect." He smiled, stood and stretched, then came to stand by her side. "I was not mistaken. You, Lady Pullington, are most definitely the muse I have been seeking."

"Beatrice," she whispered. It seemed absurd that the man attempting, as he'd said, to capture her true spirit on canvas should use her formal title. But her request was improper. She was a lady, he an artist. Use of her title was an acknowledgement of that gap.

He knew it, too—she saw the serious consideration in his eyes. "Beatrice," he repeated slowly.

He stood close. Too close. Close enough for her to know the woodsy scent of his soap mingled perfectly with their surroundings.

"What am I doing here?" she whispered.

He tilted his head and the corner of his mouth lifted in a half smile. "Call it . . . *un coup de coeur.*"

A spontaneous attraction. She could hardly deny that.

His eyes went dark, but she couldn't drag her gaze away from that fathomless blue.

This was more than she had bargained for. Flirtation, yes, and the flattery of being the subject of his beautiful artwork. But never . . . *this.* This intense need to have him *know* her, care for her.

He was an artist, a Frenchman, and a known seducer of women. Hardly a man to whom she could trust her heart.

This was desire, this was passion—nothing else. But, oh, Lord, she'd never felt the sort of heady rush she did when he looked at her like that, and her heart argued to be given its chance.

He leaned in.

There was no stopping this. She would rather die than pull away now.

His lips grazed her temple, a light touch. Warm. He drew back just long enough to meet her gaze.

He would see her acceptance, her pleading, the same way he always saw through her, to the core of what she felt. Bea knew it and looked him in the eye anyway.

Never breaking her gaze, he set the sketchbook and charcoal tin on the edge of the basin. The tin slipped and clattered to the bottom, ignored by both.

He captured her face with strong hands, barely a moment before his mouth fused to hers. Slanting, again and again. This was no light caress. Her lips parted under the pressure, and he drove inside, gripping her tight with hands that sought to possess, rather than pose her.

Bea was drowning. Her hands slid to the wall of his chest, stroking, seeking. Waves of sensation crashed over her as his tongue plundered her mouth, exploring, then thrusting, mating with hers.

He drew her closer yet, his hand at the small of her back, until their hips met, her thigh nestled between his legs. His lips moved to her neck, and her head tipped back at this new pleasure.

His tongue traced the line of her throat, down to her collarbone. Her back arched, her body wantonly seeking more. The movement brought her in direct contact with his arousal.

Bea pulled back sharply. Dear God, what was she doing?

Philippe dropped his hands, his breathing labored.

"Did you lure me into the woods to paint me or to seduce me?" The question slipped out before Bea could consider the wisdom of asking it.

Philippe frowned, the intimacy of the moment shattered. "You English are so . . . orderly. No mixing of business with pleasure. Why is this so? The French do not see it thus—though, whatever you may have heard, I do not make a habit of seducing my subjects."

She waited.

He sighed. "I intend to paint you. And I made a promise not to do anything you did not desire. *Je suis désolé.* I apologize. I shall not kiss you again—unless you wish me to do so."

"It was my fault as well," Bea acknowledged softly. "But it would be better if it does not happen again."

"Better?" Philippe echoed with a rough laugh. "An odd choice of word. Safer. More proper, perhaps. But I would not say it will be *better.*"

Once more, Bea could think of no appropriate rejoinder.

He chuckled, but the sound held a note of regret. "No matter. I believe I've enough sketches for this day. Let us go. With luck, Lady Bainbridge will be recovered enough for the return journey."

He did not offer his arm as he had before, so Bea

trudged silently behind him as they retraced the path through the woods. Never in her life, and especially never in her brief marriage, had she felt that desperate leap of desire she'd experienced at the touch of Jean Philippe Durand.

From the moment she'd agreed to this outing, she'd sensed it would be dangerous. Now she knew why.

Philippe arrived late to the Wilbournes' on Wednesday night. The trip to Montgrave had yielded an ideal setting for his next work, but had also consumed the full afternoon and evening. The estate might be close to London by the ton's standards for country homes, but it would not lend itself to daily trips back and forth.

Had the rose garden been any less perfect, he'd have been tempted to find something closer. But it *was* perfect—Bea and he had both felt it. Philippe had felt a great deal more, too, during the outing, but it was too soon to speculate about the implications of that.

The Wilbournes, Philippe was learning, thrived in the role of host and hostess. Tonight they'd planned a card party. Fortunately, such events never really got started until late in the evening, making his tardiness excusable.

The added benefit, Philippe reflected as he strode up the steps to their home after a quick stop at the hotel for fresh attire, was that since he played abominably, missing a few rounds would do him no harm.

He greeted his hosts and those few faces he

recalled from other events, then stood back, keenly aware he was out of place in this crowd. He was not English, nor titled, nor even a skilled player. He possessed the temperament to make himself at home in nearly any situation, but the session with Beatrice at the abandoned rose garden had left him unsettled.

Then again, he wasn't at home anywhere these days. His mother's revelation had robbed him of the identity he'd grown up with. Until he met with Lord Owen—a task he'd delayed due to his sudden obsession with a certain Englishwoman—he would have no answers.

His inquiries had yielded an address in Kent. If he could tear himself away from Beatrice, he could make the trip this weekend. Two days—three at the most. After all, it wasn't as though he'd be an invited guest.

A man at Lord Wilbourne's card table stood and excused himself, prompting Lord Wilbourne to beckon toward Philippe. "Monsieur, won't you join us? We've need of a fourth. The game is whist."

"I am afraid any partner of mine would be terribly disappointed," Philippe answered.

"Very well then, gents," Lord Wilbourne addressed the others at the table, "what say you we switch to Five-Card Loo?"

The men nodded, and Wilbourne beckoned once more to Philippe.

He'd run out of excuses. One could hardly accept an invitation to a card party and then expect not to play. He took a seat. A footman set a fresh wineglass by his side, peering at him with interest.

Curious. Servants were generally trained never to display facial expressions.

Lord Wilbourne dealt, introducing the two other participants as Lords Garrett and Stockton.

A tinkle of laughter sounded from across the room, where a table of women bent their heads together, clearly engaged in gossipy intrigue. Lord Garrett glanced their way. "Normally we'd balance the tables a bit better," he told Philippe, "but the opportunity to challenge Stockton and Wilbourne here was too great to pass up."

Philippe saw no ring on Garrett's hand and guessed him a bachelor—though he could think of no good reason an unmarried man would choose a table of men over the prettily-attired group across the room.

But the reason became clear as the men picked up their cards, placed their first bets, and began playing in earnest.

Merde. How had he landed at the table containing three of the most skilled—and, it seemed, wealthy—gamblers in London? It would take all his concentration to keep from losing his shirt. Unfortunately, Lord Wilbourne seemed inclined toward desultory conversation while staking what, to Philippe at least, were staggering sums.

"I hope you don't mind me saying that, although you are known to be one for effect, you truly outdid yourself at the salon," Lord Wilbourne told him. "Why, it has been the talk of London ever since. My wife couldn't be any more pleased."

Philippe, endeavoring to be gracious, nodded. "I assure you, my actions that night were not merely for effect."

"Then you are pursuing Lady Pullington? That is," he coughed, "as a subject?"

He smiled. "*Absolument.* My rose of England. She is . . . *très belle.*"

How odd. The Wilbournes' footman had now been lurking in the corner for some time—and was it Philippe's imagination, or had the man's eyes flared at the mention of Lady Pullington?

The corner was not an obtrusive position by any means, but most servants had mastered the art of appearing only when needed. Philippe had built his career upon observing people, then capturing those observations on canvas. Something about this particular footman struck him as unusual, though he couldn't pinpoint anything beyond the man's lingering presence.

He forced his attention back to the men at the table.

"Lord and Lady Bainbridge have offered the use of a site on the grounds of Montgrave as the setting. I believe the result will be captivating."

"Ah, yes. Lovely estate." Wilbourne nodded. "The duke's sister is a close friend of my wife. As is Lady Pullington, for that matter."

Philippe smiled. "It was Lady Pullington who identified the site, in fact. I have never before worked on English soil, but the lady seemed to know just what would suit. Her delicate features set amongst the first green of spring—I am thinking a tender palette will suit her shy nature, though the dark of her hair, the shadows . . . it will still have impact."

"Her shy nature?" Lord Garrett repeated. "Lady Pullington?"

"No? Am I wrong?" Philippe asked, unaccountably eager to learn more about Bea from men who had known her longer.

Garrett shrugged. "Just never thought of her as shy. She attends most of Society's events, and she always seems a companionable sort."

"Intriguing." Philippe pondered the Englishman's words. He could easily see Bea as a "companionable sort"—and yet, one could maintain appearances in Society without ever revealing one's deeper thoughts or true nature. And it was Bea's nature that held his attention. The last time he'd seen her, the lovely widow had intuitively led him to the perfect setting in which to paint her, then quoted poetry as she stood there.

He'd called her a muse upon first sighting her at the salon, but he hadn't known the word contained as much truth as flattery. If only she didn't shy away every time he got close—mentally *or* physically.

Philippe chuckled as he laid down his latest set of losing cards. "Getting me talking about art is one of the surest ways of distracting me. I believe you mean to empty my coffers while we hold this conversation," he joked.

Lord Wilbourne laughed. "Consider it a more civil method of waging war on France."

Philippe chuckled in return. Having met the Wilbournes in his home country during their extended stay, he knew they bore France no ill will.

The first round ended, Philippe having surrendered a fair sum to Lord Stockton. The older lord dealt next, and Philippe tried to focus on the game rather than remember the sweet taste of the lips of his muse. He shouldn't have kissed her. But it was difficult—no, impossible—to summon even a hint of regret for his actions.

The footman passed by again, and Philippe frowned, frustrated with his inability to ignore the man—or at least discern why he *could* ignore a high-stakes card game but not an inconsequential servant.

"You lose again, monsieur," Lord Wilbourne pointed out, drawing the cards in to prepare for a new round.

Philippe shook himself and grinned ruefully. "*Pardon.* I was distracted."

"The first rule of cards," Lord Garrett remarked in a lighthearted tone, "is never to become distracted."

"A terrible fault of mine, to be sure. I have never had much skill at card games," Philippe averred. "It is only that I find it difficult to focus on small marked pieces of paper when I have the opportunity to observe the people playing with them."

The incredulity on Lords Stockton and Garrett's faces made it clear they did not share the same problem.

"Take care not to let that fault be too widely known, or Englishmen will be lining up for the opportunity to fleece a wealthy Frenchman," Wilbourne advised.

"Duly noted. Though if I must compete, I prefer to do so in a fencing ring, where my penchant for observing people is a boon to me, rather than to my opponent."

Garrett waved a hand, relaxing visibly at this confirmation that the Frenchman did have *something* in common with them after all. "Very good. Enjoy the sport myself. Don't let Wilbourne scare you. We're all friends here. No bad blood."

"Of course, of course," Lord Wilbourne said. "Never would have invited you otherwise. All in good fun, right? A fencer, you say—have you had the opportunity for a match at Angelo's yet?"

"I'm afraid not, though now that I am extending my stay in your country, the possibility holds appeal."

One of the other tables broke up, two ladies making their way toward the refreshment board, while a third headed to the table where the men played, clearly looking for a new game to join.

Philippe stood. "By all means," he said, indicating his chair. "Gentlemen, I hope you'll forgive me." He smiled. "I admit defeat—and I confess to the desire to end tonight with a portion of my holdings still intact."

Lord Wilbourne held up two hands in a gesture of peace. "Certainly. I respect a man who knows when to leave the game far more than a man who stays when he shouldn't."

Lord Garrett nodded, his expression more solemn than usual for the normally gregarious young lord. Interesting. Philippe wondered what experience had prompted the conviction.

He excused himself and selected a glass of alcohol-laden punch from a nearby buffet, content to lean casually against the wall and observe. The lurking footman seemed finally to have disappeared. Lord Garrett traded places with another lady, evening the distribution of genders at each table. As the new players took their seats and the next round of cards began, Philippe's thoughts drifted inevitably back to Beatrice Pullington.

He'd felt inspiration before—he always chose subjects that inspired him. But never before had he felt this strange connection, that she was somehow sensing him, leading him down a path—both literal and figurative—he wanted to travel but might never have discovered otherwise. It was disconcerting.

He'd had his fair share of women—though perhaps not quite the number the gossips liked to attribute to him. And he did intend to have Beatrice Pullington. She might not yet realize it, but he sensed the inevitable—this connection of theirs would flame into a passion strong enough they both would surrender. A matter not of choice, but of fate.

Philippe grimaced, disgusted with his line of thought. Making love to a woman was one thing, but *fate*? Was he somehow under a spell, and his sense of control, the decisions he made, only an illusion? No. He was master of his own destiny.

But then, what *did* one do when a muse such as Beatrice Pullington walked into one's life?

Chapter 6

After considerable internal debate, Bea's curiosity won out on Saturday night. There was a chance she'd misinterpreted everything, but if she didn't at least test her theory about the mysterious note, she would die wondering.

If the note had been meant for someone's lover, she just *had* to help. Her own chances at finding true love had been knocked awry by an arranged marriage and early widowhood. The loneliness she'd felt in those years made Bea loathe to thwart someone else's budding romance.

There would be the inevitable awkward explanation of how she'd come by the note, but that was better than simply allowing some poor man to wonder, perhaps for years, why his lover had abandoned him.

Bea couldn't say exactly when she'd developed this inability to leave well enough alone. Perhaps the excitement with Philippe Durand had given her courage, or the fact that she'd spent the last year watching her best friend step outside all the normal bounds of propriety, and, as a result, Elizabeth was now happier than ever.

But Elizabeth had good reason to be more cautious these days, so Bea had asked Charity to accompany her tonight. Her friend's sister, always up for an adventure, had readily accepted.

As the two young women strolled through the entry to Vauxhall Gardens, strains of music could be heard from the pavilions, and the scents of the vendors' baked confections wafted through the air. Dusk had already fallen, and thousands of glass lamps lit the main walks, lending an air of magic to the scene.

"You're the best chaperone ever." Charity turned to Bea, her grin full of mischief. "With Mother and Elizabeth, all I ever do is attend balls and teas where I meet the same gentlemen I've known my entire life—only now their mamas are pressuring them to ask for my hand in marriage."

"Oh my. What a very dreadful existence," Bea teased.

"You've no idea," Charity declared, raising a hand to her forehead dramatically.

Bea laughed. "Of course, if your mother or sister find out the real purpose of our outing this evening, I am likely to lose my chaperoning privileges."

"My lips are sealed." Charity pinched them together for effect, then dropped her hand. "What *is* the real purpose of our outing tonight? More than Vauxhall's normal entertainment, I presume, since we have already missed the supper?" Her eyes lit up. "Ooh, have you planned a romantic assignation? If you wish to sneak off, I could stand watch."

"I do love you, Charity." Bea laughed again. Her

friend's little sister was the *perfect* companion for such an evening. "Actually, there is a liaison planned tonight. But I don't know with whom, or whether there is romance involved. And we aren't exactly invited."

"An intrigue," Charity breathed. "Even better. Tell me everything."

Bea explained about the note, and the message she'd gleaned from it.

"What? That happened at the salon, and you didn't tell me?"

"It occurred at the very end, and I didn't know what it was until even later. Besides, I'm telling you now."

"True. And making me your accomplice." Charity was appeased. "Who do you think it is? And where is this assignation to take place?"

"I have no idea who . . . though whoever it is must have attended the salon. As to where, I would guess the Druids' Walk, though again, it may be that my imagination has gotten the better of me in conjecturing this entire scenario."

Charity waved that idea away. "The Druids' Walk," she mused. "A favorite of lovers for decades." She giggled. "Though tonight, at least one lover is likely to be lonesome, for if you hold the note intended for his sweetheart, she will not know to show up."

Bea led Charity down the main walk, toward the more secluded paths, slowing as they drew near. The lamps were placed sparingly here, and a few yards ahead, they disappeared entirely. It was still a few minutes before ten o'clock. Bea and Charity slipped behind a row of tall shrubs, wary of revealing themselves to a party who might not be pleased to see them.

Another minute passed. A few revelers wandered within sight, but gave no indication of stopping. A middle-aged woman paused at the edge of the light. "Sarah?" she called. "Where have you gotten off to?" When there was no response, she continued on her way.

Bea winked. "Bet Sarah's having some fun," she whispered.

Charity grinned, then suddenly her expression changed—her eyes widened and she grabbed Bea's arm with one hand and pointed with the other.

Two men converged, one coming from the area of the pavilions, the other from the direction of the music room. They fell into step, then paused just beyond the entrance to the unlit portion of the paths.

Two *men?* Bea eyed Charity in their hiding spot in the bushes. This was some matter of business, then, rather than a lovers' rendezvous.

She returned her gaze to the duo, neither of whom she recognized. Their hats were pulled low, their clothing dark. Indistinguishable, which in itself was unusual, for Vauxhall was often hailed as a place where people indulged their tastes in exotic and outrageous fashions.

One of the men pulled out a pocket watch, glanced at it, then nodded to his companion. In accord, they moved deeper into the dark.

Bea frowned.

"There is a path that runs parallel to the one they are on," Charity whispered. "Shall we follow?"

Bea nodded, deciding this was not the time to

question why Charity, who had only just made her bow before Society, knew Vauxhall's dark paths so well.

The two ladies rose as quietly as possible, glancing around first to ensure no one saw them extracting themselves from the bushes. Their slippers made little noise as they hurried down the path Charity indicated.

"There," Bea whispered. Though greenery obscured the view, she could hear the low voices of men, speaking in French. Excitement rushed to her head. Their choice of language, their studied movements—just shy of furtive—all but confirmed she'd interpreted the note correctly. Or mostly so. It had been setting up a rendezvous. Just not a romantic one. She pulled Charity into a small enclave to wait once more.

"My French is abominable," Charity whispered. "I can't make out anything they're saying."

Bea held a finger to her lips, straining to hear. Her French was fine, but the men's low voices made it difficult. Clearly they'd no desire to be overheard—or recognized—which made Bea more determined than ever.

"*Elle est en retard,*" one of them murmured. *She is late.* Bea closed her eyes, focused only on translating.

"Do you think she'll come? She hasn't been discovered, has she?"

"It matters not. We cannot wait. The ship leaves tomorrow. Any reports must be on board."

The first man murmured something Bea couldn't make out, and the second dropped his voice as well. She continued to strain her ears, making out a phrase or two whenever the intensity of the discussion rose. What she heard did nothing to settle her unease.

As the conversation wore on, Bea could sense Charity's frustration. Finally, the men dispersed, one disappearing into the overgrown paths while the other headed back toward the pavilions.

Bea placed a hand on Charity's sleeve, signaling she wanted to wait until both were out of sight before emerging themselves.

"Bea," Charity said hesitantly, once they were back on the main path, "I could be wrong here, and I hope I am, but did those men strike you as, well, sinister?"

Charity's French may have been terrible, but her intuition worked just fine. "In what way?" Bea asked, wanting to hear her friend's thoughts before solidifying her own.

"Here are two men, missing their third, a woman perhaps, who meet in secret, communicate in code when writing, and are, presumably, French. I could not follow their conversation, but I know it was not about pastries, or the superiority of French wines. I caught the term 'Congress,' and 'Emperor,' and I have read, and heard, enough of the news to know war is looming once more."

"Yes." Bea pressed her lips together and gave a slow nod. The "Congress" the men had referred to was the Congress of Vienna—the group of ambassadors whose countries were dedicated to ending the second reign of Napoleon Bonaparte.

"I share your concern," Bea told her in a hushed voice, suddenly uncomfortable in her surroundings, "but let us wait until we return to my carriage to discuss it any further." She had the feeling she and Charity had just wandered into an intrigue far more grave than she'd anticipated. She only hoped their presence in the gardens had gone unnoticed.

Once they were safely enclosed in the carriage, Charity said, "I know you understood more of that than I did. Be honest with me. Were they spies?"

Bea hesitated. "It is possible."

"One of them seemed familiar." Charity frowned and shook her head. "The shorter one. But I can't place where I've seen him."

"Do try and remember," Bea urged.

The younger woman thought, then shook her head again. "I can't. What do you think we should do?" Charity tugged at a carefully arranged curl, worry evident in her tone.

Bea closed her eyes, her thoughts muddled. In matters like this, she was as inexperienced as her companion. "I suppose we could approach the authorities. The Foreign Office, maybe? Or the War Office? But what would we tell them? Oh, Charity, I'm so very sorry to have dragged you into this."

"Don't fret so," Charity reassured her. "We're both unharmed. We simply need to decide what action to take. Do you still have that note?"

"Yes. At my house. I can show you." She tapped on the window, then redirected the driver not to drop off Charity first.

When they reached Bea's house, she went once more to the desk, pulled the note from its drawer, and handed it to Charity, who stared at it, the tip of her tongue visible between her lips as she struggled with the translation.

"I cannot believe you not only read this, but discovered a whole second meaning."

Bea took back the paper. It seemed heavier in her hand now than it had when she'd thought it merely a lovers' clever game. But this was no ordinary missive . . . some mischief was afoot.

Somehow, she had been the accidental recipient of a note written in French, and in code. And tonight had provided ample evidence that while French was often considered the language of romance, in this case, it was the language of war.

News of Napoleon Bonaparte's escape from exile, followed by his march to Paris, had flooded the papers for the past weeks. If there was even the remotest relationship between those events and the slip of paper she held, or the conversation she'd witnessed tonight, the implications were more than she could comprehend.

Bea could pretend it had never happened, pretend she hadn't been intelligent enough to discern anything beyond a discussion of gardening in the note. But that would make her both dishonest and disloyal.

No. "We need to take this note to someone who will know what to do with it."

"Who?" Charity asked.

A good question. Who could she trust?

Philippe? She gave a half laugh. Simply because the letter was in French, she'd thought of him first. Or perhaps he was already at the forefront of her mind. Her body stirred at the mere memory of the last time they'd met, the way they'd kissed.

But in truth, she did not know the charming

French painter well enough to engage him in a political game of intrigue and subterfuge.

"You mentioned the Foreign Office," Charity prompted.

"True. But how does one go about reporting such a matter? If it is what we think, we cannot simply arrive at their offices and reveal everything to the first person who opens the door."

"They might not take you seriously. But if you enlist the support of someone they respect . . . Bea, could you take the letter to Alex?"

Of course. "Charity, that's perfect."

Elizabeth's husband would know what to do, and his title and connections gave him the power to take any necessary action. Relief flooded her. Bea may have stepped into the middle of an intrigue, but she had no desire to remain mired in it. One taste had been enough.

One taste of the smooth French painter, however, had *not* been enough. Beatrice could not stop thinking about him.

Their last parting had been awkward, true. Upon returning to Montgrave from the abandoned rose garden, the tension between Bea and Philippe had been palpable. Though if their "chaperone" had noticed it, she'd mercifully chosen not to mention it. Instead, the duchess had claimed a full recovery from her earlier ailment—no surprise to either Philippe or Bea—and filled the ride home with pleasant but meaningless prattle. She was thrilled to hear they'd chosen a site on Montgrave for the painting, and Bea was relieved to let her steer the conversation.

Philippe had been characteristically enigmatic—answering questions about his work with enthusiasm, but leaving Bea to wonder if the same chaotic emotions she was feeling seethed under that charming façade. But perhaps he'd not been so affected.

The only hint at his feelings came in the fact that he'd insisted on working out the details of their next meeting—the meeting she was desperately preparing for now—before delivering her home.

He'd wanted a witness, Bea thought, so she wouldn't be able to wiggle out of seeing him again.

Philippe had asked Bea to look over his sketches this afternoon, so that they might select one to develop into the final painting. She was thrilled that he valued her artistic input—yet panicked at the idea of being near him once again. He fascinated her, but his talent, his public success, was intimidating.

Her maid held up a muslin day dress in spring green. Bea shook her head. "Not that one."

"My lady, this is the fourth gown you've passed up, all of which look quite fetching on you, if I may be allowed to say," her maid pointed out. "But if you tell me what look it is you're set on achieving, perhaps I might do better in finding a gown that will suit."

"I'm sorry, Maeve," Bea said. The older woman had been her maid since she'd been out of the nursery. She was Irish, hired by Bea's mother, Lady Margaret Russell, when Bea and her sisters were young. When Bea had married, Maeve's cheerful loyalty had earned her a permanent place on the staff, even when it became fashionable to hire French ladies maids.

The maid bustled back into the closets, and Bea returned to worrying over Philippe—in spite of telling herself to stop. After all, it was just a kiss—and from a man who'd clearly done a good deal of kissing. One needn't read too much into it.

She ground her teeth in frustration as Maeve returned with a gown in each arm, then smiled apologetically when she realized the poor maid thought her frustrated expression a reaction to the new gowns.

"The pink, I think," Bea said, indicating the gown in Maeve's left arm. Her harried servant looked relieved. Bea cocked her head, considering the gown. She'd been wearing pink—well, rose—the night of the salon. Her life hadn't been the same since.

It was in Bea's nature to analyze, to overthink. In some cases—as with the note she'd translated—her interpretation was quite valid. But in matters of the heart, she wasn't so sure.

Maeve pulled the gown over Bea's chemise and stays, adjusting until everything was in place, then picked up a hairbrush. "Relax, my lady," she soothed, brushing long strokes. "I thought if we put your hair up—just so—and wind this ribbon through, to set off your dress?"

Bea nodded assent.

"You'll look ever so fetching, my lady."

But looks were not what had Bea worrying. Did Philippe value her artistic opinion—value *her*—enough for her to risk sharing her soul?

For the first time in her life, she was working with someone who not only understood the act of

creation—creation of art, that is—but actively
imbued those creations with emotion, with intimacy.

For years, she had longed to do the same. To let
her pen pour out the thoughts and feelings so long
pent up.

In school, they'd been expected to study poems
and sermons, then mimic what they read in their
own rudimentary efforts at composition.

Bea had quickly figured out that all the great poets
alluded to deeper matters of love, loss, even death.
Some addressed them outright. But her teachers
always insisted the students limit themselves to
topics appropriate to their delicate sensibilities—
nature, perhaps, or moral education.

But even nature abounded with opportunities
for allusion to romantic love—that is, until Bea's
teacher had figured out her intent, and, red-faced,
humiliated her in front of the other young ladies
who'd attended the lesson. To make matters worse,
he'd suggested the work wasn't even hers—that
she'd stolen it, copied from some other, more talented poet.

For the remainder of her time at the finishing
academy, Bea had submitted only topically-
appropriate assignments devoid of anything
deeper than surface observations.

She'd received passing marks on each, and left
the academy subdued—but not beaten.

Someone tapped on the door, and Bea heard the
butler announce, "Lady Elizabeth Bainbridge has
arrived."

A moment later, the door cracked open and
Elizabeth's crown of red hair poked through. Her
eyes widened. "Bea, is something wrong? You are

always the prompter of the two of us—and I believe Monsieur Durand was arriving just behind me."

Maeve's fingers working her hair kept Bea from shaking her head. "Nothing is wrong."

They heard the door open below, and the low murmur of male voices. Elizabeth peeked over her shoulder. "He's here!" She slipped fully into Bea's room and closed the door.

"Oh, dear." Bea's fingers fretted at the trim on her sleeves. "Do you think this gown suits?"

Elizabeth glanced up at Maeve, who was now working feverishly to pin up the rest of Bea's thick brunette hair. "You look beautiful. And I think your dear maid might stick me with a pin if I suggested you change."

Bea let out a choked laugh. "You are no help at all. E., please be a dear and entertain him while I finish getting ready?"

"Of course." Elizabeth left once again, but not without a look that told Bea they'd be discussing this later.

She took a deep breath, willing herself to relax as her thoughts drifted back to the pattern they'd held before her friend had come in. It was no crime to keep a gentleman waiting, even if it was not something she normally did.

When she'd first married, Bea had still harbored the ideal that, even if she didn't love her husband, they might develop a "lasting fondness" for one another. After all, that was the advice most young ladies received when entering into advantageous but loveless marriages. She'd hoped to build some common ground, some depth of understanding for one another.

With those hopes, she'd told Lord Pullington she was a poet. And she'd been dismissed as though she were a child.

Oh, he hadn't actively disparaged her work. He'd just never read it. He'd said, "Of course you're a poet. All young ladies are," as though she'd informed him she'd taken pianoforte lessons in school. He'd simply never considered that it might mean more to her than the standard education and "minor accomplishments" of most genteel young women. He hadn't been interested in *her.*

After that, she'd learned to keep her passion to herself.

But with Philippe, she had the sense things were different . . . that he might be someone who *could* understand. After all, what he did with a brush was the same thing she tried to do with a pen.

But Philippe Durand was famous, and she a nobody. Last fall, she'd seen one of her poems published in *The New Monthly Magazine.* Not that anyone else knew it was hers. It had taken all her courage just to send in the work anonymously. She'd known a moment of secret warmth when an acquaintance, hoping to impress her with his cultural awareness, had praised the poem during a dinner she'd attended. Even then she hadn't revealed herself as the author.

Bea's temptation to share, to tell Philippe of her work and seek that understanding between souls, was tempered by fear. If the French artist looked at her as an amateur, no different than any other woman who dabbled at the arts to pass the daylight hours, she would be devastated.

For now, perhaps, it was best to wait. Philippe was interested in her as a model, a muse. Until she knew him better, she could be content with that.

Maeve pinned the last of Bea's hair into place and adjusted the ribbon. "There, my lady. I am sorry if we kept the French monsieur waiting, but I do believe the effect is worth it."

"As do I," Bea assured her—but truthfully, keeping Philippe waiting was less about the effect of her hair, and more about not letting him know just how much effect he had on *her.*

"Lady Pullington, what a pleasure." Philippe rose as Bea finally entered the formal salon. He took two long steps to meet her, then bowed lavishly over her hand. "I declare, your beauty grows more abundant with each renewal of our acquaintance."

Bea stifled—barely—the urge to giggle and simper, managing instead a gracious smile. "And you, monsieur, are charming as always."

She thought she detected the faintest arch of Elizabeth's brow at their interaction, but then her friend simply smiled.

"Here." Philippe gestured toward the large windows, where the curtains were pulled back. "Come over where the light is best, if you will, my lady. I was just about to set out the sketches I began the other day. I have worked on them since, and while I have my thoughts, I would like to hear yours as well. It is important that my subject be pleased with the work meant to honor her, no?"

"You are too kind—I am sure an artiste of your experience needs no input from an untrained eye such as mine," Bea replied, determined to match his charm and flattery.

"*Au contraire,*" he argued, extracting a sheaf of papers from a leather satchel and spreading them across the long narrow table near the window. "I am told you have an eye for fashion—is that not, in its own way, also art?"

"Perhaps," she allowed, leaning over the papers. She forgot all about their banter at that moment, as her mind was drawn back to the rose garden at Montgrave. The sketches were rough, but the talent behind them undeniable. The images popped from the page as though living. She could see where he'd experimented with angles and perspectives, rough charcoal strokes overlapping in the quest to breathe life onto paper.

"You choose," he prompted.

"Me?"

"*Oui.*" A smile played at his lips as he watched her eyes rove over the sketches.

He stood close. Bea inhaled the male scents of leather and sandalwood. Suddenly it was difficult to concentrate, knowing he was watching her study his work. The intensity emanating from the man was just as evident in his sketches. How could so much passion be present in one human?

She straightened her shoulders, forcing herself to view the sketches with a judgmental eye.

One *did* stand out above the rest. Her paper self stood at the stone basin, an expression of delight on her face as her fingertips grazed the twigs of a tiny bird's nest, nestled in the branches of a just-budding sapling. She recalled the moment precisely—she'd been looking for the source of the broken robin's egg at the basin's bottom. She just hadn't expected Philippe's sketches to capture the occasion so completely.

The choice was clear, but Bea hesitated nonetheless in making it. What if there was something magical about one of the others that she could not see? Would her choice disappoint him? Finally she pointed. "That one," she whispered.

His smile broke out in full, and he nodded approvingly. "*Bon.* That is my favorite, too."

A bubble of pleasure, absurdly large, rose in her.

Elizabeth peered over her shoulder. "Oh, how lovely."

Philippe picked up the chosen drawing and motioned Bea to the settee. When she sat, he joined her, keeping enough distance to prevent them from "accidentally" touching, but close enough for both to study the sketch he propped on his knee.

Would she ever have the opportunity to kiss this man again?

Philippe swept a finger across the drawing, indicating the angle of light he hoped to affect in the final painting.

What had he just said? Bea bit her tongue, hard, and tried to gather her foolish thoughts back to the task at hand.

Elizabeth sat serenely, seemingly absorbed in embroidering a tiny pillowcase. Since Bea knew how much her friend despised the monotony of embroidery, this was either testimony to her joy at impending motherhood, or a sham designed to allow her to observe Bea and Philippe without seeming like an overbearing chaperone.

Could she sense the tension between them, or Bea's barely-quelled desire to touch Philippe, to scoot closer, or touch his arm as they discussed various aspects of the sketch? How obvious were they? She probably could; Elizabeth, Bea knew, was no stranger to passion.

Philippe, she did not doubt, knew exactly what she was feeling. He always seemed to know.

Fortunately, he did not press her on those feelings, as he had when they were alone. Instead, he maintained a professional focus that Bea had trouble matching.

"I would like to rework this sketch on a larger scale," the Frenchman said, "with greater detail, before setting paint to canvas."

At this, Elizabeth spoke up. "I have already informed the staff at Montgrave that you are using a site on the grounds as the setting of your next work, and that you may come and go at will. They are ever so pleased to have the notable Monsieur Durand as a regular guest, and I am certain you will find them eager to accommodate any need."

"Your Grace, you are beyond kind," Philippe declared. He turned to Bea. "I am at your disposal, Lady Pullington. I must travel briefly to Kent during the early part of the week, but should return on Thursday. I hope not to delay too long beyond that, for the season is nearly perfect to begin the full-scale work on canvas."

Bea blinked. "I am happy to oblige, Monsieur Durand, although I must consult my schedule . . ."

"Saturday?" Elizabeth suggested brightly. "I can't

think of a thing going on in town—at least during daylight hours—on Saturday, save for Lord Sidmouth's cousin's recital, and I dare say no one should be sad to miss that."

"*Oui*, perfect. If that would suit Lady Pullington?" Philippe glanced back at Bea, eyebrows raised.

"Saturday, then," she confirmed, wondering if Elizabeth's suggestion indicated her friend was once again offering the services of a companion.

Philippe took her hand as he bid her farewell— and pressed a tiny, folded square of paper into her palm. Bea's heart began to pound as she clenched her fingers around it. For the second time since meeting him, she'd received a secret note—though this time, she knew from whom. But what could the normally flamboyant Frenchman wish to tell her that he dared not say in front of Elizabeth?

Somehow, she maintained a calm façade as Philippe exited the room. She turned to Elizabeth, heart still racing as she resumed her seat and surreptitiously slipped the square of paper between the cushion and the back of the settee, praying it had escaped her friend's notice. And praying, as a second thought occurred to her, that this note was in no way related to the first, more nefarious one she'd received.

"So . . ." Elizabeth's grin was impish. "Monsieur Durand is very . . . intense, is he not? And quite taken with you."

"Oh. Well. Yes, I suppose he is quite intense . . . I cannot say about me, but he pursues his *art* with great passion."

"Great passion, hmm?"

Flames engulfed Bea's neck and face, but it was too late to take back the revealing words.

"Oh, Bea, you know I will not judge. You remember better than anyone how much trouble I was in before Alex and I were married. If he pleases you, let him pursue you—I've no doubt he will anyway. And you deserve to have some fun. You've been a dutiful wife and a respectable widow long enough."

It was true—Elizabeth had broken nearly every rule of propriety, including running from home, hiding from her family, and taking Alex as a lover— though only Bea knew that this last was true. It had taken every ounce of her friends' and family's influence, and London's respect and fear of the duke, to put her back in Society's good graces. Bea wasn't ready to go quite *that* far . . . But Elizabeth was right. She *was* ready to have some fun.

"Some chaperone you are," Bea teased.

"Me?" Elizabeth placed a hand on her hip, mocking the expression of one offended. "I've no intention of playing at chaperone, my dear friend. I'm playing at matchmaker."

Bea stifled a groan. Heaven help her now.

Chapter 7

By the time Beatrice was finally able to retrieve Philippe's note from where she'd crammed it into the settee, her heart had near worn itself out from nervous fluttering. She unfolded the little square, her fingers clumsy in haste.

Dearest Beatrice,

Lord and Lady Wilbourne have graciously offered me the use of two seats in their theater box at the Royal Haymarket this Friday evening. Love Laughs at Locksmiths *is playing—a comic opera that I am told is quite enjoyable. I plan to attend, and would like very much if you would consent to accompany me. If you are amenable, I shall send a carriage for you prior to the show.*

Veuillez agréer, Madame, l'assurance de mes sentiments distingués,

Philippe

Bea twirled in a circle, and just barely stifled the urge to jump for joy. He wanted to see her again!

Just for herself, not anything to do with his work. She hurried over to the desk drawer where she'd stashed the first note he'd sent. Then, he'd addressed her formally. Not so now.

Under Philippe's note lay the more sinister, coded message the spies had used. She couldn't wait to be rid of it. She pulled it out as well, heart thudding as she laid it side by side with the letters from Philippe. She had to be sure.

The handwriting was not a match.

Her smile stretched wider, and she snatched up a pen and paper to answer the charismatic Frenchman in the affirmative.

If Alex Bainbridge found it odd that Lady Beatrice Pullington and his sister-in-law, Charity, requested a meeting with him outside the presence of his wife, he kept his thoughts to himself.

That is, until Bea explained that no, she and Charity were *not* there to conspire with him about a surprise celebration of Elizabeth's impending motherhood. Indeed, they were there to discuss a conspiracy of a very different sort. Bea told him what had happened at Vauxhall Gardens.

"You did *what*?" His dark brows drew together and he stood, the massive oak desk in his study forming an imposing barrier between himself and the two women. "With *Charity*?"

Bea suppressed the urge to shiver at his tone. Most often she thought of Alex Bainbridge as the duke who loved her best friend to distraction, but now his expression reminded her that to many, he was a ruthless and powerful man, feared in business and politics. "I'm truly sorry. Had I thought it anything more than a harmless adventure, I'd never have brought Charity."

"But you'd have gone yourself?" he demanded.

Bea lifted her chin. If the duke sensed his prey was weak, he would eat her alive. She couldn't allow that to happen. Instead, she summoned her sauciest look and replied, "Your Grace, the last time I checked, I do not answer to you for my own actions."

She held her breath. The response bordered on disrespectful, but she'd rather be defiant than dismissed.

He sighed. "No wonder you and my wife are such close friends. All right, never mind. The important question is what we do now."

"Exactly." Bea smiled.

Alex eyed the note she'd turned over to him when she and Charity had first arrived. "I read French well enough, but I have to commend you on deciphering the hidden message here. How did you do it?"

Bea shrugged. "It arrived under unusual circumstances, so my curiosity was naturally aroused. I surmised there had to be more than what I read on the surface. I have always loved to read and interpret poetry—this was not so different." Bea carefully omitted the fact that her passion for poems extended to authorship . . . what mattered here was her ability to *interpret* words, not write them.

"Poetry? Interesting." He set down the note. "About this gathering you observed—I assume you did not recognize either man?"

"No," the two women answered in unison.

"What did they look like?"

Bea thought. "It was dark, and their clothing

was nondescript—intentionally so, I would say. One was short, not much taller than me. The other, more average."

"Their faces?" the duke prompted. "Any detail, no matter how slight, could prove useful."

Bea held out her hands apologetically. "Their hats were pulled low."

"The shorter one had a beakish nose," Charity put in.

Alex perked up, glancing between Bea and Charity. "Could you draw them?"

"I am a poet, not an artist," Bea said—then sucked in a breath as she realized she'd just admitted to *being* a poet, not just an admirer of poetry.

"I can," Charity offered, distracting Alex and saving Bea from further explanation. "I'm no Philippe Durand, but I have a steady hand. And it will make me feel useful, instead of just dragged along. Only Bea could have interpreted that note, and my skills at French are too weak to translate exactly what transpired, but I *do* remember what those men looked like."

"Good. When you've sketched them out, and Beatrice has written as much of their conversation as she can recall, we will take all of this to Castlereagh."

"The *head* of the Foreign Office?" Bea worried aloud. "What if all this comes to nothing? I've no wish to appear a fool in front of Viscount Castlereagh. Do you know of anyone in a lower office who handles this sort of thing?"

Alex gave an amused grunt. "This may come as a surprise to you, Bea, but I have no previous dealings in espionage. I have no idea how far this network of French spies extends, or what offices they may have infiltrated. I do, however, know Castlereagh, and have reasonable confidence that he will handle the matter appropriately. He has worked ceaselessly, particularly this past year, to bring the Congress of Vienna together and bring peace to Europe."

"I see, and I apologize."

"No matter," Alex replied. "Ladies, I trust you understand the seriousness of this matter. Napoleon's return has thrown all of Europe into turmoil. If this note, and this meeting you observed, are indeed related to the rogue Emperor's campaign, we cannot afford to dally. Charity, can you complete those drawings this afternoon?"

"Yes, absolutely," she told him.

"Good. I'll have to ask a few questions, but I want you both to be prepared to meet at the Foreign Office on the morrow. Bea, you may have stumbled upon something that could affect the very future of our country."

Richard Durand had never been plagued by guilt. But now, more than ever, he was convinced he was doing the right thing. He tapped his foot as he awaited the messenger from London. When he'd envisioned climbing the ladder of success—or at least following Napoleon Bonaparte as he did so— Richard had never thought to spend this much time in dark alleys and dirty cafés.

Tonight's meeting location was in an alley behind an apothecary. Richard shifted uncomfortably at the sound of rats scuttling in the darkness, gnawing on garbage.

But the discomfort was worth it. Just look how

the armies of France had rallied at the Emperor's return. The people held no love for Louis XVIII . . . where were the King's followers now?

He shook his head. Would Bonaparte's charisma be enough, when his supporters were faced with a coalition army of 600,000?

In truth, the numbers would be fewer. The Austrians and the Russians had further to travel and posed no immediate threat, though if France survived the first wave of the coalition, they would eventually have to deal with these other armies. England, Richard's sources informed him, was offering in funds what they could not supply in trained soldiers.

Nonetheless, the threat was grave. Louis XVIII had allowed the French army to deteriorate. Less than 60,000 soldiers had remained by the time the Emperor had returned. Many more had enlisted in the short weeks since then, but Napoleon would need a great many more men beyond the current levels to ensure success.

Unfortunately, Richard's plan to help him was not proceeding smoothly. There was no time for error—and yet a key informant had missed their last meeting.

The man Richard had waited for sidled up in the darkness: André Denis—or whatever name he was using these days. Richard identified him by the cigar he kept habitually clamped in the convenient gap where two teeth had been knocked from his mouth in a long-ago fistfight.

"What did you find out?"

"We contacted her. She never received the summons."

A partial relief—their informant hadn't turned

against them, or been caught. Still, they'd been careless. "How is that possible?"

André swallowed. "We believe the message, ah, went astray, though our man swears he placed it in the designated location."

"Pardon?"

"It is possible he identified her garment—the note was to be pinned inside—incorrectly. But, monsieur, there is little danger. The message was not intentionally intercepted, simply misdelivered. And because it was in code, there is little chance whoever ended up with it had any idea of what they received, assuming they noticed it at all."

Richard was not reassured. "Loose ends are what nooses are made from—and I've no desire to hang." He paused, letting the words sink in. "Do you know for certain in whose hands the missive ended up?"

"No."

"The plan was specific. Is there a chance the misplacement was intentional?"

"No," André declared. "Peters is not intelligent enough to act as a double agent."

Having never met the man, Richard could only take Denis's word. As much as he hated having only secondhand knowledge, it was prudent, for now, to remain behind the scenes—a puppeteer controlling the marionettes' actions, but ready to cut the strings—or tighten them into a noose—if need be.

"It is essential we trace that note. Your people know who attended the salon that evening. Whose cloak was a close enough match to have been mistaken for that of our contact?"

"That was two weeks ago," his man protested.

Richard gave him an icy glare. "I care not if it was two years ago. Figure it out."

Family dinners at the Russell home were a weekly affair, one Bea usually attended with little fanfare. But this week, it seemed everyone's focus was on her.

"How goes the painting?" her sister, Sarah, asked. She gestured to their mother and her other two sisters. "We are all ever so jealous."

"Very well. Monsieur Durand has done several sketches and hopes to begin on canvas soon. He is very . . . thorough." Bea hoped the lighting was dim enough that no one would notice the telltale flush creeping up her neck.

"Has he a studio here in town, then?" Sarah asked.

"I don't believe so. We chose a site on Montgrave as the painting's setting. An old garden, ever so lovely. When Monsieur Durand begins work in earnest, I imagine most of our time will be spent there."

"Lady Bainbridge is in residence?" her mother asked. "Why would she choose to stay in the country during the height of the Season?"

"Ah, no."

Lady Russell's eyes bulged. "You cannot go out there alone," she declared. "Here in town it is one thing, but—"

Bea suppressed a sigh. "I have no intention of going to Montgrave alone."

Lady Russell ceased bristling, though still she sat with arched brows, awaiting an explanation.

"I have in mind a paid companion."

Bea was spared the necessity of elaborating on the merits of this nonexistent good woman, for her father cleared his throat. "Beatrice, I'm not certain this is the best time to involve yourself with anyone French."

Bea bit her lip. Thank goodness her father was referring only to Philippe—and that he had no idea how "involved" she was in French matters far more weighty than a single kiss. If he knew of her escapade at Vauxhall, or the note she'd turned over to Alex Bainbridge, he'd likely convince her mother and sisters to move in with her—guaranteeing Bea would never again have a private moment, let alone get to know Philippe.

She said only, "Monsieur Durand is an artiste, Father, and far removed from such political matters."

"Perhaps, but what of his family?"

"His mother has passed on." Bea shrugged. "I know little of his other relatives."

"An inquiry might not be without merit. These are tricky times. Already the Duke of Wellington is mustering his forces, and Parliament has committed a hefty portion of England's coffers to defeating General Bonaparte. England's position is clear, and it is essential that we support our country."

"Papa, Bea is only posing for a portrait," Sarah pointed out.

Bea did her best not to squirm, praying her father would not find out she was scheduled to meet with the head of the Foreign Office the very next day.

Lord Pullington heaved a sigh. As head of a houseful of women, he was no stranger to their pleadings. "True. All I'm suggesting, Beatrice, is caution. You've always been a responsible girl. You'll do the right thing."

* * *

Lord Henry Owen's home in Kent was stately, but not imposing. His butler was the same. Philippe had been able to secure the nobleman's country address with relative ease—Owen was a recluse, it seemed, but not in hiding. As to his alter ego, the elusive artist Henri Gaudet, Philippe did not yet know what to think.

He'd gotten so caught up in his desire to paint Beatrice Pullington—not to mention his desire *for* that same lady—he'd neglected his original purpose in traveling to England. That is, until guilt had finally gotten the better of him. It was bad form to take a deathbed promise lightly.

Philippe waited now in a drawing room with deep burgundy walls, whose color was nearly obscured by the many paintings and bookshelves lining the walls. A pianoforte stood in one corner, collecting dust. A comfortable room, though devoid of a woman's touch.

Philippe turned toward the large fireplace, lit to ward off the spring chill, then sucked in a breath at the painting hanging above the mantel.

A pair of young lovers walking on a Paris street. Standard fare for every aspiring painter.

Except that *this* was the work of a master. The couple's features were beautifully rendered, the glow of their affection evident in each detail, down to the possessive rest of the man's hand at the small of his lover's back.

Philippe studied the work, absorbed in each brushstroke, until he heard the soft pad of footfalls on thick carpet behind him. He turned.

An older man, tall but leaning lightly on a polished cane, stood a few feet back, his gaze trained on the same spot Philippe's had been a moment ago. Lord Owen.

Philippe cleared his throat, nodded toward the painting. "One of yours."

"Mine?"

"I'd recognize a Gaudet anywhere."

"Ah, I understand. As would I. Yes, that particular painting is a favorite."

Philippe belatedly remembered his manners. "Forgive me, my lord. I am Jean Philippe Durand."

"Yes." Lord Owen nodded. "I understand you are an artiste as well. I saw mention of your arrival in the papers. I had not anticipated the opportunity to meet you, as I rarely travel to London. Although, if this situation with France worsens, it may be prudent to return to Parliament."

"*Oui,* I am an artiste. Painting is my profession, and my passion."

"A pleasure, then, to welcome you into my home." The English lord adjusted his grip on his cane.

Philippe sensed his underlying questions, but admired his restraint in not asking.

The two men paused in silent accord, returning their gaze to the painting above the mantel. A servant entered, set a tea tray on a table, and left unobtrusively.

Now that he was here, Philippe, too, felt no hurry to confront the deeper matters that had brought him to England. Instead he examined the remainder of the room more closely. It was well furnished, and he recognized the work of several artists, but no piece drew his eye like the one before him. He indicated it. "Are there others?"

"No. Unfortunately, the one above the mantel is the only one I have."

Surprise made Philippe turn to face the older man. "You have only one of your own works? How can that be?"

"My own?" An odd expression flickered across his features. "No, I'm afraid you're mistaken. I've not wielded a paintbrush since I was a lad in the schoolroom."

Philippe took an uncertain step back, glancing once more at the Gaudet hanging above the hearth. Had all this been for naught? Disappointment flooded him. "I am sorry. My mother told me . . . but perhaps she was mistaken. Her last months were not kind to her body or mind."

The old man's keen blue stare fixed on him. "Who is your mother?"

"Solange Durand. Her maiden name was La-Claire."

"Solange." Lord Owen breathed the word, almost reverently, as a visible change overcame him, and he moved unsteadily for a large chair at the edge of the carpet.

Philippe's spine prickled. "You knew her."

"Oh, yes." The man paused, lowered himself into his seat. "Yes, I knew her. Your mother was the only woman I ever truly loved."

Philippe swallowed. How did one respond to such a declaration?

The older man nodded. "I wondered, of course, what would bring a well-known *artiste* such as yourself to my remote home. Now I begin to understand."

"I fear I cannot say the same." Why, after thirty years, would his mother suddenly find it so crucial for him to meet this man—so crucial she would concoct a lie connecting him to Gaudet? How many lies had there been? What had she hoped to accomplish? A happy or tearful reunion? But one could not reunite two people who had never met.

"I know what you're thinking." Lord Owen spoke. "If I so loved your mother, why did I not remain with her?" He shook his head. "I have no good reason, beyond the foolishness of youth." Pain, regret, thickened his voice.

Philippe moved awkwardly to a chair across from the one Lord Owen occupied. "You owe me no explanation."

"Perhaps I do." Lord Owen studied him intently. "I am old, but not yet blind. I see the blueness of your eyes gazing back at me. That and the fact Solange sent you here . . . it is enough."

He tipped back his head to rest against the chair and closed his eyes. "Oh, Solange." It was a cry, rendered from somewhere deep and painful.

Philippe sat in silence, allowing the man whatever time he needed. Finally Lord Owen opened his eyes and leaned forward. "You are my son, are you not?"

"*Oui*, my lord. I believe I am," he answered quietly. "I did not know either, until shortly before my mother's death."

The Englishman gave a harsh laugh. "There's no one who can keep a secret like a woman. And Solange was more than just a woman."

"My lord?"

"Monsieur Durand . . . may I call you Philippe?"

"*Évidemment.*" Given the intimate nature of their

conversation, it seemed foolish to insist they stand on ceremony.

"How well did you know your mother?"

Philippe didn't know whether to be offended. "She was closer to me than anyone. I was her only child. She doted on me."

Lord Owen smiled. "I've no doubt she knew you. But did *you* know her? Do you know why she sent you here?"

Philippe knew what he was getting at. It was the same sensation he'd felt when she'd first told him to come to England. "I know she had her secrets. I admit I was angry, unsettled when she told me, but I believe I understand why. It seems the circumstances of my birth were . . . unconventional." Philippe had never been shy, but even he found it awkward to speak of such matters to a man he'd just met—no matter how intimately involved in those matters that man had been.

"Yes. There is that." Lord Owen paused, rubbing his chin as though deciding on something. "I suppose I owe you an apology. For a grave offense, though one I did not realize I had committed."

Philippe waved a hand. "A matter long since past. And not one that has hindered me."

"Not you, perhaps. But most certainly one that affected Solange, and for that, the depth of my regret is immeasurable." He swallowed visibly. "I'd heard that she married, soon after we . . . soon after I left. I took that as confirmation of my decision, as evidence that I had not, after all, meant so much to her. Now I understand her decision in a very different light."

Shame filled Philippe for his selfishness. When

his mother had revealed his true parentage, he realized he'd thought only of himself. He'd never considered his mother's difficult position—though he'd always wondered how she'd come to be paired with Richard Durand, the remote and ambitious man he'd known as a father. "She must have been frightened."

"Frightened," Lord Owen confirmed, "and anxious to prove herself worthy of an advantageous marriage—an offer I failed to make to her, believing the difference in our class too great. I inherited my title rather suddenly, upon my brother's death, and my determination to live up to his memory included the misguided notion that I must marry someone of similar social standing.

"Durand, for all his ambition, recognized what I did not—that Solange's beauty, her *talent*, were of far greater importance than her family's circumstances."

"Her talent?" Philippe asked. "I know she took pride in hosting my father's—or stepfather's, that is—many guests." But there was something in the way the older man across from him had emphasized the word "talent" that went beyond the duties of a good hostess.

"A responsibility I imagine she handled with grace. True, Durand forced her to channel that talent for his own purposes. A terrible loss to the world of art."

"My lord?"

The old man closed his eyes and rubbed his temples. Finally he opened his eyes. Leaning forward, he met Philippe's gaze with an intensity that chilled him.

"Solange sent you here, to me, no? From that I can only surmise that she wanted you to know—though why she preferred I do the telling, I cannot guess. Clearly," he eyed Philippe, "I am missing large parts of the tale.

"In spite of the fact that it was I who left Solange, I could not simply let go of the passion we'd shared. Could not let go of *her.* For some time I kept track of her. I stopped when I learned she had given up painting."

Philippe was glad he was sitting, or the flood of understanding might have swept him away. "Gaudet," he breathed.

"Yes."

"Mon Dieu."

Lord Owen glanced at the teapot, now grown cold. "The hour is early, but I believe I need something stronger than tea. You will forgive me if I pour a brandy?"

"If you pour me one as well."

He chuckled and reached for the decanter.

Philippe tossed back his first drink with nary a thought to its fine quality. Was there no end to his mother's deceit? He hadn't known her at all. Certain things made sense, though . . . the way she'd helped him learn things like perspective when he first began to paint, or the connections she'd used to help him gain recognition as he grew older. He'd simply attributed such things to a keen eye and years of social and political acquaintances gathered as the wife of Richard Durand. Hah.

Lord Owen poured him a second brandy, then placed the stopper back in the decanter. "Although I can hardly claim any fatherly responsibility, I would like to continue our acquaintance, if you are agreeable. It seems we have much to discuss, though I think enough has been said for one morning."

"*Bien sûr.*" Of course. How else was he to learn about the life of the artist he'd long admired, now that she'd passed on? Henry Owen, he sensed, was not a man who hurried things.

"How long do you intend to remain in England?" Lord Owen asked.

"I had intended only a short visit, but I have begun a new work and must extend my stay."

"A new painting?"

"*Oui.* The subject, and the setting, are English."

"A woman," the old man said sagely. "Your eyes grow softer at the mention of this new subject."

Perceptive old man. "*Oui,* a woman," Philippe confirmed. As for his eyes growing soft, well, he felt a certain attachment to all his subjects—why else expend the effort to capture them in art? Except that he'd *kissed* Beatrice Pullington. Thoroughly enough to learn that his proper English widow kissed with searing intensity. And that it frightened her. Intriguing.

Lord Owen, thankfully, let the matter drop. He looked at Philippe again and shook his head. "A son," he murmured, his head lowering. "If only I had known."

"It's not your fault."

Lord Owen looked up sharply. "It most certainly *is.* I cannot make amends with Solange. But know this: I shall do my utmost to find a way to make it up to you."

Chapter 8

"You are in luck, Monsieur Durand."

"Oui?" Richard raised an eyebrow.

André Denis nodded. "We have a strong lead on the information you requested. Some days had passed since the salon featuring your son's paintings, and we nearly despaired of finding anyone who recalled which other ladies might have worn a pink pelisse that evening—especially without knowing why we were asking the question, which, of course, we could not reveal."

Patience was a virtue—and information was power. As much as Richard wished his lead operative would hurry up and provide a name, he understood the value in having the complete picture. André's vast network of shadowy connections had proven useful more than once over the years.

Richard squirmed as he waited. The stench of ale, fish, and unwashed sailors permeated the tavern near the docks. He'd attempted to dress the part, but it was André, with the gap in his teeth and two-day-old beard, who appeared right at home.

"As luck would have it," the other man finally continued, "the actions of your son led us to our answer, though he may not know it. At the salon, Philippe took the extraordinary step of singling out one guest, a woman, and asking permission to paint her. This, of course, drew the attention of the other guests to the woman in question—a woman who was reportedly wearing a rose-colored gown."

He propped his elbows on the rough table and pressed his fingertips together, satisfaction in his tone. "Her name is Lady Beatrice Pullington. English. A bit of research into Lady Pullington reveals her as a woman who is always fashionable and polished. It is entirely reasonable to presume her outer garment that evening matched the hue of her gown."

"Was she the only one?"

André rubbed a thumb along the stubble at his chin. "It's possible there were others, monsieur. The salon was well-attended. But Lady Pullington is of similar size to our agent."

"How are you planning to handle this?" If Lady Pullington was a member of Society, she could not merely be threatened—or made to disappear.

"Future communications among our people will be handled with the utmost care. As for Lady Pullington, we've set a watch on her. If she mentions the note to anyone, or behaves in any suspicious manner, we'll know."

"I am not a spy," Bea protested.

Robert Stewart, Viscount Castlereagh, arched a brow. "Perhaps not one in the official employ of the

British government. But you were, in fact, spying. And doing a rather fine job of it."

"Oh."

"It's all right, Lady Pullington. You are a rather intrepid woman, and I cannot say I'd approve of such risk-taking in general, but you did the right thing in bringing this information here. We are grateful to have it."

Bea stiffened at the combination of compliment and chastisement. Darn Elizabeth's husband for leaving her in here alone.

Alex and Charity had accompanied her to see the Foreign Secretary. Bea had relayed their story, and Charity had confirmed it, offering up her sketches. As soon as Charity had presented her piece, the duke had escorted her out, saying, "I'll not take Miss Medford's involvement in this matter any further."

He'd made no such offer to spare Bea—but then, Bea reminded herself as she fidgeted, she *had* made a point to Alex that she did not answer to him. She could not fault him now for respecting that.

The viscount looked again at Bea's now-crumpled note. He frowned. "These men may be working on Napoleon's behalf," he mused, "but they are taking direction from someone else. We've intercepted many of Napoleon's communications during previous engagements. Usually, his ciphers are far more complex, mathematical in nature."

Bea gave a questioning shrug, unable to offer any insight to a matter where the Foreign Secretary clearly knew more than she.

"Tell me again how you came by the note," the

viscount requested. "The duke said it was some sort of art salon?"

"Yes, a salon hosted by Lord Robert and Lady Alicia Wilbourne, in honor of the French artiste Jean Philippe Durand," Bea confirmed.

The viscount bent his head as his pen scratched across a sheet of paper. Bea strained to read his scrawl upside down. *Lord and Lady Wilbourne. Msr. Jean Philippe Durand.* A list of names.

"Are you going to question them?" Bea asked.

"No. We don't want to alert them, yet, to what we know—just in case." He sat back. "We will watch them. If they are involved, we may gain valuable information as to how they operate—and for whom they work—before we shut them down."

Bea couldn't imagine that her friends the Wilbournes, or Philippe, for that matter, would knowingly engage in such activities. Defending Philippe on such short acquaintance was perhaps a stretch, but loyalty compelled her to at least speak on behalf of the couple. "Lord Castlereagh, it is simply unthinkable to me to hold the Wilbournes under such suspicion."

"You may be correct, but we must remain open to all possibilities. Your friends did, after all, take an extended trip to France last year. If nothing else, we know that whoever placed that note had access to the Wilbournes' cloakroom during the salon."

"What about these men?" Bea indicated the sketches Charity had drawn.

"I'll deliver the drawings to our intelligence office to see if they match any records of known or suspected foreign agents. We'll also share the images with our own agents on duty in London. If

Miss Medford's depictions are accurate, there is a reasonable chance we will locate them."

"It seems awfully little to go on. And Phili—that is, Monsieur Durand and the Wilbournes—how will you watch them without them knowing?"

Viscount Castlereagh pressed the tips of his fingers together. "Well, my dear, given your penchant for investigative work, and your unique tie to both the Frenchman and the Wilbournes, it seems *you* are in the best position to find out what we need to know."

Richard almost passed by the disheveled drunk propped against the back wall of the smoky tavern. That is, until he heard the tune the man hummed, barely audible above the clank of glasses and the low rumble of other patrons' conversation. It was the right tune. One whose revolutionary associations made it an unlikely choice in these parts, unless the man were truly drunk. Or unless he was waiting to speak to Richard.

Richard slid onto the bench across from the drunk, whose clear eyes and shrewdly assessing look testified to the farce of his appearance. An unfamiliar messenger tonight, but he'd expected that. André Denis had returned to England to monitor the progress of their plan more closely.

Richard did not ask the new man's name. He only waved a hand, indicating the messenger should proceed.

"I have good news, and bad."

Richard waited, though not patiently. Rain had driven them indoors this evening, and he was anxious to leave the smoky tavern before he was recognized. Though perhaps his fear of recognition was an unnecessary conceit. Having spent so much of his career in the shadow of those greater than he, the chance of someone knowing his face was slim.

"Lady Pullington was seen entering the building that houses the British Foreign Office this morning. The good news is, this strongly indicates she was indeed the recipient of the missive that went astray. The man watching her has not been wasting his time."

"You mentioned bad news?"

"If she's meeting with the Foreign Office, she must have broken the code."

Merde. Richard had known it wasn't the most secure method, but time was of the essence— they'd needed to pass messages quickly, and he'd believed the references vague enough that *if* a message should fall into the wrong hands, the reader would quickly dismiss it. Of course, Lady Pullington hadn't exactly stumbled across the note—finding it pinned in her coat would naturally arouse her curiosity. It was just their bad luck she'd been intelligent enough to figure out what she was looking at.

"Two people accompanied Lady Pullington to the Foreign Office," the messenger added. "A man—the Duke of Beaufort, we believe—and another young lady."

"Their involvement?"

"No known involvement—though we will continue to monitor the situation. For now, whatever the duke and the young lady know has most likely come from Lady Pullington."

"I see. How much does *she* know?" Richard asked.

If the lady was savvy enough to decipher their message, *and* take it to the British government, they could not afford to discount her as a threat.

"I cannot say for sure."

"We need to find out."

"Of course."

"Bea, you simply must tell me what happened with the Foreign Secretary," Charity pled.

She and Elizabeth were having tea at Bea's home. The moment Elizabeth had excused herself to make use of the retiring room, Charity had seized the opportunity, rounding on Bea with the zeal of a cat about to sink its claws into juicy prey.

"Alex wouldn't say a word after pulling me from the room," Charity complained. "My family's inclination to protect me like a child means I am always left out of the choicest bits of intrigue." She blew a stray strand of hair from her face. "It is ever so aggravating."

As tempting as it was to confide in someone, Bea knew the duke had removed his headstrong young sister-in-law from that meeting for a reason. "In truth, you heard most of it, Charity. After all, you were at both the salon and the gardens with me. Viscount Castlereagh asked me to go over the details once more, took a few additional notes, and that was it."

Charity cocked her head. "He didn't share his thoughts with you? What did he think those men were after? Did he mention any names?" she prompted.

"You are incorrigible." She really *ought* to be

more disapproving of Charity's antics. But the younger woman's enthusiasm was so infectious, Bea found herself laughing alongside her. "I suppose you already know that. No, he did not reveal any suspicions—if anything, I think he wanted to gather more information before acting. He did ask that if we think of any missed detail, or happen upon any other relevant information, we report it immediately. Beyond that, the matter is now in capable hands." There. What she'd said was true—she just didn't need to tell Charity that those "capable hands" included her own.

But Charity was not dissuaded. A thoughtful gleam lit her eye. "And where do you think we might 'happen upon any other relevant information?' Any ideas?"

Bea rolled her eyes. "No. Alex would have both our heads if we thought to pull another stunt like last week's. Charity, it's the middle of the Season. Why aren't you off with your friends, chattering about fashion plates and eligible bachelors?"

"Why aren't *you*?" Charity shot back. "You are just as eligible as I." She shrugged. "I do enjoy balls and such, though they promise little more than an evening's entertainment. You and Elizabeth, though, lead much more interesting lives."

"You are too fanciful," Bea protested. "You've known me for years. When, before these last two weeks, have you ever thought my life interesting?"

"Hmm." Charity appeared to give the matter consideration. "Lady Beatrice Pullington, respected member of the ton, a young widow who lives quietly—if unusually—alone. It is true I would not have looked beyond that until recently. But now that I have, Bea, I'm beginning to think you had us all fooled."

"Fanciful," Bea repeated, though she couldn't help but smile. "I'll be returning to Montgrave soon, to pose for Monsieur Durand. Do us all a favor while I'm gone, Charity, please? Don't go looking for further trouble."

Bea's fingers trembled as she clasped a sapphire necklace around her throat. Maeve had pinned her hair into a mass of curls at the crown of her head, leaving her neck and décolletage exposed by the low cut of her deep blue silk gown. Silver embroidery sparkled in a band just below her bosom, and again at the gown's hem.

She always dressed to suit the current fashion— but tonight was the first time in years she could recall dressing to suit a man.

Would Philippe notice? Compared to the Parisian fashions worn by the ladies of his acquaintance, her attire was nothing remarkable.

Bea lifted her chin. Those others mattered not. *She* was the one who held his interest now. She just had to be witty and urbane enough to keep it.

And in case that wasn't enough of a challenge, there was one other small matter—making sure the Frenchman never learned that every moment she spent attempting to charm him was also a moment spent spying on him.

Bea swallowed the bubble of hysterical laughter rising in her throat. What had she been thinking, to agree to Viscount Castlereagh's plan? She couldn't do this. Everyone would see right through her—or if not everyone, Philippe most certainly would.

But the artist had—unknowingly, she hoped—provided her the perfect opportunity to do the Foreign Secretary's bidding. When she attended the theater this evening, she could observe both the Wilbournes and Philippe.

She was confused enough about her feelings toward the French artist without having to question his every move. Did he have an ulterior motive beyond the one she already suspected—beyond, that is, seducing her? If he did, could she keep her wits about her enough to discern that motive?

If he kissed her again, it would take every ounce of rationality Bea possessed to remember her duty to England.

Oh, lord. She really was a spy now. Charity would have gleefully jumped at this chance—which was probably why the duke had pulled her away from the meeting with the Foreign Secretary before the idea occurred to her.

She arranged a silky shawl around her shoulders. The evening was warm enough to leave heavier coats behind. She took one last glance in the mirror. Ready.

Philippe was due to arrive any minute. She wouldn't add insult to injury—not that he would know—by keeping him waiting.

To Bea, the idea of spying on people she knew and liked held an undercurrent of disloyalty. Whatever faults she might have, she'd always considered herself a steadfast friend. She prayed her observations would quickly prove them all innocent. Then the pursuit of the men she'd seen at Vauxhall Gardens could be left to those trained in such business.

Bea was nearly certain it was not the Wilbournes themselves, but one of their servants who was involved—who else would have had access to pin the note into her pelisse the night of the art salon? It would have drawn far too much notice for the lord or lady hosting the event to go poking around the coat room. Perhaps he was even one of the men she'd seen that night at Vauxhall. But she was not familiar enough with the Wilbournes' staff to match the faces she'd seen with a name or position.

Philippe's carriage arrived, plain black but well-appointed. She saw it from the window and, though her heart leapt with the urge to run and meet him, she managed to wait just long enough to be seemly—but not a second more. Bea stepped out to the waiting vehicle and allowed the footman to assist her up.

She sensed him before she saw him in the dim light. For a moment he said nothing as she took a seat and the door closed. Slowly her vision adjusted to the shadows.

"Beatrice," he finally greeted her, and she thought she heard a thousand meanings in the one word.

"Philippe."

His eyes, blue even in the darkness, mesmerized her. He reached across the carriage to take her hand.

"I would have come to the door, you know." He sounded amused.

She would carry out her duty to England. Later. Now, she was going to kiss Jean Philippe Durand. He appeared to share her need, for the moment the carriage wheels set in motion, his grip on her hand tightened and he hauled her across the space separating them. A gasp of startled laughter escaped her as she landed half on his lap, half on the seat beside him.

But her laughter faded a second later as his mouth fused to hers.

Yes, oh, yes. She'd longed for this since that afternoon at Montgrave.

She kissed him back, her lips parting willingly beneath the pressure from his. Her hands gripped his shoulders, clinging to him for balance amidst the sensations swarming her.

His tongue dipped in to explore. A little sound of need escaped her as she touched her own tongue to his, desperate to make him feel the same pleasure he offered her.

The kiss exploded. He plundered her mouth, stroking over and over, harder, faster. Bea matched him stroke for stroke, reveling in his taste, his touch, as he tipped her backward until she was half-lying on the seat, Philippe above her, their torsos pressed intimately.

Still she craved more of this heady sensation she'd read of in poems, yet lived so long without. She arched her back, seeking, and heard the Frenchman groan. He tore his lips from hers to trail kisses down her throat, her collarbone, until he reached the swell of her breasts above her gown. One hand slid up to cup her breast as he pressed a slow kiss to the top.

Oh . . . *oh*. Pleasure flooded her. Never had anyone kissed her like this, as though they could continue until all reason was abandoned.

Bea twisted, needing, and was rewarded as his thumb brushed over the crest of her breast, stroking as her nipple beaded and strained against the fabric of her gown. He tugged at the already low neckline, finally finding the hook that loosened the bodice enough to bare her chest. She shivered at the sudden sensation of exposure, but then his lips replaced his fingers, closing around her nipple, suckling. He used his mouth to tug, gently, and Bea cried out as pleasure streaked down her core and she arched further, pressing into his mouth for more.

His hips rocked against hers, startling her from her haze of pleasure as she registered Philippe's arousal. She knew what came next—she'd been married. And while her friend Elizabeth had tried to convince her that intimate relations could be pleasurable, Bea, knowing only the experience of her own marriage, remained unconvinced.

But tonight those old memories did not matter. She and Philippe would be at the theater in minutes. There was little threat of their kisses, however impassioned, going too far.

Philippe lifted his head, sensing her hesitation. "Are you all right, *chérie*?"

Bea relaxed. "I'm fine," she told him, and pulled his head down to begin the kiss anew.

Philippe grinned. Beatrice had not been entirely successful in her efforts to restore order to her hair and gown before they entered the theater. She looked delightful. Doubtless she'd be mortified if she'd witnessed the exchange of glances he'd shared with Lord Wilbourne upon their arrival.

Thankfully, the other man was too well-mannered to draw attention to her state of disarray, and Beatrice remained blissfully unaware.

The Wilbournes led them to their box, and Philippe settled Bea into one of the plush seats before taking the one next to her, the married couple on his other side.

Beatrice leaned across to address the Wilbournes, and Philippe stifled the urge to pull her into his lap once more.

"It is very kind of you to offer these seats to Monsieur Durand and I," she said.

"Our pleasure, of course," Alicia Wilbourne answered. "Theater is so much more enjoyable when one attends with friends." She shot Philippe what he would have sworn was a conspiratorial glance, then lifted her opera glasses to innocently survey the audience.

"It is especially enjoyable," Philippe joked, eyeing Robert Wilbourne, "when one is attempting to appease one's guilt after badly fleecing the friend in question at cards."

Robert laughed. At Bea's inquisitive look, Philippe confided, "I am a terrible player."

"Really?" Bea smiled, openly curious. "Most games are simply a matter of strategy, proper counting. And luck, of course."

Philippe shrugged. "I lose focus. I would far rather analyze the features of my partner . . ." He let his gaze fall to her lips. He heard the slightest catch in her breath before he gave her a wink and continued, "Or wonder just what blend of dyes was used to color the silk of his waistcoat, than attempt to calculate the value of the cards he might be holding."

"You *are* bad at cards. How fascinating—the august artiste is human after all." She laughed, casting him a sideways glance—flirtatious, with a mere hint of her usual shyness.

He returned her smile, the rest of his body responding to her in ways he hoped were less obvious. "Who ever said I wasn't human?"

Moments later, the curtains separated and the stage lamps lit as the orchestra launched into the overture. The players took their places, and the drama began to unfold. Beside him, Beatrice smiled.

He'd hoped to ease her nerves tonight by taking her to a purely social event where, unlike their previous encounters, she was not an object of scrutiny. Not that he'd been disappointed in their earlier meetings, but he sensed so much more potential in his chosen muse, if only she would open up to him. If the carriage ride to the theater—or her easy laughter at discovering that his talent did not extend to the card table—were any indication, the plan was already working.

Though he'd sensed a moment of hesitation in the carriage, Bea had not closed up, not shown the same bewildered trepidation as when they'd first kissed in the rose garden.

The theater served as a distraction for him as well, for he'd not yet sorted out the things he'd learned from Lord Owen. It was too great a betrayal to believe that his mother, his closest confidante, had kept from him a secret so great—especially knowing the desperation with which he'd sought to find Henri Gaudet. Why had she hidden the truth from him? Could she not trust her son? Neither of his parents had turned out to be the persons he thought them. They'd raised him well, yet he'd been thoroughly deceived. And where did that leave him now, if his own identity had been built on lies?

Philippe forced his mind back to the present. *Now,* it left him sitting beside a woman who was shy, perhaps tainted by a passionless marriage—but at least *her* past was not shrouded in painful deceit. And despite Bea's reputation for respectability, they'd shared kisses that spoke volumes about her capacity for passionate desire. Once he managed to melt her reserve, she would not let him down.

His gaze roved the audience as the play continued—he was drawn, as always, to observing the full spectrum of humanity, not just that arranged for display on the stage. He rarely painted group scenes such as the one before him, preferring to focus on a single, unique subject. But it entertained him to think of how he would do it—how he would go about getting the colors just so, the contrast of light and shadow, the expressions of the audience—some entranced, others bored, and still others more engrossed by the company beside them than by the performance. It might make for an interesting painting, if he were so inclined.

The show was well attended tonight, though he recognized but a few faces. Lord Garrett, with whom he'd played cards, with a group in the box next to theirs. The Earl of Haverford, seated beside a buxom blonde that, given the rather obvious display of her charms, Philippe strongly suspected was not the earl's wife.

Beatrice Pullington was far more lovely, more subtle . . . her charms a mystery waiting to be solved.

He felt for her hand next to him, heard her soft intake of breath as his fingers wrapped around hers.

She didn't pull away. He drew satisfaction from that, especially knowing the theater, while dim, was not so dark as to guarantee they would escape notice. He stroked her palm, noting the softness of her skin. His own fingers were calloused and often paint-flecked—a reminder that in spite of his great success, he worked for a living.

Below him, the main floor was filled with others who worked for a living—though perhaps not as comfortable of a living as that which Philippe enjoyed. Londoners from all walks of life who could spare a few shillings for general admission had crowded in for the popular show.

Wait. Philippe leaned forward.

Unless he was mistaken, the Wilbournes' servant— the one he'd noticed at their card party—had chosen to attend the theater the same evening as the couple he served.

Assuming the man had no duties this evening, there was nothing untoward about his choice of entertainment. Yet his presence was discomforting. Philippe frowned. Why did he keep finding himself distracted by a mere footman, a man with whom he'd never directly exchanged words?

He leaned toward Robert Wilbourne to point out the man's presence, then reconsidered. If the servant *was* skipping out on his duties, Philippe had no desire to tattle on him. Working men ought to look out for one another, he figured, whether they stood with the commoners or sat in well-appointed theater boxes as guests of the nobility.

Beside him, Bea had leaned forward as well. Her

shawl had slipped back, offering him—if he tilted his head just so—an enticing view of the hollow between her breasts. Philippe relaxed. Much better. Why waste attention on the man below when he could put his mind to far better use by focusing on the woman inches away? What would it take, he wondered, for Lady Beatrice Pullington to relax to the point she would allow him . . . or better yet, *beg* him, to remove her shawl and gown entirely?

She seemed intent on the scene before them. She shifted, obscuring the view Philippe had been enjoying. With regret, he turned his focus back to the stage.

When intermission came, he stood, but not as quickly as Bea. She brushed past, forcing him to jump back to avoid being run over as she continued past the Wilbournes.

"Terribly sorry," she called back as she disappeared in a swish of silk and sparkling silver, with no further explanation.

Philippe cocked his head. How very unlike her. Either Beatrice had urgent need of the retiring room, or the lady was up to something.

Beatrice barely registered the astonished looks on the faces of Philippe and the Wilbournes as she blew past them in her rush to follow the man she recognized from Vauxhall.

She'd spotted him during the second act and had been fidgeting ever since. It *had* to be the same man. He was already on his feet as well, heading for the lobby. She could beat him there, if she was quick—the main floor was crowded.

As for her friends, she'd have to come up with an excuse for her behavior when she returned. It couldn't be helped now.

She didn't dare confront the man, but by following him, perhaps she'd discover a clue to his identity. Though she would need more than that to satisfy the Foreign Secretary.

She'd racked her brain to remember anything the men at Vauxhall had said. Some kind of papers . . . a plan? She couldn't be sure.

Was it too much to hope her questions would be answered tonight? Or did the spy simply enjoy theater? *Love Laughs at Locksmiths* was popular, true, but somehow, she hadn't pegged the man she followed now as a patron of the arts.

She reached the lobby and paused in an alcove as people streamed in through the theater doors. Though her heart beat quickly, her mind felt strangely clear, focused on her mission. He'd been wearing brown and—*there.*

The man in question appeared, alone, just behind an elderly couple. The older duo moved slowly, and Bea could nearly feel the waves of frustration radiating from her prey as he finally spotted an opening and dodged around them. He strode toward the side of the lobby, moving quickly now, looking only ahead.

If he knew Bea was following him, he gave no indication.

She slipped through the crowd, weaving past several familiar faces but avoiding eye contact. If she paused to chat, she would lose him.

They reached the edge of the lobby, the spy a few yards farther to the back of the building than she. He threw a quick glance around, then pulled the knob of a door Bea had never before noticed and disappeared inside. She hesitated.

No. She couldn't hesitate. She ran forward and caught the door with the toe of her slipper just before it closed.

Inside, the corridor was dark. Had anyone seen her enter?

Oh, Lord. Oh, Lord. The Foreign Secretary had reassured her she'd be doing nothing more than paying closer attention to people with whom she already associated. So what was she doing sneaking into the back corridor of the theater, following a man she'd never met?

But if the real objective was to discover the spies' plan, this was an opportunity not to be missed.

The man turned a corner, following the corridor to a back entrance near the dressing rooms used by the players. Bea hung back at the corner. There was no other place to hide.

She heard the faint creak of a door opening, then the soft *snick* as it closed.

Then a woman's voice. "Have the weeds grown tall?" The question was asked in French.

Bea's heart was in her throat—could it be the woman who'd been missing that night at Vauxhall? The one whose note she'd received?

"Nay, the garden is well-groomed," the man replied. *"Bonsoir."*

"Evening," the woman's voice replied, this time in English.

Bea dared a quick peek around the corner, then pulled back. Rose Kettridge. The *actress.* Moments before, she'd been watching this woman on stage.

Bea struggled to remember the night of the

salon. Had Miss Kettridge been present? Actresses were not commonly invited to ton events, but a salon honoring an artist was different—particularly considering Monsieur Durand's broad appeal to the full spectrum of Society. But would she have come as someone's guest? Or at the direct invitation of the Wilbournes? And if she was directly invited, did that implicate Bea's friends?

"We move forward, then?" Miss Kettridge asked.

"Yes," the man told her. "Msr. Denis has given us one more chance. We must not be careless again."

"No. I shudder to think of the consequences. Your progress?"

"My placement is not as advantageous as yours." He sounded frustrated. "Rarely can I abandon the duties of my position without drawing the notice of the butler, or the nobles themselves. I may pass messages, but it is to you we must turn if we are to accomplish this."

"Oh?" Her voice held a calculating note. "It seems you are fortunate to have me."

"Huh. He said you would ask."

Bea's heart beat a rapid tattoo as she peered around the corner once more, in time to see the man pass a small purse to the actress.

"Now," the man said. "Have you secured our interests with the major?"

"He stands ready to assist—though he does not know it."

"You are sleeping with him."

The actress shrugged. "It is not displeasing. He cuts rather a fine figure in his uniform."

Bea's cheeks burned as she pressed back against the wall. She shouldn't be here. It was too dangerous. When the pair of spies ended their conversation, what would happen? Miss Kettridge would return to the dressing rooms, but the man? Unless the corridor held an exit she hadn't seen, he would be forced to retrace his steps—bringing him directly to where she now stood.

Slowly, she inched away, listening for any cues to suggest their conversation was at an end, and it was time to run. Blood pounded in her ears, and she had to strain even harder to make out their words.

"Have you access to his office?"

"I'm sure I could persuade him using the guise of a midday . . . distraction."

"I do not doubt your skills in that area," he told her. His tone held a faint note of distaste. "But can you remove any items of interest and escape notice?"

"There is no need," she said softly, her own tone one of superiority and satisfaction. "Remember what I do for a living? I can memorize anything I see."

"That is all very well," the man replied, "but do you believe he will allow you sufficient time to sit, in a government office, mind you, and read the entire plan, as well as commit it to memory?"

Bea had heard enough. She moved swiftly, staying on the balls of her feet to avoid making noise. Had the corridor been this long before? Almost there.

She came to the door, fumbling in the darkness for the knob. Finally she found it and pulled.

"Lady Pullington?"

Bea gasped.

Chapter 9

Just on the other side of the door stood none other than Monsieur Jean Philippe Durand.

"Are you all right?"

Bea nodded, the movement making her dizzy.

He peered at her closely. "You look pale."

Undoubtedly. All the blood had rushed from her head the moment he'd spoken her name. "It is nothing."

He glanced at the door she'd just passed through. "Were you lost?"

"No," she answered, before realizing he'd handed her the perfect excuse. "I—I mean, yes!"

His expression was clearly one of disbelief.

"If you were not lost, Beatrice, then have you a secret lover?"

"No!" Some of the blood flooded back to her face at the wildly invasive question.

His lips quirked as though he were amused by the vehemence of her denial.

Finally she gathered her wits—enough to register that it seemed oddly coincidental that Philippe had been waiting at the door to the corridor. That is, unless he'd been guarding it.

Before she could question him, the cursed door opened once more, and the man she'd been eavesdropping on walked past, paying neither of them any attention. He crossed the lobby and exited, not into the theater, but out to the streets.

Philippe followed his departure with narrowed eyes.

Bea watched Philippe's reaction to the man she knew as a spy—and saw recognition in those depths of blue. Her chest felt tight. "What are *you* doing here, anyhow?"

He gave her a bemused look as his charm slipped back into place. "Why, looking for my lost lady, of course." He proffered an arm.

Bea placed her hand on it and allowed him to lead her back to the Wilbournes' theater box, the unanswered questions roiling between them like clouds building before a storm.

Once they were seated, he did not take her hand again during the last acts of the play. Bea felt the withdrawal of his affection like the ache of an open wound. Yet she could not help but wonder: what else, besides affection, might he be keeping from her?

The carriage ride home was equally awkward—more so because the formal distance they maintained stood in stark contrast to the intimacy they'd shared during the earlier ride before the show.

By the time Philippe bid her a reserved good night at her door, Bea was more confused than ever. She had precious few hours to sort out her thoughts, though, for tomorrow held their appointed return to Montgrave.

Elizabeth and Charity arrived at Bea's house the next morning, long before Bea was ready to face the day. In fact, she'd only just begun composing a letter to the Foreign Secretary, relating her observations from last night's theater performance, when a flurry of colorful skirts appeared in the doorway and the sisters popped in.

"Morning, Bea!"

"Oh! You're early." Bea hastily shoved the letter into the drawer of the writing desk and went to greet them.

"Charity's fault," Elizabeth claimed. "She complained of being left out—so she not only invited herself along, she then proceeded to usher me out the door well before a civil hour."

"Charity not wanting to be left out?" Bea asked drolly. "Heavens, that's difficult to imagine."

"Oh, lay off, you two," Charity responded, clearly not taking their teasing too seriously. "Of course, I wanted to go. Meeting Monsieur Durand at the salon was entertaining, but the opportunity to actually see the famous artiste at work—that is ever so much more appealing than spending another dull day strolling about Hyde Park."

Bea cocked her head and asked Elizabeth, "Has she renewed her tendre for Monsieur Durand, then?"

"Not at all," Charity answered. "I simply thought it sounded like fun."

"Of course, you are welcome along," Bea told her, meaning it. The more people besides herself and Philippe, the better. She couldn't trust him. Or maybe it was that she couldn't trust *herself* around him.

Unfortunately, she could hardly explain to her chipper friends the events of last night that had her so out of sorts. Alex Bainbridge had been angry enough that Bea had dragged Charity into the spy mess. She didn't dare aggravate him further by involving his pregnant wife as well—no matter how close a friend she was.

Instead, she did her best to mirror her friends' enthusiasm for the upcoming outing.

"Will Monsieur Durand begin on canvas straightaway, when this last sketch is complete?" Elizabeth asked.

"Very soon, I should think, since he hopes to capture the spring season just before its peak." Unless he was too busy moonlighting as a spy. Before she could dwell on that dark thought, Bea shoved it from her mind. Elizabeth's question had reminded her of another dilemma. "E.," she said, "I am ever grateful for your company, but when Monsieur Durand does begin on canvas, I expect we will need quite some days at Montgrave for him to work, and I feel terrible for infringing on your generosity for so long."

Elizabeth smiled. "You needn't worry a bit. I am a true friend, for I am two steps ahead of you. The moment Monsieur Durand selected Montgrave, I anticipated you might wish to make an extended stay and avoid the frequent travel. So I wrote to my cousin, inviting her for a stay as well."

"Your cousin?"

"Yes, on my mother's side. Her father was a country

squire, and Lily herself was married for several years, poor woman, but lost her husband at sea."

"Oh, my."

"She's agreeable enough, and takes on any number of odd positions to get by, and I thought—"

"Wait," Charity interrupted. "E., did you say Lily? As in Lily Moffett? Our *cousin* Lily Moffett?"

Charity's incredulous tone earned her a warning look from her sister—and aroused Bea's curiosity.

"It's just," Elizabeth explained hastily, "Lily hasn't always had an easy time of it. I'm afraid she wasn't at her best the last time Charity saw her. But that was some time ago. Her health has quite recovered."

"I see," Bea said. She looked at Charity, whose lips were clamped shut. Since she'd never known the girl to refrain from voicing her objections, Bea assumed there was nothing further to say, and let the matter drop.

"I hope I haven't presumed too much," Elizabeth said, clasping her hands anxiously. "I do think the two of you would get on rather well."

"No need to worry," Bea told her. "I would be happy to have Mrs. Moffett as a companion." Widows often took paid positions as companions to their wealthier counterparts, and Bea counted herself lucky to be in the situation of needing a companion rather than hiring on as one. If she could help a relative of her best friend, even better. Bea knew Elizabeth held a special admiration for women forced to work for a living—she'd done so herself for several months before her marriage to the Duke of Beaufort.

Bea laughed. "Actually, I suggested this very solution—bringing along a companion—to my mother. She expressed concern that if Monsieur Durand and I spent too long at Montgrave, it would give the appearance of impropriety. However, at the time I offered up the idea, I had yet to identify the companion I promised to have."

"See? This will work perfectly," Elizabeth said brightly.

"Wait." Bea cocked her head. "You said you were two steps ahead of me. What is the other one?"

"Well, I assumed you would agree this was the perfect solution—as you just did—and Mrs. Moffett has already arrived."

"Here?"

"No, silly, she is at Montgrave. You shall meet her today. In fact, if you and Monsieur Durand become caught up in your project, there is no need to come back to London at all." Elizabeth frowned. "Bea, dear, I am about to be terribly rude, but . . . are you planning to wear *that* to Montgrave?"

Bea glanced down at her traveling costume. Normally she'd have worn a morning gown, but given their planned departure early in the day, such attire would only have necessitated the need for a change, so she'd donned the traveling clothes when she'd risen. "Is there something wrong with it?"

"It's only—didn't you wear that the last time we went to Montgrave?" Elizabeth asked.

"I don't think I did," Bea replied, confused. Her maid would never have laid out the same attire for two outings in such close succession.

"Maybe one of similar color, then, or cut," Elizabeth suggested. "At any rate, we can't have Monsieur Durand thinking your wardrobe so dull." She giggled. "He finds you alluring, mystical even—and so you must look the part." She bounced up, surprisingly energetic for a woman whose mornings had been given to illness the past few weeks. "Come, I'll help you pick something out."

Bea followed her friend in bewilderment. Her traveling costume was perfectly serviceable. But maybe that was the problem. Bea narrowed her eyes. If this sudden scrutiny from Elizabeth had anything to do with her matchmaking ideas, Bea suspected her attire was about to be replaced by a frock whose appeal had little to do with serviceability.

"Charity, are you coming?" Elizabeth called as they headed toward the stairs.

"In a moment," Charity called back. "I'm just going to—to finish this divine scone."

The moment they were gone, though, Charity dropped the scone as though it were last week's fish. She hurried to Bea's writing desk. What was it Bea had so hastily shoved into a drawer when she and Elizabeth had come in? She hadn't missed the telltale flush on Bea's face, and she'd been wondering about it ever since. A love letter? Something to do with the spies? She had to find out.

Charity briefly—and to no avail—tried to summon the appropriate guilt for snooping. If people would just *tell* her things, she reasoned, there would be no need to snoop.

Quietly, she slid open the drawer. A sheet of paper lay atop the remaining contents, but Charity needed to look no further. It was addressed to Viscount Castlereagh. Aha! Bea had been doing some snooping—or was it spying?—again herself.

That sneak! Charity had *known* there'd been more to that meeting with the Foreign Secretary. It must have been Bea's skill in uncovering the hidden meaning in that message that had earned her Castlereagh's respect—and, apparently, another assignment. Charity had sketched the men they'd observed that night, to be sure, but almost anyone could do that. Ugh. If only she had the talent Bea had, she, too, might have been included.

Charity scanned the letter.

While at the theater, I recognized a man in the audience as one of the same Miss Medford and I observed at Vauxhall.

She could barely breathe as she read—this wasn't just snooping, it contained mention of *her*!

He is a servant, as I later overheard, for I followed him to a most interesting conversation with the actress, Miss Kettridge—

Here the letter cut off. It must have been the point where she and Elizabeth had arrived, Charity realized. Drat. If only she knew—oh. Oh! A servant. The *Wilbournes'* servant. She *knew* she'd recognized the shorter of the two men at Vauxhall—she just hadn't been able to place him until now. But she was almost sure of it. Almost.

Quickly, Charity closed the drawer containing the half-finished letter, then hurried upstairs to join her sister and Bea, hoping her absence hadn't seemed unusually long. Now, she just needed to think up an excuse as to why she'd suddenly changed her mind about accompanying them to Montgrave.

* * *

Philippe arrived promptly at the designated hour, showing no hesitation about resuming their project. And though Bea sensed a latent tension in the artist's long, lean frame, there was no further mention of the awkward moment at the theater. Even when Elizabeth innocently asked how he'd enjoyed the show, his enthusiastic description of the actors and plot soon had Bea wondering if she'd simply blown out of proportion the whole incident during intermission.

At Elizabeth's urging, Philippe and Bea arranged to have their trunks packed and sent after them. Charity, displaying a typical bout of flightiness, had suddenly recalled a picnic she'd promised to attend and begged off the trip to Montgrave. The remaining trio was soon on the way to the estate, where Mrs. Lily Moffett, the companion thoughtfully provided by Elizabeth, waited.

When they arrived, Philippe excused himself. "If you ladies do not mind, I wish to stretch my legs after the journey. I understand you may wish to refresh yourselves and greet this cousin of Lady Bainbridge's. Would my absence be inexcusably rude? I shall not dally."

"Please, do as you wish," Elizabeth told him. "I genuinely meant you should use these grounds freely—do not feel you must attend to us. We shan't be long either." She led Beatrice inside, where the butler informed them Mrs. Moffett was reading in the library.

"I first kissed Alex in a library," Elizabeth whis-

pered to Bea as they approached the room. "I'm
rather fond of them now."

Bea stifled a giggle as they opened the door. A
woman seated on one of the chaises leapt up. "Elizabeth! That is, Your Grace!" She dropped her book
and hurried over.

Lily Moffett shared her cousin Elizabeth's brilliant red hair, but the resemblance ended there.
Her skin was freckled, her figure plump, and her
clothes that of a country widow. But her eyes were
merry and her smile wide.

"A pleasure to meet you, Lady Pullington." She
curtsied. "I hope I can offer some companionship
during your stay."

Bea smiled. "Elizabeth is my closest friend. If she
has invited you here for my benefit, I am sure we
shall get on splendidly."

"I do hope so." Lily gave Bea a brief rundown of
her previous employment—a smattering of odd
jobs—and ended proudly with, "I can produce references if you wish, my lady." She clasped her
hands as though anxious to please.

"No, no need," Bea replied. "This is not an interview; I simply wanted to meet you before starting
on the day's work. I trust Elizabeth's judgment."

Elizabeth flushed. "Right. So, ah, what else can
I tell you to help you two ladies get to know one
another? I do so hope you will be comfortable together once I return to London."

Someone tapped on the door. Philippe poked his
head in. "Lady Pullington? If you are refreshed,
shall we begin?"

Elizabeth looked relieved—more so, Bea thought,
than was merited by the minor awkwardness of

introducing Bea to Lily. But there was likely nothing to it. In Elizabeth's delicate condition, all her emotions seemed stronger than usual.

"Why don't the two of you get started, while Lily and I see to the arrangements for your stay?" Elizabeth suggested.

"Yes, thank you." Bea smiled, but something in Elizabeth's tone—or maybe the smirk she couldn't quite hide—tipped Bea off. The moment Philippe's head disappeared from the doorway, she turned to her friend and hissed, "You aren't still playing at matchmaker, are you?"

"Me?" Elizabeth placed a hand to her heart. "What opportunity would I have? I return to London on the morrow," she said, neatly avoiding the question.

Bea quirked a disbelieving brow, then went to follow Philippe. "Mrs. Moffett," she requested as she left, "when you and Elizabeth are finished, please do join us—Elizabeth can direct you to the rose garden."

"Thank you, my lady," her new companion replied.

Elizabeth followed Bea to the door. "You are pleased with my cousin as a companion, then?"

"Yes, I think she will suit." Lily Moffett seemed cheery and agreeable, and after all, the relationship was only to last a week or two.

"Wonderful." Elizabeth grinned and made a shooing motion. "Best not keep Monsieur Durand waiting—I understand artistes can be quite temperamental."

"Hmm." Bea exited, walking toward the hall entryway where Philippe stood waiting. Why did it seem, these days, that everyone from the highest government officials to her girlhood friends had secret agendas? Except perhaps Mrs. Moffett, who appeared genuinely grateful for the position of companion.

Lucky for Bea, she was not in the room to hear Elizabeth's final words to her cousin. When the two women were once again seated, Elizabeth met Lily's eye.

"Lily, I know things haven't always been easy for you." Her cousin flushed, probably wondering how much Elizabeth knew—which was enough to know Lily's last two positions hadn't lasted long. Elizabeth softened her tone. "I think you'll find your time here to be an exception. Bea—Lady Pullington—is a respectable widow. She'd never come out here to be painted without a companion for propriety, though I doubt you'll have too much to do besides enjoy one another's company."

Of course, if her dearest friend returned to London *still* a proper, respectable widow, Elizabeth would be ever so disappointed. Fortunately, she knew one way to ensure Bea and her handsome French painter weren't monitored too closely. She hesitated only a moment before mentioning it. After all, what harm could it do?

"Oh, and Lily?" she said casually, "please consider Montgrave your home during your stay. The house and grounds are entirely open to you—though," she paused as if just remembering something, "if you don't mind forgoing my husband's brandy collection—the cabinet just through the door to the study, there—I'm sure you'll find the wines served with meals are perfectly pleasing to the palate."

"Of course, Your Grace." Lily said, her gaze darting to the open study door and back to Elizabeth. She nodded, eyes wide. "I shall go nowhere near it."

Elizabeth gave her a smile. "I knew we'd reach an understanding. I believe I'll go have a bit of a lie-down. Traveling tires me of late. But I'm certain Monsieur Durand and Lady Pullington will be happy to have you join them. The garden is just a little way into the wood, down the path and to the left."

Elizabeth's smile grew smug as she shut the door. She'd chosen the perfect chaperone. She knew Lily well. If pointing her cousin toward the liquor cabinet didn't do the trick, nothing would.

Lily stared at the door that closed behind her cousin, unable to believe her good luck. Satisfied she was alone, she jumped to her feet, spun in a circle, and chortled with glee.

Who would have thought Miss Elizabeth Medford would one day be Lady Bainbridge, Duchess of Beaufort? And now *she,* Lily Moffett, a widow of limited means, was going to get to spend the next two weeks playing at being a great lady.

She went to the window, where the view of the fine spring day reflected her sunny mood. From here, she could just make out the path leading into the woods. Somewhere within, Monsieur Durand and Lady Pullington waited—but there was no hurry. She'd already made a brief exploration of the house upon arriving, since no one but the staff had been present to greet her—not that she'd expected a duke or duchess to drop what they were doing and rush out to the country on her account. Just being here—the only family member besides Elizabeth's sister, Charity, to garner such an invitation—was enough.

Lily's self-guided tour of Montgrave had not, however, included the study. She wandered toward it now.

She paused at the door. A man's space, definitely, with a massive desk and heavy chairs, though the tall hearth and thick rug managed to convey warmth. And just inside, the cabinet that held the duke's brandy collection.

Lily swallowed, her throat inexplicably dry, her gaze focused on the cabinet. Her hand lifted as though controlled by another. She caressed the polished wood.

Realizing what she was doing, she snatched back her hand and turned in a quick circle. She let out a breath. Still alone.

She touched the wood again, her heart pounding. What sort of brandy did a duke collect? Surely it would do no harm just to *look.*

The cabinet door gave a soft *snick* as she eased it open.

She sucked in a breath. Ah. Before her stood bottle upon bottle of fine spirits. Commoners like her couldn't afford whisky or brandy—the taxes had driven all but a few distilleries out of legal operation. The duke's collection, however, extended well beyond anything she'd seen before. French brandy, Scottish whisky . . . smugglers were more than willing to ensure England's aristocracy did not go without.

She squatted to see the bottles better. The ones in the shadowed corners of the cabinet were too hard to read, but it didn't matter. The ones in front told her all she needed to know. A week's wages would not purchase the least of these bottles.

She sank to her knees. One finger stroked the closest bottle lovingly. No. What was she doing?

But to be so close, and not even learn what such fine brandy *smelled* like?

Her fingers closed around the bottle. She drew it to her, cradled it as she removed the stopper. She inhaled deeply and let her head fall back, her eyes closed as the aroma penetrated her nostrils.

Lord have mercy, but that was fine.

"Shall we begin, Lady Pullington? You know already where to stand." Philippe waved a hand.

Bea moved toward the basin at the center of the abandoned rose garden, swallowing her disappointment at his use of her formal title, rather than the *"ma chérie"* she'd grown accustomed to when they were alone. She adjusted her skirts, then readopted the pose she'd held in the sketch they'd both selected.

The latent tension she'd sensed in Philippe earlier was back, but she kept quiet as his charcoal scratched across the paper. He, too, worked in silence, sometimes nodding as though in approval, other times frowning at something on the paper, rubbing at it with the heel of his hand.

She held the pose until her arms grew tired, and the temptation to move, to use one slippered foot to scratch the itch on the opposite calf, was driving her mad.

Suddenly he thrust the papers away. "This isn't working."

Bea sucked in a breath. "Am I standing wrong? I'm sorry. I thought—"

"You are in position. It isn't that. I cannot concentrate." He paced, frustration evident in every feature, every movement.

"Monsieur?" Never had Bea met a man who expressed himself as fully, as freely, as Philippe, and yet the force of that expression had some of her old nerves rising to the surface. She dropped the pose and cautiously asked, "Is something bothering you?"

"*Oui.*" He rounded on her. "Beatrice." She thought she heard frustration, but not anger, in his tone. And something else. Pleading? "About last night."

She swallowed. She'd known this was coming.

"I can think of no good reason for a lady such as yourself to be slipping through the back corridors of the Royal Haymarket Theater. If your hurry to escape me during intermission was not due to an illicit rendezvous with a lover, then what *were* you doing?"

This time, she was prepared. "Foolish man." She batted her eyelashes, and offered up a half truth. "I have no lover. I followed someone I thought I knew . . . but it turned out I was mistaken."

He folded his arms. "You thought you knew the Wilbournes' footman?"

Her heart skipped a beat. "Their footman?" she repeated.

"The man who exited after you. He works for them."

She tried not to let her excitement show at what he'd just confirmed. "I . . . no, I did not realize that. As I said, it was all a mistake. Are you certain that man works for the Wilbournes?"

Philippe nodded. "He served us at their card party last week. I tend to remember faces."

"A benefit to someone in your profession, I should think." Bea exhaled slowly, some of her nerves receding at his logical explanation. Philippe knew the servant-spy because he'd been served at a party, and because as an artist, he *noticed* people— not because he'd dealt with the man in any other forum.

"Indeed." But Philippe was not to be dissuaded from his topic. "Beatrice, you are an intelligent woman. Please do not ask me to believe you make a habit of following strange men into dark places."

"No. I was—I was caught up in the moment," Bea explained, sticking to at least a portion of truth. She laid a hand on his forearm. Every muscle was taut. "He reminded me of—of a favorite cousin, whom my family thought was lost at sea some years ago. Foolish, I know. In fact, I had just reconsidered the wisdom of my actions, which is when you saw me emerging." Bea was amazed how easily the lies rolled off her tongue. Perhaps she ought to write novels, rather than poetry.

Philippe met her gaze directly, holding it for a long moment. Finally he seemed to accept her answer, for she felt his muscles relax. "I am glad," he told her, his eyes darkening, "for it was driving me mad to think of another man doing this."

"Doing wh—"

Bea's remaining words were lost against the crush of his lips.

The kiss was fierce, the onslaught on her senses complete as his arms closed around her like steel bands, hauling her inch for inch against his form. Her head tipped back against the pressure, and his tongue drove into her mouth. All she could smell, all she could feel, all she could taste was Philippe, who kissed her so searingly she felt as though he was trying to brand her.

Too much. She couldn't breathe. Too much, Bea thought wildly. She pushed away, scrambled backward.

"No!" Chest heaving, she dragged in air. She scooted around the stone basin, putting it between them.

Philippe, too, breathed heavily, staring at her, then down at his hands which had so recently grasped her.

"Wh—what are you doing?" Bea asked, when she could find her voice.

"I do not know."

She heard the surprise in his voice.

"*Merde*," he swore. "That was not . . . I did not mean . . . never have I reacted so strongly to a woman . . . to you."

"I don't understand."

He leaned across the basin, his hands extended in an earnest plea. "I am so very sorry, *ma belle*. Please know that. I could not stand thinking another man had taken such liberties only minutes after what we shared in the carriage on the way to the theater. But I did not mean to frighten you. Here." He stroked her arms reassuringly, until the wild beat of the kiss dissipated, and Bea felt her heart slow.

A bird chirped, and she looked around. The rose garden remained as normal, and the look of concern on Philippe's face melted away her fear.

"I am recovered now, I think," she whispered. "It was only—I was not prepared . . ."

"Je suis si très désolé." He cupped her cheek. "I am desolate at the thought of causing you unhappiness."

"I am not unhappy," she promised him. "Only—that kiss was . . . was so *uncontrolled.*"

His brows arched, but if the Frenchman had thoughts regarding her statement, he kept them to himself. "Let us return to something simpler then, *oui?* You will pose again, while I sketch?"

"Yes." As she posed once more, Bea wondered, irreverently, how much faster she and Philippe would complete this project if they didn't get distracted with kisses each time they came out here? Although, unless one of her "companions" discovered a heretofore untapped sense of duty and actually showed up at the rose garden, she had a feeling such distractions would continue.

Philippe worked as quietly as before, but Bea sensed a change. There were fewer slashing strokes and rubbing out of lines that did not please him. Indeed, this time when he set the paper aside and stood, he was smiling.

"Much better. I am nearly done. This will be different than any work I have yet completed. I can *feel* it." His blue eyes lit with creative passion.

Bea shivered—though from the spring chill, or Philippe's intensity, she couldn't say. "Different? But what if people don't like it?"

"Do not worry, Beatrice. With your lovely face gracing my canvas, the work is sure to gain admiration from even the staunchest of my detractors. They shall love it. One moment." He retrieved his pad and made a few quick strokes with the charcoal pencil. "Or if they do not," he continued, "it does not matter. I do not paint to please the public. I never have."

Setting aside the sketch, he moved closer. His fingers brushed her neck as he tilted her chin, lingering until she held the new pose, then a moment longer.

"Ma chérie, je veux juste te faire plaisir."

My darling, I only want to please you. Bea shivered again. More dangerous words were never spoken.

"Why me? I offer nothing in return."

"Not true. It is something in your face, your eyes . . ." Philippe mused. His fingers trailed down her neck as he dropped his hand. "It is why I could never paint in the stiff and formal styles of old, for it shutters out the soul. People are drawn to faces—after all, is it not said that the eyes are the windows to the soul? It is our nature, that desire to connect with other human beings, to be recognized. To be loved."

Her flesh tingled where his fingers had so recently rested. Foolishness.

"You are a master of flattery," Bea whispered. She knew better than to fall for such words. Even Charity had seen his act for what it was. He might not be a spy, but he was definitely a seducer.

"Of course." He laughed. "But do not think for a moment, *ma chérie,* that I am insincere."

He held her gaze, and her breath caught at the intensity burning there.

Heat flooded her senses, and she forgot she was supposed to be holding a pose as her hand moved instinctively toward him, tentatively brushing the front of his jacket. His fingers caught hers, guiding them to his lips.

"I can make you feel . . ." he murmured, his accent growing thick, "what it is you seek."

"What I seek?" she echoed. She drew her hand away from his lips, reluctant to relinquish his touch. What was she doing? She had to think this through.

He wasn't going to let her. "You want to be kissed, do you not?"

Bea had no answer to the bold question. Denial was impossible, but admitting it would be an even greater folly.

The corner of those sensual lips quirked upward, acknowledging her dilemma. "You do."

"Arrogant beast." But there was no malice in Bea's tone.

He laughed. "Ah, *chérie*. Accept that you wish me to kiss you, and stop worrying about what will happen if I do."

"What will happen?"

"Shh." He placed a finger over her lips. "Only this."

He replaced the finger with his lips. A gentle brush. Not the fierce branding of before, but a tender caress. When she didn't pull away, he returned, molding his lips to hers, the pressure firm, yet not demanding.

"I will not frighten you this time," he whispered, his breath warm against hers.

But Bea wasn't frightened—she was kissing him

back. Oh, yes. Forget thinking things through. She *needed* him to touch her, taste her like that.

His hands slipped into her hair, cupping the back of her head as he deepened the kiss. Her head swam, and she held his shoulders as the rest of her surroundings fell away.

Before Bea was ready, Philippe pulled back.

"Ah, Beatrice." He slowly let out a breath. "So much fire beneath that polish. And a widow." He chuckled. "In France, you would have never remained a widow for so long."

Bea wasn't so sure—but now was not the time to mention that the flames of passion had hardly been present in her marriage, or that her widowhood had been quiet, respectable, and equally passionless.

He leaned in again, and Bea met him willingly. This time he took a nip at her bottom lip, and when her lips parted, his tongue slipped in for a taste. The flames leapt up again, within her, and her breath caught. Her tongue met his, tasting, stroking, until a small whimper of need escaped her throat.

He broke the kiss gently, leaning his forehead against hers while they both caught their breath. "The daylight hours wane, *ma chérie*, and I have a sketch yet to complete. And, I promised not to frighten you."

Bea's every sense hummed with awareness, her lips still moist and parted. No, he hadn't frightened her—she had to bite back the temptation to wantonly ask for more. Instead, she stood still and allowed Philippe to pose her like a doll. The sensual turn of his lips as he did told

her he knew exactly what she was feeling. What
he'd made her feel.

Cool air washed over her skin as he moved away,
resuming his position at the edge of the garden as
he finished the sketch.

How could he return so calmly to his charcoals
and pad, when everything inside her tumbled like
waves breaking on a stormy beach?

What was she to do? He sensed her fears and
assuaged them, sensed her desires and offered to
fulfill them.

Except that Bea—at least when her senses were
calm—desired far more than Philippe had guessed.
A thousand melting kisses could not give the life-
long companionship, the love and understanding
she ached for deep within.

But he hadn't promised love. Only pleasure.

Bea gave him a little smile as he glanced up, then
bent his head over the pad, his artist's concentration absorbing him once more. A snatch of the
Wordsworth poem she'd quoted upon first bringing Philippe here returned to her mind, unbidden:

> *In that sweet mood when pleasant thoughts*
> *Bring sad thoughts to the mind.*

She could take the simple pleasure he offered,
tell herself it would be enough. But it would be a
lie. Her heart was already involved.

Chapter 10

Jasper urged the horses to a quicker pace as the cart bearing Lady Pullington and Monsieur Durand's trunks rolled toward Montgrave. He'd been assigned the watch on Lady Pullington—a natural choice, since Peters and Miss Kettridge both had "regular" employment that limited their flexibility.

Though they teased him for his layabout ways, Jasper considered himself a man of opportunity—when one arose, he was there to take it. Monsieur Denis knew who he could turn to. The others could laugh all they wanted. Jasper would get the job done.

Watching Lady Pullington had been easy, until a conversation with one of her footmen this morning indicated today's outing to Montgrave was not a mere day trip. Then, he'd had to scramble.

It had been easy enough to secure the job of delivering Monsieur Durand's luggage from the hotel to the estate. He'd done odd jobs for the hotel manager before. It had been even easier to convince Lady Pullington's staff that there was no sense in sending two separate vehicles for such a mundane task—he'd simply take her trunk as well.

Now, the trick was figuring out how to maintain the watch once the trunks were delivered. Rumor had it the Montgrave butler ran a tight household—there was little hope Jasper could loiter for long without attracting his notice. But Jasper's mind, while not suited to long stints of steady employment, *was* suited to creative solutions. If Lady Pullington was spying for the British, she would be in contact with the Foreign Office. And when that contact came, he would be waiting.

Richard waited as the ship docked. He sat on a bench, studying one of the Paris papers—a day old, it told him little he did not already know. Dockworkers, merchants, and laborers went about their business. No one paid him any attention.

He'd taken to spending most of his days in Calais. The port city allowed for faster communication with his men in England. Besides, Paris was—politically, at least—a mess. He'd had no messages for several days. That worried him. His goals depended on his agents in England.

Waiting, he allowed himself a moment to dream . . . soon, he would establish himself as the most loyal of Napoleon's followers. The Emperor had met with success so far, but the greatest danger—the armies of the coalition—lay ahead. Britain, Austria, Prussia, Russia . . . all were marching toward France. Napoleon would need help. Other men had rejoined his cause—but while the foot soldiers joined him blindly, men like Richard usually kept one eye turned toward a route of escape.

Fouché was one of the worst—he had the ear of the Emperor, and that burned. How could Napoleon have offered *him* the position of police minister? Everyone knew Fouché had conspired against his ruler when Napoleon had been forced to abdicate last spring—and was in all probability conspiring against him now.

Richard grimaced. Self-preservation, he understood—within limits. He'd stayed alive through France's turbulent changes in regime by carefully balancing the desire to be valued by those in power with the need to appear insignificant.

Well, he was tired of being insignificant. If he could deliver the British plans for the invasion, and *if* that was enough to give the Emperor the edge he needed—still a considerable risk, Richard knew— he would be rewarded far beyond Fouché, far beyond any measure of greatness he'd previously known.

André sidled up behind him. "The Channel crossing grows tiresome."

"Undoubtedly. Though you are well compensated for your time." Only one thing guaranteed the loyalty of men like André Denis. Gold. And Richard had staked a significant portion of his personal coffers on this endeavor. "The news?"

"Lady Pullington—the British informant— and your son were seen at the theater together in London, in the presence of Lord and Lady Wilbourne. Unfortunately, Philippe and the lady have since removed to a country estate owned by the Duke of Beaufort. Apparently, your son intends to use the grounds as a setting for painting his English fancy."

Richard resisted the urge to roll his eyes. In spite of the fact that he'd ordered Solange to stop painting after they'd married and turn her efforts to more useful pursuits, like becoming a proper hostess for a man of his station, he hadn't been able to stop Philippe from taking up the oils and brush. And now the boy had picked himself a pretty little spy to paint. He probably had no idea.

Richard eyed André. "And?"

"I must ask, monsieur . . . Whose side is your son on?"

"Philippe?" Richard scoffed. "The boy has no head for politics."

"Do you think it coincidence that he asked to paint a woman who appears to be a British informant? And who, by all reports, is now becoming remarkably close to your son?"

"The circumstances are odd," Richard admitted. "Though, knowing Philippe, I am inclined to believe it *is* mere coincidence. Is there anything to suggest Lady Pullington engaged in political activities prior to intercepting our missive?"

André shook his head. "She appears to have led a quiet, proper life. As have many of our own best agents," he added pointedly.

Richard rubbed the back of his neck. "Continue watching them. I don't care if he's painting her, or if he's sleeping with her—but I do care if he's *talking* with her. I want to know what they each know, and where their motives lie."

"The problem is, we cannot shadow them at the country estate—not closely, anyway."

"Get someone on the staff." The solution was so obvious, Richard shouldn't have had to suggest it.

Denis shook his head. "Impossible. The Duke of Beaufort is extremely selective in hiring servants. We could hardly get them to speak to us—beyond the phrase 'not hiring,' that is."

"Bribery?"

"Again, no. He pays them too well. What's more, they know it, and each and every one of his servants fears the duke's wrath should they abuse their position."

"Merde."

The burly spy nodded, agreeing with the sentiment as he took a long pull on his ever-present cigar. "Further effort on that front would arouse suspicion. We have set one of our men in the nearest village. He can monitor any comings and goings from the estate."

"In the meantime, our primary objective remains the same," Richard reminded him. "Time runs short. We must deliver the plans."

It could already be too late. Forces were amassing on the Continent, and information was only useful if one had time to react to it. Bonaparte had survived the battles at Ferrara, and then at Tolentino— but those were child's play compared to what awaited.

"I want to know where the coalition is gathering, and how soon they will be ready. Most importantly, seek any document, any overheard whisper, that references *tactics,*" Richard instructed.

"Of course, monsieur."

"Bonaparte will have informants monitoring the proceedings of the Congress of Vienna, but it's

Wellington's plans I want. The other armies must march across vast distances to reach France. Their intentions will be known long before they reach us. Not so with the Brits. If this confrontation turns into a drawn-out battle, with one army slogging away at the other, Napoleon Bonaparte will eventually, inevitably, be defeated. But the Emperor has a known flair for tactics . . . especially when his enemy's intentions are scripted before him."

André's lip had flattened into a thin line during the course of his employer's lecture. Richard bit back the remainder of his impassioned rant. "All right. Just tell me. Where do we stand?"

"Close, monsieur. Very close. There is an officer on the planning council who loses his reason when distracted by Miss Kettridge's considerable charms. And he is not immune to mixing business with pleasure. She has access to his offices."

"Good. Continue working that angle, and any other that may prove fruitful."

Having received orders, André adjusted the brim of his hat in a gesture that implied he was getting ready to leave.

Richard stopped him. "One more question. How much risk do we assume by leaving my son to dally in the forest with the English spy?"

André cocked his head, a gleam in his eye. "Very little—to our primary goal, that is. Judging from the behavior we observed, I think the only risk you need concern yourself with is how soon you will have bastard grandchildren running about England."

Richard shot him a dark look.

"Unless he marries the chit, of course," the burly agent quickly amended.

"Hardly better." Then he'd have a defector in the family. The English were enemies . . . surely Philippe, for all his political naivety, knew *that* much.

"A passing fancy, most like." André waved his cigar as though Philippe could just as easily be dismissed, studied the glowing tip a moment, then clamped the unlit end back into its usual spot. "Although," he mused, "have you considered that this, ah, *relationship* between your son and the Englishwoman, not to mention his relationship with the Wilbourne couple, may prove . . . useful?"

Shrewd eyes studied Richard for a reaction, but Richard allowed no expression to reflect on his features.

André nodded. "Just a thought."

Lily hurried along the path into the woods. How much time had passed since her cousin had left her in the library? Enough that Monsieur Durand and Lady Pullington had surely noticed her absence. She prayed they weren't angry.

She'd re-stoppered the brandy in the duke's cabinet—oh, so very hard to do, then wandered down to the kitchen.

"Did your interview go well, mum?" Betsy, one of the kitchen maids, had asked.

"It did. I shall be staying on." Her hands had trembled as she'd asked, "Is it possible to trouble you for a glass of wine? Just something to settle my nerves."

Betsy had looked sympathetic. "I was terrified when I firs' came on here—the duke holds 'is standards high, but you'll get used to it. I haven't access to the wine cellar, but let me ask Cook for you, mum, an' I'm sure he'll see to it."

"Thank you."

Two glasses of fine red wine later, the trembling had stopped, and Lily had *almost* forgotten the alluring scent of fine brandy. She'd also almost forgotten her position as companion—which was what had her hurrying toward the abandoned rose garden now.

Ah, here it was. Lily edged up to the clearing. The spot was secluded, with a wild sort of prettiness. The perfect place for a tryst. But the couple seemed to have no such intentions. Lady Pullington stood at a stone basin, holding very still, while Monsieur Durand sat some distance away, absorbed in sketching her. Both were doing exactly what they'd come to Montgrave for—offering no hint of any other motives, in spite of the romantic setting.

Lady Pullington spotted her and flashed a quick smile. If she wondered where Lily had been all this time, she gave no indication.

Lily laughed to herself and thought longingly of the duke's brandy. Chaperoning these two, it appeared, would be as easy as helping herself to the estate's fine libations.

Had someone informed Bea a month ago that she'd be secluded on a vast estate with a world-renowned artist and a flighty woman she'd never before met as her only companions, Bea would have dismissed the idea as absurd. Yet here they were. An odd lot, perhaps, but with a common purpose.

Before she could devote herself to that purpose, though, there was one matter she had to see to: the Foreign Secretary expected a report. Nearly a week had passed since their meeting, and he'd been very clear about the urgency of the matter.

Thanks to Elizabeth and Charity's early arrival the previous morn, she'd had to postpone the missive. She'd managed to grab the half-finished effort just before leaving for Montgrave, though with the gown Elizabeth had insisted she change into— a wispy frock that was most definitely *not* a traveling costume—she'd been challenged for a place to stow it. She'd managed to slip it between her chemise and stays, then found herself constantly patting the area to reassure herself of the paper's presence. Finally, they'd reached Montgrave and she'd had a moment to tuck it away in a safer place.

The remainder of their arrival day had been too full to pry a moment alone. But Elizabeth, seeing that Bea was satisfied with Lily as a companion, had claimed she missed Alex dreadfully, and decided to return to London the following morn.

After seeing off her emotional friend, Bea returned to the lovely suite the staff had readied for her. She could delay no longer. She pulled out the now-rumpled letter to Viscount Castlereagh, picked up a pen, then stopped.

Something wasn't right. She crumpled the letter and tossed it into the fire.

She'd originally planned to entrust the note to a member of her own staff, but now it would have to be delivered via an unfamiliar messenger. If this note were read by the wrong eyes, she didn't like to think of the consequences.

After careful consideration, she composed a new missive in Italian, figuring the foreign language, less common in England than French, offered a layer of caution. Even if the messenger broke the seal, it was unlikely he would read Italian well enough to grasp the significance of what she wrote. Lord Castlereagh, she judged, would have no such difficulty.

In the letter, she offered up the actress, Miss Kettridge, by name, and warned of her intentions toward an unnamed but apparently attractive major. Bea hoped the description would mean something more to the Foreign Secretary. As for the male spy, her argument with Philippe had confirmed the man was a servant of Lord and Lady Wilbourne. She relayed this as well, then closed the letter with:

> *My current commitment to sitting for Monsieur Durand requires my presence at Montgrave. Thus, I am unable to make further observations of anyone, save, of course, Monsieur Durand, though nothing leads me to believe he is involved. Should I happen upon any further information through unexpected means, I will not hesitate to report it to you.*

There. She sealed the letter with wax and slowly let out a breath. She'd done her duty to England. The only piece she'd left out was Philippe's role at the theater that night. Perhaps the omission was self-serving, but she couldn't bear to implicate him in the same fashion as those she *knew* were involved. Her loyalty to England was strong, but not strong enough to ignore the inexorable tug of loyalty to the man she was beginning to suspect held her heart.

The hours spent traveling to and from Montgrave, the hours in the rose garden, the hours at meals and later in the evenings, when they'd laughed over poetry or stories of each other's childhoods . . . more and more she was drawn to him. How could she spy against him?

She'd tossed and turned for hours last night, torn between her growing connection with Philippe, and the Foreign Secretary's identification of him as a person of interest. True, she could not account for Philippe's every waking moment, but Bea had spent more time with him than anyone, and there was just nothing, beyond his nationality, to link him to the spies.

At the theater she'd been suspicious, but both times he'd confronted her about the incident, his only concern was jealousy, that she might be meeting another man. No hint of concern she could have been in danger, or *en*dangering some ulterior motive of his own. There had been those days when he'd traveled to Kent, but he'd told her the brief journey had been to pay a call on an old friend of his mother's, a request she'd made shortly before her death. Why shouldn't she believe him?

If she was wrong, if Philippe was working for Napoleon's men, she herself could be in great danger if she betrayed him. But Bea couldn't manage to summon any fear over that possibility—because truth be told, she'd never seen Philippe take an interest in anything beyond art, the theater, and *her.*

She refused to harbor further doubts. Doing so would only destroy her chance at romance with the one man who'd ever shown signs he might understand her, understand their shared need to observe the world and create their own interpretations, whether with words or paints.

It was a risk—and Bea was not by nature a risk-taker. But for once, she had to follow her heart and pray it did not lead her astray.

As for the letter, she needed someone to carry it to Lord Castlereagh. Unfortunately, as Elizabeth had already left, Bea could not simply send the note with her. She trusted her friend implicitly—though, at least this way, Bea would not have to answer her friend's questions about *why* she was delivering a note addressed to one of the prominent political figures in Britain.

Instead, Bea carried the note to Montgrave's butler, and asked that he recommend a reliable messenger. One Mr. Reilly, an earnest looking footman, was brought forward.

"You know the route?" she asked him.

"Yes, my lady. I have run messages from Montgrave to London before."

"It is of considerable importance to me this message be delivered promptly," Bea said, tempted to use stronger words, but stayed by the fear of tipping off the servant. If anyone had a trustworthy staff, it was the Duke of Beaufort—but then again, one could never be too sure.

"I shall make no delay," Reilly promised her.

"Good." She handed him the letter, trying not to

let her fingers tremble. "Here is some coin for your trouble, and to cover any expenses you incur." She handed him a small pouch.

"With your permission, my lady, I can leave immediately."

"Granted." Bea breathed a sigh of relief as Reilly bowed and exited. Moments later, she saw him crossing the grounds, heading toward the stables. Good.

She hoped the Foreign Secretary was satisfied. For now, the matter was out of her hands.

Jasper tipped back his mug of ale to swallow the last drops.

"More?" the owner of The Cock and Crown asked.

He shook his head.

"Traveling far today?"

He shook his head again. "Waitin' on word from the boss," he said. It was the intentionally vague excuse he'd invented to justify lingering for a day or two. Delivering the trunks to Montgrave had been easy, but afterward he'd retreated to the nearby village, where the tavern keeper turned out to be a talkative sort.

"What sort of business are you in, mister?"

"Trade," Jasper replied noncommittally.

The other man nodded, picked up a rag, and began polishing mugs.

Jasper stood and stretched, tossed a few coins onto the table, and went out into the yard.

Damn it. How was he to keep the watch now? Sneak

into the woods and spy on the site Monsieur Durand had chosen for his next painting?

Jasper spat. He'd already done that yesterday, while en route to delivering the trunks, but from what he'd observed, the lanky artist and his English chit were more interested in getting to know one another than in extracting secrets of national consequence.

Then, earlier this morning, a carriage emblazoned with the Beaufort crest of arms had passed him by on the road. The duchess, he guessed, returning to London. Though her husband the duke had accompanied Lady Pullington to the British Foreign Secretary's office, he had no evidence to suggest the lady spy was communicating through Lady Bainbridge. Jasper had chosen not to interrupt the duchess's travels. He hoped he hadn't missed his chance. She was too prominent a figure in London Society to be accosted on a whim.

He frowned. There· *had* to be more he could do—Monsieur Denis had said if they were successful, the reward would be great. Jasper didn't need much, just enough to set himself up. He hadn't been to France in years—not since he was a boy, and his mother dragged him, crying, across the Channel to this gray land where she'd eked out a living making buttons. She'd told him to be thankful for his safety, because his father had not been so fortunate in the turbulent times following the Revolution.

But how could he feel lucky when he had to steal to feed his teenage appetite, when every Brit who heard his accent made it perfectly clear his presence on their soil was not welcomed, but merely tolerated?

It hadn't taken him long to lose his accent, though along with it, he'd lost his identity. For years he'd struggled to find his path. It wasn't until meeting André Denis at a boxing match—a real one, not the kind that took place at the gentlemen's clubs—that he'd discovered a way to get even, and if things went well, to never need an odd job again.

Leaving the cart in the inn yard, Jasper led his horse back toward the road leading to Montgrave. When he reached the woods, he left the road, intending to work his way to the other side of the estate where the rose garden lay.

Before long, though, he heard a cheerful whistling and the clop of hooves on dirt. His own horse nickered and he placed a hand on the animal's neck to still it. A man on horseback rode along the road, coming from the direction of the duke's estate. Jasper narrowed his eyes. A lone man on a horse . . . a messenger? He couldn't be sure, though the rider's clothing identified him as a member of the lower classes.

He eased out of the woods to the edge of the road, still leading his horse.

Upon seeing him, the other man pulled up. "Morning."

"An' a good morning to you," Jasper replied.

The man's gaze took in the fact that Jasper stood on the ground. "Horse trouble?"

"No, jus' out looking for mushrooms. I have a lady friend who fancies them," he said with a conspiratorial wink.

"Bit early in the season, don't you think?"

Jasper put a finger to his nose and wagged it. "Right on, you are. But my lady friend is in a delicate way, as it were, and mere reason cannot satisfy her."

The man astride the horse chuckled. "I see. Then I hope your efforts are rewarded—though you should know, if you wander much farther in, you will be treading on grounds belonging to the Duke of Beaufort."

Jasper mustered a look of surprise. "Beaufort? I hadn't realized I'd come so far." He nodded gravely. "Thank you, stranger, for the warning. I shouldn't like to trespass."

"No thanks necessary."

Having established trust, Jasper moved on instinct. "You mind if I fall in with you for a bit, then? Follow the road out away from the duke's grounds?"

"Not at all."

Jasper swung onto his horse, and the men moved off.

"You work for the duke?" he asked casually.

A nod. "I serve at Montgrave."

Just as he'd hoped. A few paces later, Jasper asked casually, "What brings you out today?"

The servant hesitated—and that moment's pause, more than the words that followed, told Jasper what he needed to know. "A task my master entrusted to me."

"Ah. A man of importance, you are. Say no more."

Jasper looked down the road. If he were going to act, it would have to be soon. Already they drew near the village.

He eyed his prey, never turning his head. They

were of similar size, but Jasper held the element of surprise—an advantage not to be discounted. He started whistling.

His companion never saw the blow coming. Jasper pulled his horse close in, just behind the other man, simultaneously pulling a sock filled with pebbles from his saddlebag.

By the time the other man started to turn in question, the makeshift cosh connected with the side of his skull.

The messenger emitted a grunt and slid from the saddle. Jasper dismounted as well. For good measure, he swung the homemade weapon once more. The man ceased moving. Jasper rummaged through the saddlebags of the messenger's horse. Nothing of interest.

Damn. They could be interrupted at any moment. He had to hurry.

He turned his attention to the prone form of the messenger. He used his boot to roll the man onto his back, then slid his hands inside his jacket. His fingertips brushed paper.

Ah. He extracted a sealed envelope. His eyes bugged out as he made out the London address. Unbelievable. After days of watching Lady Pullington's routine—which was no different than any other pampered woman of the Quality—he'd almost believed this assignment pointless.

It looked as though his luck had changed.

Hastily, he shoved the letter, along with the cosh, to the bottom of his own saddlebag.

Next, Jasper slid his arms beneath the messenger's shoulders and dragged his limp form into the woods, well away from the road. There. No one had seen him. But the horse still presented a problem. If he turned it loose, it would return to Montgrave, signaling the staff that all was not well.

Merde. He hated messy work. Though, at least this time, the duke's servant provided an unwitting source of clean clothing when the job was done.

He retrieved a knife from the saddle scabbard on his own mount, then led the other horse back through the trees to where his master lay.

Minutes later, Jasper emerged from the woods, mounted up, and rode for London.

Philippe waited impatiently for Beatrice to emerge from her suite. Already much of the morning had been eaten away—first with seeing off Lady Bainbridge, after which his lovely muse had disappeared into her room without explanation. Rather than stalk the corridor of the guest wing, he'd gathered his materials, including a lightweight easel he'd acquired recently in London, and retreated to the library to wait. He'd toyed with a few sketches, but they didn't hold his attention. He would focus when they reached the rose garden, *if* the subject of the painting would be kind enough to join him.

At long last, he heard voices in the corridor. Shortly after, the door leading to the study opened, and Beatrice came through, followed by the freckled companion provided for her stay.

"Ladies." He stood and swept them both a gallant bow.

Beatrice smiled benignly. Her companion—Mrs.

Lily Moffett, he recalled—giggled and dropped an awkward curtsy.

"Are you ready to begin? I've asked the staff to pack a picnic lunch, that we may work uninterrupted." Not only that, it would give him an excuse to send Lily off to fetch it when they were ready. Though she seemed an agreeable sort, Philippe was not anxious to share the abandoned rose garden with anyone other than Beatrice.

"Lovely," Bea said. She offered no excuse for the lengthy delay in her room. Interesting. He knew ladies had need of privacy at times, but his Beatrice was turning out to be more mysterious than he'd first anticipated.

"Ooh, a picnic. How fun." Lily's eyes were bright—unusually so.

"Are you certain you are feeling well, Mrs. Moffett?" Philippe asked. Barring the possibility she was feverish, he had a fairly good idea what caused such a physical reaction—not that he'd stoop to calling her on it in front of others.

She giggled again, this time, he thought, nervously. "Oh, yes, Monsieur. Let us go."

He nodded, gathered up his things, and led the way out the door and toward the path, keeping an eye on both women. Until recently, he'd thought himself fairly adept with the ladies; in France and Italy, he understood their passion, their sultriness and sulkiness. But England was teaching him a great deal. He'd had to come to this odd country to discover his own mother was not the person he'd thought she was. And the English women were something new, as well. They were . . . quirky.

Quirky meant unpredictable—which could be a

problem, given what Philippe hoped to accomplish this day. It might take all his powers of persuasion to get Beatrice to agree, but if she did, the result would be worth it—the difference between a good painting and one that approached the transcendental.

They reached the rose garden, and Philippe set down his satchel on the bench, then propped his easel against it.

"Where shall I sit, that I will not be in the way?" Mrs. Moffett asked.

Back at the house, Philippe thought dryly—though he bore her no real ill will. But Beatrice pointed the woman to an unobtrusive spot, where she settled in, watching Philippe and Bea with curiosity.

Philippe took his time setting up easel and canvas. It had made an awkward load to carry all at once. For future sittings, he thought, the assistance of a footman might be useful.

Eventually, Lily Moffett lost interest in the slow proceedings and opened a book. A few minutes after that, her eyes drooped, and her chin bobbed forward. *Bon.* Luck was with him. It would be hard enough to convince Bea to do what he wanted without the looming judgment of another female.

By the time everything was ready, Bea, too, had drifted into daydreams—though unlike her companion, her eyes remained open. She reclined on the bench, her head tipped up to the patch of blue sky above the treetops. Her lips were softly parted, her features peaceful. For a moment, he wished this was how he'd chosen to paint her. He approached quietly, kneeling until they were level and he could speak quietly. "So, *ma belle* Beatrice, the sketches are done, and I have prepared the canvas. It is ready to begin. But there is one matter we have not yet discussed."

"Yes?" Bea asked, a soft smile playing at her lips.

She looked soft, pliable. Open to persuasion. He kept his tone light, almost teasing. "I know *where* I will paint you, and how you will be posed . . . but what will you be wearing?"

"Oh." Bea sat up. "I suppose we haven't discussed that. I can't imagine why it hasn't come up. I should have asked."

Philippe knew exactly why *he* hadn't raised the topic—he'd wanted the proper widow completely at ease with him first. Finally, she seemed to have reached that state.

"Do you need me in the same thing each sitting?" Bea asked. "I have gowns in a great many colors," she offered. "I am certain that if you tell me what you are thinking, I can produce one that will suit."

He considered her for a moment. She might have closet upon closet of gowns—but he doubted very much any of them bore the slightest resemblance to what he had in mind. One corner of his mouth quirked up in a half smile. "No, I don't think you can."

"Monsieur?"

"Do not take offense, beautiful Beatrice. From what I have seen of your wardrobe, each and every garment is both lovely and fashionable. Unfortunately, each and every garment is also quite proper."

Her eyes widened, and her tongue darted out to moisten her lips. He smiled, resisting the urge to taste them as she just had. Instead, he used his hands, gesturing as he told her his vision for this painting, hoping she would see the same thing.

"I intend to portray you not as a London socialite, but as a muse, an enchantress—like the women painted by the Italian masters of old. As to what a muse should wear, I envision something transcendent, almost . . . translucent."

"Oh, Lady Pullington, you must. It sounds so lovely."

Philippe stifled a groan at the sound of Lily's voice—he'd thought her well asleep. Although, it appeared she was on his side—hardly what he would have expected, but then, the Duchess of Beaufort *had* chosen her, and he was beginning to suspect Bea's closest friend had a rather unusual perception of the duties of both chaperones and companions.

Bea appeared to be considering the idea.

"Mrs. Moffett," Philippe requested, "would you be so kind as to check with the staff about our picnic? And ask them to add some extra lemonade—the weather is turning quite warm."

"Of course, monsieur." Lily jumped up, then took a moment to steady herself, as though she'd risen too fast, before hurrying down the path. Unless he missed his mark, she would not hurry nearly so much in returning to them.

Philippe smiled. "Beatrice, will you trust me?"

Eyes still wide, she gave him a solemn nod.

He stood and moved to the bags in which he'd carried his supplies. From one, he withdrew a folded length of cloth.

Turning to her, he shook it out.

* * *

Bea gasped as rays of sunlight danced off the most beautiful fabric she'd ever seen. A pale rose color, shot through with gold threads, the silk was incredibly fine—and incredibly sheer.

I intend to portray you . . . as a muse, an enchantress, he'd said, his face alight with creative possibility.

Bea could picture it, too, and the very decadence of the image aroused more than her artistic sensibilities. Heat pooled at her woman's core. She didn't know if she could be so daring, but she took a wicked thrill in the idea of it—the idea of standing in the woods, clad in something akin to gossamer fairy wings, with Philippe close by, capturing her every curve with the skilled strokes of his brush.

She stood, drawn to the shimmering fabric as though it held some strange power over her. She fingered it lightly. "Beautiful," she whispered.

Philippe rose as well, holding the sheer curtain of material between them, and in the depths of his blue eyes she saw the intense hope that she would share this vision of his—that she would allow him to paint her in this magical fabric.

There was a problem, though. "It is beautiful," she repeated. "But the fabric is uncut. To have it sewn into a gown would surely take too long."

Philippe chuckled. "Indeed, it would." He held the length against her shoulders. "But I do not think the ancient muses wore proper English gowns. If it were draped, just so, with a few pins to hold it . . ."

Bea drew in a shaky breath. He wanted her clad in a sheer swath of fabric with naught but a few pins to keep it in place? Oh, if only her sense of propriety were stronger than her imagination, she could say "no." But now that she understood his vision, now that it had sunk in, she knew nothing else would suffice.

"Will you trust me, Beatrice?" he asked again.

The question jarred her from the fantasy—but only slightly. Philippe's question referred only to art, to the matter of her attire. Not to weightier matters of trust, like treason or espionage. Or love. And thankfully, this interlude at Montgrave had given her no further cause to believe Philippe anything other than an artist—one whose vision for her was so captivating, she simply had to help make it reality.

"Yes," she whispered, placing a hand over his that still held the fabric against her. "Show me how you wish me to begin."

Chapter 11

Lily Moffett was not a fool. A souse, perhaps, she admitted to herself as she ambled toward the manor house. But not a fool. Jean Philippe Durand couldn't have cared less whether their picnic lunch was ready. He just wanted Lily away from the rose garden. Well, she didn't mind obliging him.

The picnic would undoubtedly be waiting the moment she inquired—the duke's staff never missed a beat. But after all, there was no hurry . . .

Cousin Elizabeth had not misled her—the wine meant for meals was entirely pleasing to the palate. Yet it could not staunch the craving for something more intense. Something she knew was within reach, waiting for her, calling her from the cabinet in the study. She felt it the moment she set foot in the house—as though invisible, silent arms stretched out and drew her inexorably toward the brandy.

The glassware was conveniently stored on a shelf just above the bottles, waiting for her. She plucked a short glass from the first row. She could always wash and replace it—no one had to know.

Next, she picked a bottle that was already open and poured just the tiniest taste. Why, that was barely half a finger. But brandy such as this practically *required* a proper mouthful to truly be appreciated. She poured a tad more.

Lily inhaled deeply before taking that first sip. Oh, yes. Yes, yes. She knew women who were fools over men. But this was far more satisfying than any man—not to mention more reliable. Some might call her a sot, but truly, she had a passion for fine spirits.

The liquor flooded her veins, working its magic like always, softening the edges of a capricious world. She relaxed into the haze, allowing herself just one more pour when the first disappeared all too soon. But then she stopped. She could not afford to lose her wits completely.

Would the duke notice that the bottle held a bit less than before, the next time he selected it? Likely not. That could be months from now. Still, to be on the safe side, she poured a measure of water into the bottle. There. To the eye, if not the tongue, the bottle appeared no different than before she'd first touched it.

Even better, this lovely little trick would work just as well on the remaining bottles as it had on the first. Thank you, cousin Elizabeth. For once in her life, Lily Moffett was in for a good time.

"What do you think has happened to Mrs. Moffett?" Philippe asked, voicing the question on both their minds.

The sun rode high in the sky, filtering through

the trees to warm the little clearing where Bea and Philippe stood.

"I'm sure I don't know," Bea told him honestly. They'd been waiting for her companion's return for some minutes—ever since Bea had realized she would need someone to assist her with changing out of her own structured garments and into the beautiful folds of gold-shot rose Philippe had shown her.

After that realization she'd stood nervously, trying not to think how much of her body would soon be bared before Philippe's eyes. It was one thing to get caught up in a kiss, to touch him in the dark safety of an enclosed carriage. It was quite another to freely, knowingly expose herself in the clear light of day.

A wicked thrill shot through her as she met his eye now. "Likely she'll return at any moment," Bea said. "Are you hungry?"

"Starving," the Frenchman averred. At the raw heat in his voice, Bea's throat went dry. He wasn't talking about food.

Bea gazed back at the path. Where was Lily? If she were here to assist, it might calm the tension sparking between artist and muse. Perhaps infuse some sensibility back into Bea, for she seemed to be losing her own.

Unfortunately Lily—not to mention the picnic lunch—was nowhere to be seen. Bea could find no overtly objectionable qualities to Elizabeth's cousin. She was ever cheerful and friendly. But she was also turning out to be nearly as unreliable, at least when it came to the usual duties of a companion, as Elizabeth herself had been.

Finally they heard footsteps on the path, accompanied by humming. But the face that appeared seconds later belonged to a young woman Bea recognized as one of the kitchen maids. Since the night she and Charity had visited Vauxhall Gardens, she'd begun paying unusual attention to the faces of the servant class.

The maid held up a large basket, attempting a curtsy but wobbling under the container's weight. "My lady, and monsieur, your luncheon."

"Please, set it just over there." Bea cast a hand toward the bench.

The maid hurried over and gratefully relinquished her burden. "Cook prepared a lovely spread. Shall I set it all out for you?"

"That won't be necessary," Bea said. "But you *can* tell me—did you happen to see Mrs. Moffett on your way?"

The maid's eager smile drooped and she shuffled her feet.

Philippe cocked a brow, plainly curious at her reaction.

She looked between her superiors, finally focusing on Bea, and answered, "I did, at that. I'm right sorry to tell you, my lady, your companion felt a trifle . . . indisposed, when I left her. She says she's terrible sorry, and hopes you'll be able to continue without her this afternoon."

"Oh, dear. Does she need assistance?"

"No, no," the maid hastily assured her. "She's in good hands."

Philippe folded his arms but held his tongue. Bea would have dearly loved to know his thoughts on this newest development.

"Is there aught else I can do for you, my lady?" the maid questioned.

"No, thank you. You may return to your other duties."

The girl curtsied again and went tripping down the path.

Bea turned to Philippe. In unison, they eyed the picnic basket, then the length of fabric Philippe had left resting on the edge of the stone basin.

Bea took measure of the sun once more, and made her decision. He would see her, study her every curve, soon enough. It seemed silly to insist upon modesty now.

"I am not so very hungry after all. Better we make use of this fine afternoon," she said softly. She gestured to the back of her gown. "I cannot manage the hooks myself," she told him. "If we are to begin today, you will have to do it."

His eyes darkened. "You're sure? I could catch that maid if I hurry."

"Yes, I'm sure." To confirm it, she turned her back to him, suppressing a shiver as he began working to undo her clothing.

His fingers were deft but not hurried, his breath warm on her neck.

"Beatrice." His usual smooth tone had been replaced by one deeper, huskier.

She turned her head, slightly, toward him.

His fingers stilled. "If you do not wish your skin to be caressed as it is bared, you should find a maid and ask her to do this chore." He cleared his throat. "I can promise that once you are draped in the silk, I shall be once again caught up with the need to capture your image, to do justice to your beauty, your spirit, with my paints. I am, first and foremost, an artiste." He blew out a breath. "But I am also a man. To ask me to unclothe, yet not touch, you . . . I cannot promise such restraint."

He was giving her a choice. But she'd already made her decision.

"I do not wish a maid to do this for me."

His hands exerted gentle pressure on her shoulders, turning her until she met his eyes. Her knees grew weak at the intensity she saw there, the acknowledgement of her choice and all it meant.

His fingers returned to the hooks, still unhurried, and this time she longed for him to complete the task, so she might feel his touch on her bare skin, as he'd promised. He worked the bodice loose, until her sleeves slipped down and the rest of the high-waisted gown billowed to the ground at her feet. He paused to press a kiss to her bare shoulder, then pushed the thin straps of her chemise over her shoulders, sending that garment down to meet her gown.

Her breath came faster at the feel of the spring air, the dappling of sunshine, in places never before exposed to such elements. How very wild she'd become.

Next went her stays. She hadn't been daring enough to go without them—but after today, she might reconsider. She'd have little left to fear after this.

"*Ah, belle,*" Philippe murmured, his breath sending pleasurable little shivers across her skin. He skimmed her shoulder blades and bent in to kiss her neck while his thumbs came together to stroke down her spine, past the small of her back, stopping only when they came to her bottom. He took her into his arms, pulling her close, until she felt the solid wall of his chest at her back, the thrill of his erection brushing against her buttocks.

She wiggled against him, then felt her body rocked by the jolt of pleasure that shot through her as he used one hand to haul her tighter against his hips, the other to cup her breast, brushing over her peaked nipple.

Oh, God, she needed him to keep doing that. She arched into his hand. When had she become such a wanton?

She heard his breath grow as ragged as her own. Finally he turned her to face him, the force of his movement setting her off balance as his mouth swooped down to claim hers, tasting, plundering, until she could think of nothing but her need for him—to touch him, to explore and offer him the same mindless pleasure she felt at his touch.

But he was still fully clothed.

She felt the strength of his back, his lean torso, even slid her hands over his bottom, then beneath the hem of his shirt until her fingers met warm, taut skin. Never had she dreamt of touching a man this way, of *desiring* to touch a man this way, yet now she whimpered at how good it felt. She lifted the shirt, expecting him to rip it off and toss it away. But he paused, just long enough to rasp, "Beatrice, if you do that—and dear God, I want you to, I must warn you, I *will* lose control."

Her breath caught. She pulled back to meet his gaze, though her hands continued to roam his back, unwilling to cease touching, seeking. But if he was about to lose control . . . "Shall I stop?"

He shook his head slowly, a smile playing at his lips. "No. Control is indeed a worthy accomplishment, *mon coeur*, but it is only when one relinquishes control that one is truly able to experience passion. To experience *life*." The smile grew. "It is not a bad thing, *chérie*, to lose control. Not if you accept it is what you want. What we both want."

She heard truth in his words, for she had enough experience to know she'd been missing something for most of her life. In her marriage, "relations" had consisted of a few mercifully short encounters in the bedroom. The difference was literally night and day. Now she stood gloriously naked, no bedroom in sight, and she hoped desperately this encounter would *not* be short-lived.

As for what was surely about to happen, as for physical intimacy . . . Bea had been so wrong about everything else, it only stood to reason she had a lot to learn where *that* was concerned, too.

At her lengthy pause, Philippe gave a low chuckle and pulled her close. "Stop thinking so hard."

That did it. At the touch of her breasts to his chest, the feel of his erection pressing toward her, nestling against her hips, desire raced through her anew. "All right."

She tipped back her head, surrendering to the sensation of Philippe kissing her neck, trailing his tongue down her throat, her collarbone, until he drew one peaked nipple into his mouth and tugged.

She cried out, arching toward him. The pleasure was unbearable—and yet she needed so much more.

He released her, just long enough to toss the picnic blanket across a grassy spot and divest himself of shirt and trousers. He pulled her to the ground with him, lying atop the blanket.

He rolled her onto her back and hovered over her, murmuring French endearments she only half-registered between kisses, between his tongue doing maddening things to her breasts while his fingers dipped between the folds of her sex.

Bea mindlessly opened further for him—never had she imagined such need, such pleasure.

"*Mon Dieu,* Beatrice," he rasped. "*Tres belle. Chérie,* you drive a man to madness. I can wait no longer." He positioned himself at her entry. Bea braced herself.

"Relax, my sweet," he murmured. "You are so wet, *oui,* so ready. This will be only good."

He pushed forward, and Bea arched up at this new onslaught of pleasure. Never had she felt like *this*. He drew back, then drove in again, and she lifted her hips to meet him. "Yes, oh, yes."

His thrusts formed a rhythm, growing faster as he teased her nipples, his other arm bracing his weight just above her. Her hands dug into his back, pulling him closer again and again as the pleasure built into a desperate need, a need indefinable, undeniable.

He thrust deep, just as his mouth closed again over hers, and Bea came undone, the answer to her need coming in a shower of sensation that left her trembling. He sensed it and drove into her once, twice more, his head lifting, falling back as he gave into his own desire and she felt him coursing inside her.

He collapsed, rolling to the side and pulling her with him. He cradled her head to his chest, his heart thundering nearly as much as her own. What was he thinking? Ought she say something? She lacked the sophistication of her Parisian counterparts . . . though she had learned one thing.

"You were right," she told him. "Never have I experienced such passion—or even imagined such utter abandonment of control."

He laughed and squeezed her tight.

The breeze blew across her skin, reminding Bea she was lying naked in the woods. As though of the same mind, Philippe shifted next to her, propping himself up on an elbow. "Beautiful Beatrice," he murmured. "Perhaps we should dress?" He eyed the picnic basket. "And also eat? I am famished."

"How like a man," she teased him, attempting to keep the mood light and cozy. As desperately as she wanted to know his deeper thoughts, she wasn't sure she could bear it if they did not match her own—if what they'd just done had not meant as much to him as it had to her.

She allowed him to help her dress, at least to a point of half-modesty. There was no point redoing all those buttons if she were going to be clad in the rose silk after they'd eaten. She laid out the luncheon. The staff had thoughtfully sent both lemonade and wine. She chose and poured the wine, preferring to soften the remaining edges of the day. When they sat, Bea was surprised to discover she was just as ravenous as Philippe, and they both ate heartily. She let her gaze wander as she bit into herbed pheasant and spiced cucumbers.

Philippe's paints still sat at the edge of the rose garden, virtually unused this day. The afternoon had not yet waned. She only hoped that if Lily returned, her companion didn't question too closely the lack of progress on the painting. Bea felt heat creep up her cheeks.

How very much her life had changed in a few short weeks. As for her brief foray into the world of espionage, she was glad that was over. But everything else, everything since meeting Philippe—she wouldn't change for the world. Of course, eventually he *would* complete his painting, and what then? She didn't want to look that far ahead. Because Bea knew she could never go back.

Going back meant the endless procession of teas and soirees that left her mind full of meaningless chatter and her heart an empty void. She *couldn't* go back to that life, which had really been no life at all. Not now that she'd known the first taste of passion. To do so would be naught but a slow death.

She was in over her head already. Because as much as Bea knew she could never go back, she feared what would become of her if she gave herself over, fully, to this desire. No flame could burn so hot and last for long.

He would paint her, consume her with that passion of his. And when he was done, she'd be alone again, left clinging to memories in the face of a bleak future.

Chapter 12

The note consisted of two lines:

Network compromised. Being watched.
Must act soon.

Merde. Richard crumpled the scrap of paper.
Matters were getting out of hand. André had promised him they were close, but the fact was, Richard
did not yet have the British war plans in hand.

He kept his breath controlled. Panic was unac-
ceptable. And "being watched" was not the same as
being caught. Richard strode to his closets, grabbed
the bag he always kept ready, and summoned his
carriage and driver.

"Le port de Calais," he told the coachman, and
settled in for the short journey to the port.

There was a slight chance—depending on how
much had been leaked—he could salvage this. Or
rather, he could salvage himself. There was no
pride in going down with a sinking ship.

But there was no pride in the action he was

considering, either. Richard had never been close to his son, never understood his complete disinterest in world affairs, but he'd always stopped short of using him as a pawn in those affairs.

The stakes, however, had risen. The future of France was at risk. Philippe, whether he knew it or not, was already involved. Richard's network hadn't been able to prove Philippe was intentionally conspiring with the light-skirted British informant he'd chosen as the subject of his work, but the likelihood grew stronger with every day Philippe remained in England. It appeared his son had fallen prey to the long tradition of female informants who used their charms to accomplish their mission. The boy had told him he was planning only a short visit to the country, "as a favor to *Maman*." Now, it seemed, he was in no hurry to leave.

Philippe's presence there, and his activities, presented Richard with an opportunity he could not ignore. Because if he didn't take action, the name Richard Durand would soon be linked with whatever other members of the network were known, and after that there would be no saving him. Whether by official court trial or a knife in the dark, the British would find him. There was the possibility they'd forgive a popular artist who made a mistake. There was no possibility they'd forgive a known supporter of the Emperor. And Richard did not relish the prospect of prison, exile, or death.

First things first. Richard needed to join his son in England. Then, he would see.

* * *

Bea had heard nothing. And she'd written nothing—nothing of her own, that is.

She'd been so caught up in writing and deciphering words pertaining to spies and war, she'd had no time for spring's usual words of growth and love. Yet spring held the intoxication of new beginnings, the idyllic pleasure of hours spent rediscovering nature's wonders. She felt it every time she and Philippe ventured to the rose garden, and she itched to set her thoughts to paper.

She understood, for the first time, the depth of passion that had driven the poets of old. She longed to emulate them, to infuse her own writing with her newfound wisdom.

Especially now that Bea was away from London, the threat of sinister plots, of French spies with dark purposes, seemed remote indeed. Instead, she had only the pleasurable routine of posing for Philippe—sometimes with her erstwhile companion Lily, but more often not. The abandoned rose garden became a haven, a place where no one could touch them, no one could shatter the spell Philippe wove each time he picked up a brush and paints.

Her fingers itched to follow his lead, to pick up pen and paper and capture her thoughts in verse, but it would have to wait. Philippe seemed understanding that his model was human, and therefore must shift occasionally from the pose in which he set her, but she doubted that his tolerance extended to painting her while her head was bent over a notebook.

Besides, she'd never mentioned to him that she wrote.

One other matter also kept Bea from being able to relax fully into the idylls of spring: the promise she'd made to aid the Foreign Secretary. *Why* hadn't she heard anything from him? London was not far—he should have received her note by Sunday evening. He was a busy man, but surely he would not hesitate to respond.

Until she knew for certain the matter was resolved, she could not put it completely behind her.

Alternate venues of information—sought in the absence of direct words from Viscount Castlereagh—were proving just as fruitless. The day she'd arrived at Montgrave, Bea had professed a fondness for London news to the staff. They'd seen to it she received all the notable circulars and gossip sheets, beginning that same day. She scanned each one as they came, searching for any clue as to the fate of the French spy ring, but neither Monday or Tuesday's paper contained anything useful—only a mention of Miss Kettridge's latest performance in *Love Laughs at Locksmiths*.

The fact that the actress was still performing clearly meant she hadn't been arrested. Why? Viscount Castlereagh was a clever man. Alex trusted him. Perhaps the Foreign Secretary was laying a trap, or biding his time while gathering stronger evidence. Maybe what she'd provided wasn't enough to hold up in a trial. Of course, Bea wasn't certain spies were often brought to court. In her poet's imagination, such things were handled by cloaked men in the quiet of the night.

Although she'd wanted to wash her hands of the intrigue, Bea now wished she knew what was happening. Beyond idle curiosity, she felt a responsibility to see this through. She'd turned her knowledge over to more capable hands. But she couldn't shake the sense of impending trouble.

Her sense of foreboding was confirmed on Wednesday morning, when she received a note from Viscount Castlereagh.

Actually, she received two. The first was illegible—until a second messenger arrived bearing a translation key. Then, the message became very clear . . . and very worrisome.

> *Lady Pullington,*
> *I am anxious to hear from you. My sources indicate you may have had the opportunity to make new observations. Remember that even the smallest seed can grow into a garden. The messenger who delivered the translation key for this note will await your response. Evans is trustworthy. He bears identifying papers, but as those are not always reliable, you will recognize him by the wart on his chin, from which sprout two dark hairs. Should this message arrive to you from any other source, do not respond.*

The note was not signed, but the messenger, Evans—who did indeed bear a hairy wart on his chin—showed her papers that identified both him and his employer, the Foreign Secretary.

Oh, dear. Bea pressed her fingers to her temples. This explained the lack of news in the papers—Viscount Castlereagh had never received her letter. The head of the Foreign Office was clever, though. In spite of her lack of communication, he knew where she'd been, and with whom—and the reference to the seed was clearly meant to remind her of the first French note that had started this mess.

She looked up to meet the gaze of the messenger, who had retreated some distance while she translated and read the note, but remained present and alert.

"I gather Viscount Castlereagh has received no messages from me?" she asked, needing to confirm her suspicion.

"I cannot speak to that, my lady," Evans answered. "All I can tell you is that when I left London this morning, he instructed me not to return without your response. And, begging your pardon, my lady, but I am to wait while you compose it, so that I may verify it was produced by none other than yourself."

"An understandable precaution." Bea answered politely, but her mind was whirling. What *had* happened to the letter she'd sent this past Sunday?

The Montgrave butler had recommended Mr. Reilly, the man she'd asked to make the delivery, as a trustworthy servant. When he hadn't returned, she'd assumed he'd stayed on at the Bainbridges' London house—especially knowing the couple was in residence there. Now, she wondered what fate might have befallen him.

"I sent a message some days ago," she worried aloud.

"And the man you sent it with? He promised it was delivered per your instruction?"

"I haven't seen him since," she admitted. Was she being too open? If Viscount Castlereagh trusted this man to carry his codes, surely she could speak with him. From his speech, the messenger was clearly more educated than a simple errand runner.

Evans paused. "That is distressing," he finally said. "I do not know what you can do now, besides relay that information to my employer. I can advise you, however, that when I am to deliver a message, my employer splits my payments into three parts—one before I set out, as a matter of goodwill, and the other two when I return with confirmation the job is done. This method ensures I've reason not to dally in my return."

"A well thought-out plan, indeed. I shall remember that." Bea once again appreciated the Foreign Secretary's cleverness—if only she'd had similar foresight, she might have known earlier there was a problem. She lapsed into silence for a moment.

Then, aware Evans was watching, she pulled out a fresh sheet of paper and dipped her pen in ink. "Am I to respond in the same code?" she asked.

"It is safer, my lady."

She nodded and bent her head to the paper, referring to the key for the proper mix of letters and numbers to convey what she'd tried to say before—along with the information that her lack of communication was not intentional. The code was not difficult, but without the key, she could well imagine a person spending quite a few frustrating hours trying to decipher a message. A far more clever system than what the French had used. She understood now how careless they'd been.

She, too, had been careless, Bea realized as the knot in the pit of her stomach grew larger. It was too much to hope her last message had been innocently misplaced. And the Italian language in which it was written would cause but a slight delay for someone truly determined.

She should have seen the Foreign Secretary personally, before coming to Montgrave. Her throat felt thick. She'd let her feelings for Philippe blind her good judgment—though, really, Viscount Castlereagh ought to have provided better instructions for how they were to communicate. He'd played this game long enough to know its dangers. Bea had not—though she was quickly learning.

Someone knocked on the door. Hastily she shoved her work under a large book at the side of the desk. She saw Evans's eyes widen as Philippe entered the room.

"Ah. Pardon," the artist said as his gaze took in Bea at the desk and the unfamiliar man standing across the room. "I did not realize you were occupied— I had thought we might begin early today, as it looks as though we may be in for rain later. But I have interrupted, for which I apologize. A matter of business?"

"Yes," Bea confirmed, amazed she could speak at all when her heart felt as though it had lodged in her throat. "We should conclude shortly, and I will come find you."

At this obvious dismissal, Philippe glanced curiously between Bea and Evans once more before exiting the study.

Bea took a few deep breaths, willing her heart to slow to its normal place. What in heaven's name had possessed Philippe to seek her out at this very moment? Unless he knew what she was about? No. How could he? She'd given him almost no reason to suspect . . . save for that one moment at the theater, but they'd put that behind them.

She pulled the papers back from under the book, working quickly now. She coded her remaining words, sealed the missive, and handed it to the Foreign Secretary's waiting messenger.

"Thank you, my lady," he said, tucking it into his jacket. "I will make utmost haste in delivering this."

"Do take care, Mr. Evans. Given the disappearance of my first letter and its carrier, I am given to worry."

"Do not worry overmuch, Lady Pullington." He opened one side of his coat, revealing a small pistol at his side. A glance at his boot revealed another bulge. "I have been in this business for many years."

He tipped his head toward the desk where the key lay. "If you don't mind a word of advice, burn that."

"Of course. Godspeed, Mr. Evans."

With a quick bow, the man was out the door. Bea walked to the desk, retrieved the incriminating code with the tips of her fingers, and tossed it into the fire.

Charity tucked her second favorite fan into her reticule late Wednesday morning, then went to find the coachman to take her to the Wilbournes' home. Her maid trailed dutifully behind, an unknowing accomplice in Charity's plot to confirm that the French spy—or one of them, anyway—worked for the Wilbournes.

She'd tossed around any number of far-fetched excuses for inviting herself over before settling on the simplest—that she believed she'd left her fan at their home the night of the salon and wished to search for it. That was easier than inventing a social occasion. Alicia Wilbourne was ten years older than she, and her husband a good deal older than that, so although they moved in the same circles, Charity couldn't quite count the couple among her close friends.

Today was the first opportunity she'd had to execute her plan. When she'd determined *not* to go to Montgrave with Bea and Elizabeth, her mother had taken that as an indication Charity was enjoying the success of her first Season. Thus, she'd spent the past three days being dragged to a seemingly endless series of events designed to thrust her in front of the ton's eligible bachelors, or ingratiate her with their mamas.

Finally she'd broken free, as her mother had played cards all night and awoken this morning with a headache.

When Charity arrived and was ushered in, Lady Wilbourne was unfailingly gracious to her unexpected guest. "You say you've misplaced your fan?"

"My very most favorite," Charity averred. "I was searching for it the other evening and could not locate it anywhere. I tried to think when I last had it—I know I carried it the night of the salon honoring Monsieur Durand, but could not recall having seen it since."

"How troublesome," Lady Wilbourne sympathized. "Has anything turned up?"

"I don't believe so. What did it look like?"

"It had a lovely Oriental pattern in blue." Charity gave her the description of the fan currently residing in her reticule. If necessary, she could slip it behind a piece of furniture, then "find" it. "Would it be terribly imposing to ask if I might look around?"

"Not at all. I'll even help you. I am forever losing things and know how frustrating it can be. Have you come alone, dear?"

"My maid is in the carriage. I told her I'd only be a moment."

"Very well." Lady Wilbourne glanced at the clock. "My mother-in-law is due to call soon—but perhaps we shall be lucky and find your fan quickly. Come. We'll search the ballroom first, as most of the guests mingled there during the salon."

Charity followed her. Sure enough, Alicia Wilbourne was friendly to a fault. Together they looked behind every piece of furniture and potted plant—even in one of the back rooms where items were stored when not in use. Aside from the butler who'd seen her in, and two maids busily dusting, none of whom matched her memory of the spy at Vauxhall Gardens, Charity saw no other servants.

She was desperate to shake her helpful hostess so she could accomplish the real mission she'd come here for. But if she "found" her fan, there'd be no reason to linger. So they continued the pointless search. Finally, Charity asked, "Do you suppose any of your staff who worked that evening might recall seeing my fan?"

Alicia Wilbourne shook her head. "If it was left behind and one of the servants found it, I'm certain they would have returned it to me. Reliable help is difficult to find, and Robert and I are fortunate to have an excellent staff."

"Yes, I'm sure. I didn't mean to imply otherwise,"

Charity apologized. Though, secretly she had her doubts as to the excellence—or loyalty—of that staff.

"Oh, I know you didn't." Lady Wilbourne smiled. "No offense taken, dear." A bell sounded toward the front of the house. "That must be Robert's mother. Would you excuse me a moment? You're welcome to keep looking, though I can't fathom where else your fan could be."

"Of course," Charity said. "I'll search just a minute more—and don't worry, I can see myself out. Terribly sorry to have troubled you so. 'Tis likely I misplaced it elsewhere and am too henwitted to remember." She rolled her eyes as though exasperated with her own foibles. "Oh. Before you go, my lady, might you point me in the direction of the necessary room? 'Tis possible I set it there while seeing to my hair."

"Certainly." Lady Wilbourne pointed it out. "I hope you find your fan, Charity. Tell me if you do!"

She left the room, and Charity breathed a sigh of relief. Finally.

Now, where would that footman be? If he'd pinned the note to Bea's coat, accidentally or not, it stood to reason he was an upstairs servant—the Wilbournes wouldn't have entrusted the care of their guests' belongings to the lower staff. On a hunch, she headed in the direction of the time-honored gathering place of servants—the kitchens. Or at least what she hoped was in the direction of the kitchens.

Don't go looking for trouble, Bea had implored her. Well, she wasn't. She was looking to be helpful. Bea was busy at Montgrave, being painted—and, Charity suspected, wooed by the handsome artist—

leaving Charity with a second chance to prove her value.

She moved carefully, avoiding being seen. She could always say she'd become lost, but better to avoid such an awkward situation.

She entered a corridor that was narrow and plain. Good. She'd found the servants' quarters. The rich aroma of stewing meat wafted toward her. She heard clinking sounds and the low murmur of voices.

She crept forward, but there was a problem. If she wanted to see who was talking, she would have to expose herself. Reports of her odd behavior would surely reach Lady Wilbourne, ruining her chances for future reconnaissance. Was it worth the risk? What if she learned nothing?

There had to be a better way. Charity turned to go.

"Peters," a woman's voice called. "Do me a favor— carry that silver to the storeroom and put it up? The mistress wants her newest set out instead."

"Anything for you, luv," a man's voice responded.

A moment later Charity heard footfalls coming closer. Eek! There was no place to hide—save a door to her right. Without thinking, Charity pulled it open and slipped inside.

She felt around as her eyes adjusted to the dark. The room that hid her boasted no windows. It was small, lined with shelves and . . . oh, *no*. Her chosen hiding spot was a storeroom—exactly where the servant called Peters was headed.

The footsteps stopped. Above the pounding of blood at her temples, Charity heard fumbling, and a moment later, the door cracked open.

"Bloody hell!" The man at the door dropped a

candlestick in surprise. He bent to retrieve it. Straightening, he looked her up and down. "An' who might you be?"

"I—uh, that is—I became lost . . ." Charity stammered, her heart pounding as though trying to escape the confines of her ribs. No question. This was the same man. Peters, the woman had called him. It sounded English. So did his speech. If she didn't already know, she'd never have guessed him French. Even in his surprise he'd sworn like any British commoner, with no hint of an accent. But his face was unmistakable.

Unfortunately, it was the nature of spies to be suspicious. Peters narrowed his eyes. "Long way from the main rooms, you are, miss. Surely you didn't expect to find your way back while shut in this closet." He folded his arms.

Think like a spy. Be clever, like Bea. Except Bea hadn't gotten caught. Ugh. How could she have been so stupid?

She should just leave—that's what she'd been about to do anyway. But he stood blocking the doorway. Frustration filtered through her fear . . . and with the anger, she found her strength. Who was he to challenge her? He didn't know *she* knew he wasn't just any common servant. So she lifted her nose, and in the haughtiest tone she knew, told him, "I don't believe I owe you any explanations."

She knew from the way he eyed her that he registered the difference in the quality of their attire, yet he did not move.

"You are blocking my way," she pointed out.

His brows raised. "Indeed I am. I'm simply making sure there's no trouble, here. You could be a thief, for all I know. And a servant's job is to protect the interests of his master."

"And who *is* your master?"

It was the wrong thing to say. Or maybe the wrong way to say it. Either way, Charity knew she was in trouble by the way his expression became doubly guarded.

"A yellow-haired woman of Quality, sneaking around with no good reason," he mused. "Tell me, are you acquainted with a Lady Pullington?"

She was caught. Because before she had time to answer—or to scream—his large hand clapped over her mouth. His other pulled the door closed, shutting them both within.

Chapter 13

Philippe waited for Bea to come out of the study. What was she up to? And who was that man? Not a lover—he hadn't sensed a romantic undercurrent at all. And yet her nervous reaction to his interruption told him her "business" was not merely a household matter.

The woman he'd pegged as a shy but beautiful widow was turning into a bundle of contradictions.

Meanwhile, his own matters of "business" had been far more simple. Meaning practically nonexistent. He'd received one letter from Lord Owen, originally addressed to his lodgings in London and then sent on from the hotel. The old man had written to inform him that, given the current state of politics with France's rogue Emperor, he felt it his duty to return to London to take his seat in Parliament. Philippe, he said, was welcome to set up a studio in his house on Charles Street.

A kind offer. In fact, Philippe suspected the Englishman's true motivation lay less in politics than in getting to know his son better. Philippe felt that same pull. He would never know Henri Gaudet—his mother's secrecy had ensured that. The best he could do was learn from the man who had loved and lost her.

Perhaps when he and Bea finished at Montgrave, he would trade his hotel lodgings for a stay with the father he'd never known. How awkward could that be? Philippe laughed. Good thing he'd never been the inhibited type.

As for the man who'd raised him, he'd heard nothing. Not that he expected letters from home. After all, he was a grown man, and had never been close to his stepfather. He imagined Richard was currently waist-deep in political maneuverings. Likely he hadn't spared so much as a thought for his wayward, art-loving son.

Philippe tapped his foot impatiently. Mrs. Moffett was ready to go as well, so he studied her while they waited. She sat demurely on a chair, a calm contrast to Philippe's unchanneled energy. Though he judged her to be a few years older than Bea, she had the flightiness of a much younger girl. And, unless he was mistaken, a fondness for imbibing spirits when she thought no one was looking.

Not that Mrs. Moffett wasn't agreeable—in fact, Philippe had to commend the Duchess of Beaufort on her excellent taste in companions. He was in no place to protest Beatrice's desire to give the appearance of propriety during their interlude at Montgrave, but he was infinitely relieved that such appearances did not reflect reality. When the duchess had first mentioned the presence of a widowed cousin at Montgrave, he'd pictured someone far more dour.

As usual, Philippe's thoughts turned to art. He'd never painted a freckled woman before. Not that he was interested in painting Mrs. Moffett. But it would be a challenge—capturing that sun-dappled, healthy glow, as opposed to the spotted, diseased look he feared most artists would produce.

As though she sensed his scrutiny, a pink flush grew beneath her freckles, and she trained her gaze out the window and away from Philippe.

Ah, well. If he ever found a freckled subject who intrigued him, he would rise to the challenge. But for now, he had the pleasure of painting Bea's creamy complexion, enviably smooth and oh-so lovely when her cheeks betrayed her emotions with that telltale pink flush.

Finally Bea emerged from the study. "I am sorry to have kept you both waiting," she said politely. "One quick word with the butler, and I shall be ready to proceed to the woods."

Her tone seemed unusually formal. Minutes later, as the trio traipsed toward the abandoned rose garden, Bea walked with her head bent forward, her brows knit together. She seemed withdrawn, barely responding to the animated chatter of her companion, or his own comments about the work he had planned for the day.

Adding this to the way she'd dismissed him in the study when he'd interrupted, and Philippe was discomfited. Did Bea regret their lovemaking? God, he hoped not—but women were often unpredictable about such things. The past couple afternoons had been, for him at least, a paradise of art and passion. He'd managed to get her alone a second time, though only briefly. Each taste of his beautiful English muse had but whet his appetite.

He wanted more, and he also wanted Bea to feel the same toward him. Whatever was bothering her, he would go to any length necessary to see it resolved. And then he would get her alone again.

When they reached the clearing, Bea and her companion scurried deeper into the woods, arms laden with the rose silk. Yesterday, when Mrs. Moffett had first helped Bea into the translucent costume, she'd not batted an eye at the impropriety. In fact, she'd made a rapturous comparison to the ancient Greek statues a former employer had collected. An apt comparison, if not entirely expected. But Philippe wasn't one to look a gift horse in the mouth. Lily Moffett was an *ideal* companion for Beatrice during this venture at Montgrave.

Philippe set up his easel and began mixing pigment, all the while trying not to think about Bea's naked body, the whisper of silk over a dusky nipple . . . it was no use. He'd grown hard at the first stray image that had filtered into his thoughts. The curse of a vivid imagination—he could see her smooth skin as though she already stood before him. He shifted on the stool behind his easel, then blew out an exasperated breath and stood to take a walk.

It would never do for Bea and Lily—experienced women, both—to return to the clearing and find him in such an obvious state of arousal.

He returned a few minutes later to see Bea sitting demurely on the garden bench—as demurely, at any rate, as it was possible to be when one was clad in fabric designed to be even more alluring than actual nakedness. One look at her sent a jolt straight to his groin.

Thankfully, Philippe was, as he'd promised, an artist, first and foremost. Not that it was easy to drag his mind away from the thought of unwrapping her like a treasured gift, but he *did* want to paint her. Very much.

Mrs. Moffett sat nearby, her face serenely tilted upward, toward the sun dappling through the leaves, as though it was nothing out of the ordinary for a paid companion to assist her employer into a situation any other person would surely deem compromising.

"*Je suis enchanté,*" Philippe declared as he strode back into the clearing.

Bea started and stood, the silk slipping precariously. "This is how we arranged it before, right?" she asked, grasping anxiously at the material.

Philippe chuckled. "*Oui, chérie.* Just so. Shall we?" He waved an arm toward the basin, and Bea adopted the pose they'd both become so familiar with.

Philippe settled back behind his easel, and quickly fell into the absorbing process of creation. Time slipped by unnoticed. If he could not worship her with his body at this moment, he could do so with his brush.

"Why did you choose to come to England now?"

"Pardon?" He shook his head to clear it. Bea's pose had her standing with one outstretched hand grazing the new leaves on a branch. He'd been concentrating on getting just the right angle, the right softness of touch, to replicate her pose.

He'd chosen to work on that particularly difficult piece of the painting today, because the intense concentration required kept him from focusing on other things . . . like the curve of her breast, the way the silk draped and fell, exposing one white shoulder he longed to touch.

Unfortunately, that same intense concentration had rendered him deaf to her question.

Bea repeated herself, explaining, "Your work has steadily gained in popularity these past several years, yet your travels have never before included England. Why now?"

"Ah." Philippe set down his brush and flashed the wide smile he knew had helped garner the popularity she spoke of. "You are correct. But only because I did not realize England held such fine beauty. I was told stories of gray moors, and weather-beaten old fishwives. Had someone told me instead of lovely ladies and mysterious gardens grown wild, I should have rushed across the Channel much earlier. Happily, I made the discovery anyway."

When his lighthearted answer failed to elicit a similar response from Bea, he sobered. "Actually," he told her, "I traveled mostly to cities known as great centers for the arts. London only came into my plans recently. My mother, just before passing from this world, expressed . . . a fondness for certain English things. She had traveled here in her youth, and thought I might benefit from doing the same. I came here to fulfill her wish, but I had not planned to stay long. That is, until I saw you."

It was as close to the truth as he could relay, especially with Lily Moffett sitting nearby. Not that he feared judgment—if her *laissez-faire* attitude toward safeguarding her employer's reputation were any indication, Bea's companion was not one to be judgmental.

No, it was her discretion that concerned him. Lily, he guessed, did not have a malicious bone in her body—but a careless one? Probably several. And careless words quickly became oft-repeated rumors. Philippe did not need half of England speculating about his dead mother's affairs, or whether he'd been illegitimately conceived by one of England's own nobles.

Bea seemed to accept his answer, and they lapsed once more into thoughtful silence. Philippe resumed painting, but with the disconcerting awareness that although his muse stood physically before him, her mind seemed thousands of miles away.

She noticed the smell first. When Charity awoke, she was in a place that smelled damp, and vaguely of fish. She guessed they were near the river.

Next, she noticed the cramps. God, how had she ended up in this uncomfortable position? She moved to stretch—and that was when she realized her wrists were bound. No wonder she was so miserable. She opened her mouth to scream for help—then stopped. The low murmur of voices indicated the presence of her captors. They would hear her long before a rescuer. Somehow, she doubted this was a place frequented by knights in shining armor.

As she came fully awake, the memories assaulted her. The storeroom at the Wilbournes', where the footman-spy had discovered her. She'd fought against him, but he'd cut off her breath until she went limp. He'd bound her wrists and gagged her, then left her to sit in the dark while he continued his farce as a loyal footman.

She couldn't say how long she'd remained there before he'd snuck her from the house and into a waiting vehicle. Not too long, she thought— it had still been daylight. Upon arrival at their current location, she'd been semi-conscious. He'd half-dragged her inside as she struggled to keep her feet.

Another man had opened the door, sworn when he saw her.

"What the hell? I summoned *you*—not you and a wench."

"Not just any wench. Caught her spying," the footman had grunted.

She'd been dumped in the corner where she lay now. Someone had held a foul liquid to her lips, pinched her nose until she'd swallowed. Then, nothing—until now.

Charity forced herself to remain calm in spite of the panic that threatened to rise in her chest and cut off her breath. She'd been so anxious to prove her worth that she'd acted foolishly, recklessly— and it had gotten her caught. She couldn't afford to lose her head again. Would they kill her? Not if she could convince them she was too important to risk killing—but how would she do that, when they would discover all too soon how unimportant she was?

Wait. Maybe the same foolishness that had landed her here *could* get her out. If her captors discovered her to be a vapid henwit, they'd have no reason to deem her a threat. Charity breathed easier. Maybe they'd let her go—or at least relax the guard enough for her to escape.

First, she had to figure out how to undo these ties.

Her captors didn't seem to realize she was awake. There were three of them now—at first there had only been two. Peters, the footman who'd brought her here, and the one who'd let him in. She did not know his name. He was quiet, his appearance menacing. Thickly built, his forearms looked capable of snapping the bones of anyone who crossed him. Not that many would dare—the others clearly deferred to him. He kept a cigar clamped on one side of his mouth. When he'd spoken, she'd seen that it rested in a gap where several teeth were missing.

The third man must have arrived later, while she was unconscious. Charity didn't dare keep her eyes open longer than a quick peep—but that was enough. She recognized the third spy immediately. She'd seen him before at Vauxhall.

She heard a rustle of paper, then the scrape of chairs. When next she peeked, the three men were clustered around a small table across the room, heads bent to the light of a single lamp as they conversed in rapid French. The man with the cigar pointed to something on a paper that lay between them, muttering a few words that sounded even more foreign than French. Italian, perhaps? She was in way over her head.

The contents of her reticule lay spilled upon the table. They must have taken it while she was unconscious. Fortunately, she didn't think it contained anything they could use against her.

Cigar man scrubbed a hand across his chin. "Is Rose in place? The hour grows near."

That was easy enough to understand, as was the third spy's response: *"Oui."*

For the next few minutes, Charity caught only snatches . . . "Lady spy will soon know . . . her message" . . . "Tonight. Only one chance" . . . "Castlereagh" . . . "Kettridge must flee."

Oh, why hadn't she studied harder in school? What were they talking about? *Kettridge.* She knew that name . . . it had been in Bea's letter. How much of this did Bea know? Was she the "lady spy" they referred to—and most importantly, was she in danger, too?

Charity kept her body still, straining her ears and mind to make sense of the words. But by the time her brain could translate one person's words and form an idea of what their vague references meant, she was several sentences behind in the mental chase.

That is, until one person spoke a name that stopped her cold. "Monsieur Durand."

She didn't realize she'd gasped—until the men at the table turned to face her.

"I see our little piece of fluff is awake," Peters said with a smile that gave her chills. He'd switched to English, for her benefit, Charity was sure, though she didn't waste energy taking offense at the slur to her character.

Now that they knew she was awake, there was no sense pretending. Charity pushed up awkwardly to a sitting position and looked around, blinking. "Where am I?"

"Somewhere you cannot cause trouble," the man she'd pegged as the crew's leader told her.

Charity shrank deeper into the corner. What had they been about to say concerning Monsieur

Durand? She wasn't likely to find out, because their attention was now focused in the last place she wanted it—on her.

"What should we do with her?" the third one asked.

Peters indicated their boss. "He said a yellow-haired woman went with the lady spy to see Castlereagh."

"Just so," Cigar man acknowledged. "But better make sure she's the right one."

The two lesser spies hauled Charity to her feet and escorted her to the last empty chair at the table. When she hesitated, Peters gave her a shove. She sat.

All right. She had to remain calm. Keep her head. She couldn't let them see how scared she was. But never in Charity's life had she been alone with three men—no mother, sister, chaperone, or even a maid. Let alone with three strange men who bore her definite ill will.

Cigar man led the questioning. He opened with the same question Peters had asked when he'd discovered her lurking in the Wilbournes' storeroom. "Are you acquainted with Lady Pullington?"

Charity tapped a finger on her chin. "Lady Pullington . . . oh. Oh, yes! Yes, of course. I have so very many friends, you see," she explained eagerly, "it becomes rather cumbersome at times to remember them all."

"Then perhaps you'll remember something more specific: a visit with Lady Pullington to the British Foreign Secretary's office?"

She couldn't deny it—they already knew she'd been there. "Why, yes," she said. "Oh, and what a *wonderful* adventure that was. Of course, the duke and Lady Pullington would not allow me to actually sit in on the meeting, yet it was ever so fascinating to visit the offices of such *important* people. And so many officers in uniform," she prattled on. "I *do* love a man in uniform." She sighed.

The incredulous stares of her captors told her the act was working. Thank heavens Miss Kettridge was not here to call her on what she would surely recognize as a performance.

"Did they tell you the purpose of their meeting?"

Charity frowned. "Dear me. I seem to remember something . . . was it the duke? Or possibly Lady Pullington and . . . oh, yes," she finished triumphantly, "I do recall. The meeting was about *politics.*"

The leader's lips pulled back, revealing smoke-browned teeth. It was difficult to say whether the facial movement constituted a smirk or a grimace.

"I will ask you an easier question," he said. "What is your name?"

She was amazed he didn't already know. Or maybe he did, and he was testing her. She didn't dare let him catch her in a lie. "Why, my name is Charity Medford, daughter of the late Baron Medford."

"Aristos," the third man muttered with a sneer.

A sharp look from Cigar man shut him up, but Charity made a mental note to be more careful in any mention of nobility. Clearly that was a sore spot for the Frenchman—understandable, given the terrors of the Revolution. The spy who'd spoken reminded her more of a dockworker than a displaced nobleman, but one never knew.

"Tell me, Miss Medford," her interrogator said, his tone darkening with implied threat, "if you are the innocent miss you would have us believe, why exactly were you hiding where Peters here found you?"

"Oh." She'd known this was coming. "It's rather embarrassing, really." She lowered her lashes and studied her cuticles, trying to summon a blush—no doubt successfully, given the pounding of her heart. "You see, I lost a bet." She held up a hand. "I know, I know, it is terribly unladylike to gamble, and my mother would have my head if she found out, but the other girls were . . . oh, anyway, the forfeit was, there is a . . . ahem . . . rather strapping footman who works for Lord Wilbourne—all the girls sigh over him, though, of course, he is entirely off limits—and I was to attempt to kiss him and return with a token to prove I'd done it. Unfortunately, I could not find the man, and thought perhaps I could in-vent some sort of token and avoid having to go back, for it was all so very much trouble . . ."

"You are a fool," the third man told her. "Do you not have a brother or even a cousin from whom you might have garnered your token? That's what any other female would have done—but you actually took your forfeit seriously?"

"In retrospect, it was a foolish decision," she agreed. "Of course, I had no idea it would lead to such trouble. Please, sir, I've nothing to give you. Mightn't you let me go?" Please, please, please, she prayed.

"Too risky."

A sharp rap at the door kept them from discussing the matter further. Hope flared in Charity's chest. Please, she prayed again, let it be someone looking to rescue her.

But the person outside the door began humming. A man's voice. The tune seemed vaguely familiar, but he stopped after a few bars.

Cigar man had moved toward the door, and when the humming stopped, he picked it up, completing the phrase or verse. He cracked open the door and slipped through it. Charity could catch no glimpse of the person on the other side. It didn't matter, she thought, heart sinking. The humming ritual was clearly some sort of password—not anything her fantasy rescuer would know.

The walls were too thick for her to hear anything else outside the door, assuming the men were still there.

Her remaining captors said nothing about their leader's sudden exit. One leaned forward, playing with a small knife, while the other slouched, eyes drooping nearly shut.

Minutes passed. Charity shifted uncomfortably, staring down at the ugly red welts popping up beneath the leather cord binding her wrists. By now, her family must know she'd gone missing. Someone *would* come for her. She just had to last long enough for them to find her.

The door creaked, and Cigar man returned, alone. "Time to go."

The other spies jumped up. "What do we do with her?" The third one jerked a thumb toward Charity.

Cigar man glanced at a pocket watch. "*Merde.* We should already have departed. Leave her. We act now."

Charity stood slowly, trying not to panic. What now? If they left her, could she safely find her way home? Was there anyone else out there—a guard, maybe—who would stop her?

Peters shuffled toward the door, but his companion hesitated, glancing at Charity.

"You want me to . . . ?" The spy made a motion that resembled the slicing of a throat.

Charity took an involuntary step backward, tripping over her chair and hitting the ground as true fear seized her.

She scrambled back up, just as Cigar man answered, "Not yet." He looked at her, gave a short laugh at her obvious distress. "I am not certain our little captive is as addlepated as she wishes us to think. If all goes well tonight, we shall not return. If not, she may prove of further use. So for now, just store her somewhere . . . quiet." He left, Peters at his heels.

She found her breath. They weren't going to kill her. But if they didn't come back . . .

The third man jerked his head. "All right, my pretty pet. Time to go."

Charity remembered her act and fought to buy herself more time. "Oh, yes—but wait! I seem to have misplaced my pink hair ribbon." She patted her head and scanned the floor. "I simply couldn't leave without it."

"You're concerned about a *hair* ribbon?" The disbelief in his tone made it clear he thought Charity had her priorities askew.

Which, of course, she had—sort of. She widened her eyes. "Why, yes. It was rather dear. And my mother taught me to look after my belongings." As she rummaged about, she managed to knock her handkerchief, which had been among the contents of her reticule, underneath the table. When her family came looking, the scrap of cloth couldn't tell them how to find her, but it was the best she could do.

She straightened. "Where are we going?"

He folded his arms. "A place where, if I wring your pretty little neck, there will be no one to hear you scream."

Charity swallowed thickly. She was getting to him. But the pecking order was clear—and Cigar man had directed him to let her live.

"Jasper," the leader barked. "*Maintenant.* Now."

She dared not push too far. But at least she'd learned his name. "Dear me, I don't see it anywhere. I suppose I'm ready, then." Though as she moved toward the door, she couldn't resist adding, "Terrible shame, though, Mr. Jasper. Such a lovely shade of pink."

He rolled his eyes and gave her a push out the door. Charity gulped and abandoned her act. She needed all her wits now to look for a possible escape route.

This time, Bea did not have long to wait before hearing from Viscount Castlereagh—his response arrived the very next morning. Indeed, given the time for his messenger to travel to and from Montgrave, he must have composed the newest letter in the middle of the night, and sent his man out on dark roads to deliver it.

That same urgency was reflected in the terse words of his message:

> *Thank you for your response. Very helpful observations. The news that your first letter never reached me is greatly disturbing. Though we may hope the explanation is innocent, we must assume it is not. In all likelihood, our adversaries*

now not only know the contents of that letter;
they know that you wrote it. My lady, I must
advise you to return to London. As our situation
develops, your assistance may again be needed,
and the country, while lovely, is an ineffective
location from which to operate. Additionally,
my people can offer you greater protection if
you are in town.

> *Respectfully,*
> *R.S.*

Bea read it once, then reread, noticing there
was no mention of any specifics—the French spies
were not named, not even their country. Nor was
Montgrave mentioned, though clearly the Foreign Secretary knew she was there. His initials
were the closest thing to an identifying factor in
the note.

Bea frowned. Her suspicions had been high since
the last word she'd had from the Foreign Secretary.
To date, Mr. Reilly, her first messenger, had not been
found. The Montgrave butler assured her Reilly had
no history of abdicating his duties, leaving her with
only one reasonable conclusion—and a heap of guilt
for whatever fate had befallen the poor man.

"How do I know this is truly from him?" Bea
asked. If *either* of her notes—though most likely the
first—had fallen into the wrong hands, the response
before her now could easily have been forged.

Evans shook his head. "An astute question, but
one for which I have no answer—save that I am
the same man who was sent to you before. I know
where my loyalties lie, and they are with Britain.

But I have no method of proving that to you at this moment."

She resisted the unladylike urge to pace the room. Instead, she scanned the note once more. *"My people can offer you greater protection if you are in town."* She swallowed. "Does Lord Castlereagh believe I am in danger?"

"I am very sorry, my lady. I cannot speak for his lordship. But I can tell you he does not mince words. If his letter leads you to believe you are in danger, it is most certain that you are."

Bea pressed her fingers to her lips and gazed out the window. A soft rain fell. Under the gray sky, the woods looked dark and menacing—the sort of place an enemy might lurk. Yet therein lay the rose garden, where she'd naively dreamt that art and passion might flourish untouched by the cares of the outside world. Bea clasped her hands to still their trembling. Her haven existed no longer.

Not long after the Foreign Secretary's messenger left, bearing Bea's promise to think through the best course of action and act accordingly, Alex Bainbridge arrived. He bore news far worse than his predecessor.

Bea had retreated to her rooms, the weather preventing she and Philippe from their usual artistic pursuits, and so she did not see his carriage arrive. She had not yet come to a decision on whether, or when, to follow the Foreign Secretary's advice and return to town, when a maid knocked lightly on her door and informed her that the duke awaited her in the study.

Alex wasted no time. He did not even invite her to sit before he spoke.

"An important set of British papers has gone missing." He closed his eyes. "So has Charity."

Chapter 14

"What?" Bea's insides went hollow. She felt for the chair behind her.

The duke rubbed a hand across his forehead and strode toward the liquor cabinet.

The decanter on top was empty, so he selected a bottle from within. Bea shook her head when he waved the bottle her direction, offering some, then watched him pour himself a generous amount. A few drops splashed over the edge—clearly his mind was more consumed with his sister-in-law's disappearance than the contents of his glass.

"Could she have . . . do you think there is any chance she ran off with a beau?" What had the world come to that Bea was actually *hoping* the answer to her question was "yes"?

"No."

In spite of her hopes, it was the answer she'd expected. "They don't—they don't think *she* stole the papers, do they?"

"No, no. We believe whoever took the war plans took Charity as well."

Bea bent forward, fighting a wave of dizziness and fear. "When did she disappear?"

"Yesterday."

Alex tipped his glass to his lips, his eyes still on Bea—that is, until the liquid reached his tongue and sent him sputtering. "What the devil—" he caught himself, glanced at Bea. "My apologies."

He lifted the glass, studied the remarkably clear liquid, and shook his head in disgust. "Water. When I get a hold of the staff . . ."

Sudden realization struck Bea. "Uh, actually, I don't believe you'll find the culprit among your servants. But—and I hope you'll forgive me for saying so—perhaps among your relatives."

The duke raised his brows. "Ah. I see. An interesting time you have had with your companion here?"

"She's very pleasant."

He waved a hand. "It hardly matters, especially now. Bea, we need your help. Charity disappeared from the Wilbournes' house. We think she's been taken by those bloody villains the two of you uncovered, and when the Wilbournes' staff was questioned, one of their footmen was missing. You know more about these criminals than I do."

"I know precious little, Your Grace, but I am utterly at your service. What else have you learned?"

Alex shook his head. "I can tell you more on the journey to London. The grooms are changing out my team of horses as we speak. Can you leave immediately?"

"Absolutely."

* * *

"What do you mean, you must return to London?" Philippe made no attempt to mask his surprise; Bea's proclamation, made only moments after exiting the study where Alex Bainbridge remained, was absurd. "Your portrait is only just begun."

Bea held out her hands, pleading. "Please understand—it is a matter of great importance to the duke, though I cannot explain in detail."

This made no sense. Men, especially stuffy Englishmen, did not include women in matters of business. Yet in their short stay at Montgrave, Beatrice had received multiple callers, all male. He hadn't been privy to their meetings, but he'd gathered they were not social in nature. Which was only a partial relief. And now—now she wanted to leave, just when the painting was progressing, taking the shape that had haunted his dreams since he met her?

"When?" he asked.

"Today. Preferably within the hour."

"Mon Dieu!" he exploded. "But you cannot be serious."

"I assure you I am."

She was, too—no hint of mirth marred her solemn expression. In fact, her eyes appeared wider than normal, her complexion paler. The duke's news, whatever it had been, had clearly bothered her.

"Is someone ill?" he demanded. As a painter she owed him no allegiance, but as her lover, surely he deserved *some* explanation.

"I hope not."

Her answer told him nothing.

She sighed, then cocked her head and met his gaze. "Philippe, have you by chance heard from Charity?"

"Charity?" He thought fast. "That is your friend, the duchess's sister, no? I am sorry, *ma belle,* but I have not heard from the young lady. Indeed, I have but met her twice."

She studied him intently as he answered, prompting him to a question, "*Should* I have heard from her? She would make a fetching subject—though her surface beauty does not hold a glow to your own, *mon canard.*"

The endearment—my duck—earned him a small smile.

"I am sorry, Philippe." She laid a gentle hand on his shoulder. "If you can continue in my absence, please do. I shall return as soon as I am able. But this is something I must do." She kissed him, and amidst the usual stirrings of desire he tasted confusion, fear.

"Your friend is in trouble?" he murmured against her lips.

She broke the kiss, pulled away. "I must go." Her voice caught on the words—he barely heard her as she disappeared in a swish of cherry-colored skirts.

Philippe heaved an exasperated sigh. He'd thought he understood her. A wealthy, if lonely, young widow with an eye for fashion and nature's scenery. An open book. Obviously, he'd judged too soon. She had passion that set his own desires aflame, made him long for eternities he'd never before considered. And she held more secrets than a priest taking confession. How very vexing.

Success! Richard punched a fist into the air as the ship sailed safely from the English harbor. He'd gotten in and out of England with no one the wiser. The sacrifice of two of his informants—two who'd been compromised anyway—was *nothing* compared to the value of what he was about to deliver to his Emperor.

The sacrifice of his son—well, that didn't bear dwelling on. He'd done what he had to. The maps were hidden in Philippe's hotel suite—tactical maps, with troop movements denoted by arrows. Nothing a mere painter ought to possess.

And they *would* be found, because Kettridge and Peters had their orders. The two lowly spies hadn't thought to question the instructions—there was always a plan for what an informant was to do if caught. What neither understood was that this time, the plan had included their capture. They would be angry when they realized the ship had left without them. Angry—but mostly afraid. They had a day, two at most, before Castlereagh's men would hunt them down like scurvy dogs.

"Answer no questions," he'd told them. "If they ask for names, you may give them only one." Neither agent had demonstrated surprise at the name he'd provided. That in itself had caused Richard a moment's revulsion. What had he come to, that he engaged in a business of this nature? But it was far too late to turn back. The last piece of advice he'd given the two he'd known would soon be caught: "The Brits may torture you. But if you talk, *we* will kill you."

Bea hated leaving Philippe, but she had no time to dwell on it, for moments later she was in the duke's carriage, the fresh team of horses barreling toward London.

The one good thing about her parting conversation with the artist was that she felt reasonably confident he had no involvement in Charity's disappearance. Philippe's first thought of her had been as a possible subject for a painting. Either he was an extremely accomplished liar, or a man who lived and breathed for art. She thought she knew him well enough to bet on the latter—which meant it was probably safest to leave him behind anyway. No sense embroiling yet another innocent in such dangerous intrigues.

There was so much she didn't understand. "Alex, Lord Castlereagh's messenger came to Montgrave just before you did. But he made no mention of missing papers."

"No. He would not have known at that time. The loss was only discovered this morning, after Evans was on his way to you." He dragged a hand through his hair and let his head fall back against the carriage. "So much has happened . . . the past day is but a blur.

"Do not tell anyone about the missing papers. It is essential we recover them first—or resort to an alternate plan, which is likely whether the plans are recovered or not. Were the public—let alone the rulers of other nations—to find out about the loss, Britain would lose face. Viscount Castlereagh will ensure anyone who is in a position to help is informed."

"You trust him still?"

Alex looked at her sharply. "Have I reason not to?"

"No, no," Bea assured him. "It is only that too

many people I thought I knew are turning out to be something . . . other. It has made me suspicious of everyone."

He nodded. "Speaking of trusting people, I must ask, Bea. What of Monsieur Durand?"

She shook her head. "He knows nothing of this."

"Are you certain?"

"As certain as I can be. I know the circumstances—the timing of his visit to England, his friendship with a couple who happen to have a French spy among their servants—but Philippe came to England for his art, and you and I are friends with that same couple, so that proves nothing. He is far more concerned with whether he can mix the right pigments to get the color of a new leaf, than he is with whether or not Napoleon Bonaparte will be defeated."

Alex regarded her steadily, and Bea wondered if he suspected the French artist meant more to her than she could publicly acknowledge. Finally he nodded. "I trust your judgment."

It meant a great deal, this trust both the duke and the British Foreign Secretary had placed in her. She hoped she wouldn't let them down. And perhaps, just perhaps, when they'd sorted out this mess and things were back to normal, she could summon the confidence to put more of her poems out into the world. After all, her old fears paled in comparison to what she faced now.

The duke seemed of similar mind. "Poor Beatrice. This is no fit business for a lady. But it cannot be helped now. You have a quick mind. We need you." He swallowed visibly. "Charity needs you."

"Tell me what happened," Bea asked softly.

"Right. Alicia Wilbourne was the last to see her. She said Charity stopped by in search of a fan she thought she'd misplaced. When Lady Wilbourne went to greet another caller, Charity said she'd finish up the search and see herself out. She didn't see Charity again after that, and had no idea anything was amiss until Charity's maid wearied of waiting in the carriage and came to ask after her mistress.

"Then a new search began—Lady Wilbourne and her full staff looked in every room of the house, to no avail. Somehow Charity left—alone or not—without anyone seeing her."

Bea absorbed the tale. "Wait. You said Alicia's *staff* aided in the search? But if one of her servants is in league with the French spies, how can we trust that Charity's presence wasn't just covered up?"

"Exactly. As I left for Montgrave, Lord Castlereagh had directed several constables to fully question the Wilbournes and each member of their household—though we learned that one footman was missing. A man named Peters. Claimed his mother was ill and needed help. He left, perhaps not coincidentally, yesterday afternoon."

Bea pressed a hand to her chest, where her heart had begun to beat an erratic tattoo.

"Thank God her mother had the sense to come directly to Elizabeth and I, once her daughter's terrified maid returned with Lady Wilbourne to confirm her mistress had gone missing. At the time, none of them suspected this type of foul play. Indeed, Lady Wilbourne sheepishly admitted she did not realize that anything more than a young lady's reputation was on the line. She thought to find Charity kissing a groom, perhaps on a dare." He gave a hollow laugh. "My sister-in-law is known for being reckless, but I never thought it would come to this."

Never had Bea seen Alex Bainbridge so distraught—except perhaps once, when he and Elizabeth hit a rough patch early in their marriage, in spite of the fact that he'd literally ridden to her rescue after a distant relative had abducted her in some misguided revenge for her rejection of his suit. Elizabeth had never shared the full details of what else had come between she and her heroic duke, or how the reconciliation came about, but it was known to all that the once rakish duke now loved his wife to distraction.

"Why do the women of my wife's family have the habit of disappearing—not of their own free will?" he asked rhetorically.

"We'll find her," Bea said, but the reassurance fell flat. The duke knew as well as she did that although she would try her best, she could make no promises. Alex and Elizabeth had been married only since the past fall, yet it was clear that in addition to his wife, he loved his young sister-in-law as though they'd grown up together.

And dear God, Charity was missing.

"Elizabeth knows?" Bea asked.

"She knows." If it were possible, the lines on his face etched themselves deeper, giving the normally-handsome duke a near haggard appearance. "She doesn't know the full extent, and I pray she never will. It is too risky to share any detail that might place her—or any of the others—in danger as well."

Bea took a shaky breath. "How far can this horrible business spread? Is Elizabeth all right?"

Alex lifted one shoulder in a shrug that said he knew not what else to do. "She is distraught, of course. I left her resting, with strict instructions not to leave the house. But I cannot stop her from worrying—I can only hope it does not harm the baby."

Bea let her head sink to her hands. "Oh, Lord, this is all my fault. I should never have invited Charity to Vauxhall that fateful evening." Had she had the faintest suspicion they'd be intruding on anything of this grave nature, she wouldn't have.

Alex shook his head. "You both blundered into more than you bargained for. But I daresay Charity had some role in this latest trouble—that girl has never learned to leave well enough alone. Think, Bea. That's all I ask now. Think how we can find her."

He didn't say the words "before it's too late," but Bea heard them nonetheless. She closed her eyes against the tears that welled within, and spent the remainder of the journey to London doing her best to imagine herself in Charity's shoes. She *knew* Charity hadn't left the Wilbournes' house alone. She was intelligent enough to suspect, as Bea had, that one of the spies worked for them. And she was brazen enough to go looking for him. Bea would bet anything she had found him.

Chapter 15

Philippe attempted—for about an hour—to do as Bea had suggested and continue the painting without her. After all, he needed to capture this moment, the *particular* green of the leaves at this very phase of spring, before capricious nature changed once more and forced him to work from memory alone.

Unfortunately, it was raining. And carrying a few snipped branches indoors was no help at all when his mind was transfixed not by the green of the leaves, but by the pale of Bea's face as she'd departed.

This was ridiculous. Philippe shoved his stool back and packed up his paints, muttering a few choice words in his native language. Whatever had happened to Charity Medford, it was something important. And Bea had chosen to leave him out. Why? Some misguided notion that just because he was an artist, he was too ignorant to handle weightier matters than selecting the proper mixture of pigments to replicate the colors of nature? He'd seen that reaction from his stepfather, who could not accept the idea that a person might *choose* to eschew politics in favor of art. The only reasonable explanation, to the elder Durand, was that Philippe must be incapable of understanding such matters, for surely if he understood them, he would pursue them.

Bea might not be guilty of such condescension, but she definitely was keeping something from him.

Well, he didn't need protecting, Philippe thought angrily. She'd trusted him with her body, but not her worldly cares. In the past, with other women, he'd had no problem with that. But Bea was different. With her, he wanted more. Good and bad, he wanted to *know* her.

His mother had already shut him out—he couldn't let Bea do the same thing.

Philippe headed for the stables. He didn't need a fancy conveyance—just whatever would get him to London swiftly.

He felt a slight twinge of guilt as he passed the house and thought of Lily Moffett. He'd be leaving her behind just as surely as Bea had left him. But it couldn't be helped. And Lily would get over it. The duke's liquor supply would provide whatever solace she needed.

Without knowing exactly what trouble Bea faced, he was at a loss for how to help. But when he caught up with his mysterious lover, his first task was to convince her there was more to Philippe Durand than pretty pictures and passionate kisses, convince her he was worthy of standing at her side—no matter what the trouble.

* * *

The Foreign Secretary was in a meeting with his highest officials when Alex and Bea returned to London, but he soon ushered them in.

"Were you followed?"

"I cannot say," Alex admitted.

Viscount Castlereagh shrugged. "It matters little. Your names and faces are known to them."

"Are we in danger?" Bea shook her head as soon as the question slipped out. "Of course we are."

"Only until these people are caught." The confidence in the government official's tone was reassuring. "I have observers all over the city. Discovering any detail that might lead to the war plan or Miss Medford is now their primary mission."

"And?" The muscles of Alex's face appeared so tense they were on the verge of snapping. "What can you tell us?"

"We questioned the Wilbournes' butler as to the duties of the missing servant Peters. The butler could not confirm the existence or location of the lesser servant's ill mother. What he could tell us is that Peters took on the additional duty a few months ago of helping to clear out a warehouse owned by Lord Wilbourne, which the lord was planning to sell."

"A vacant warehouse," Bea repeated. "Where?"

He gave them the directions.

"You've searched it?" Alex asked.

"Only the exterior." The Foreign Secretary folded his hands. "I know this may be difficult to understand, but the team at the warehouse was redirected—an urgent development I could not ignore, as it will likely lead to the capture of one or more of these spies—which, in turn, could lead to Miss Medford.

"We received word that the captain of a ship we've had under surveillance, which makes frequent crossings to France, has recently come into some extra money. Though it is possible he is smuggling goods, our sources indicate he ferries those who do not wish their travels documented on a ship's roster. The team at the warehouse had closest access to the water, and the timing is urgent, for the ship is scheduled to depart today."

"I still wish to search this warehouse," Alex told him.

"Absolutely," the Secretary said. "If you will but wait, I have another team of two men coming on shift. They can escort you."

The duke folded his arms. "When?"

"Two hours. Three, at the most."

"Not fast enough."

"Every other team currently on shift is on assignment. Even if I sent an aide to find and redirect them, it would take that long," Castlereagh argued.

Alex pressed his lips together then nodded. "Send them directly to my house. We will be ready the moment they arrive. Meanwhile, I must see to my wife. She is most distraught."

"Of course, of course." Viscount Castlereagh considered the duke, his eyes narrowing. "If," he said slowly, "you should, for any reason, locate the Frenchmen before my men do, please consider that they are more valuable alive than dead."

The duke frowned. He was more inclined to rip the men limb from limb, Bea surmised, than exercise restraint.

"Understandably, that is not always possible," Castlereagh admitted. He waved a hand. "Also, do not trouble yourselves over the war plans. It is essential we put a halt to the espionage, but recovery of the actual plan means little. I've already notified Clancarty—my delegate at the Congress of Vienna—and Wellington that the plan is compromised. Fortunately, our strategists never limit themselves to a single plan.

"Britain is, in my assessment, in far less danger than your young sister-in-law, Your Grace." He gave Bea a nod. "And your friend. I pray you find her unharmed. Good luck, and Godspeed."

As they exited, Bea turned to Alex. "That was odd advice . . . why would he think you might encounter the spies first?"

"Because," the duke responded grimly, "he knows full well I have no intention of waiting for his men to join us before searching that warehouse."

Upon returning to London, Philippe went first to the town house of Lord and Lady Bainbridge. But the only person he found there was the sniffling duchess, whose red nose and eyes did *not* complement the red of her hair.

The moment he entered the formal salon, she rushed to him, clutching at his arms. "Do you bring word?"

Philippe sensed the need to tread very carefully in the absence of knowledge. "I have just come from Montgrave, *madame*. Your husband was there this morning; he and Lady Pullington left for

London as soon as his carriage horses could be changed. I departed shortly thereafter."

"But no word of Charity?" Elizabeth Bainbridge wilted, fresh tears springing to her eyes as he escorted her toward a sofa. He proffered a fresh handkerchief to replace the soggy one she used to wipe her eyes, and she accepted it automatically.

"I am sorry, Your Grace," Philippe told her. "I have no news of your sister. To be honest, I know little at all, other than that she is in trouble."

"She's *missing*," Elizabeth wailed. "And I don't have the full story either. Alex promised to find her—that's why he went to fetch Bea from Montgrave. He thinks she might know something about Charity's disappearance. But why would Bea know, and not I? She's my *sister*. We've always shared everything." She collapsed in tears once more.

Philippe was not unaccustomed to dealing with women in hysterics. In France, the ladies seemed to have regular bouts of them. But hysterics weren't going to help either of them—let alone Charity Medford—right now.

"Where," he asked gently, "do you think your husband and Lady Pullington would have gone upon arriving in London?"

She sniffed and took a shaky breath. "He said he had business with Viscount Castlereagh."

It was a name even Philippe recognized. "The British Foreign Secretary?" This was getting stranger by the moment.

Luckily, the clatter of carriage wheels, followed by the rush of feet on the steps outside, saved Philippe from having to pump the young duchess for additional details.

She leapt from the couch and ran to the door of the salon, Philippe close behind her, in time to see her husband and Bea enter the front door of the home.

"Alex!" Lady Bainbridge called.

The duke shook his head at the pleading look on her face, and Philippe felt a pang of sympathy.

Bea faltered in her step upon seeing his face behind that of Elizabeth. "Philippe. What are you doing here?"

"I am not yet certain. I know only that I could not bear to sit behind, knowing my dear friends face difficulty while I dabble in paints—especially if that friend is a lady. It would be most unchivalrous."

"You never 'dabble,'" Bea said.

He gave a half laugh at her oddly loyal reply. She believed in him as an artist, but that didn't erase the memory of how easily she'd dismissed him when more critical matters were at hand.

"Nonetheless, I am here to stand by your side," he declared. "You will find I have talents beyond the canvas, I hope, should you need to call on them. Though, if either yourself or the good duke would enlighten Lady Bainbridge and I," he gestured to the weepy duchess, "it might help."

Elizabeth was not so restrained in her request for information. She swiped at her tears with the back of her hand, then thrust out her chin, her focus trained on the duke. "We had an understanding, oh husband of mine, that you would not keep important information from me, correct? *Even* when you are only trying to protect me?" Her voice, no longer tear-choked, had found strength in anger.

Alex and Elizabeth shared a long look, neither of

them paying any attention to the remaining two people in the room.

When her husband did not speak, Elizabeth clasped her hands together. "The last time you tried to keep things from me, it nearly cost us our marriage. Please, don't let it cost me my sister. I do not know if I can help, but by keeping me—and Philippe—in the dark, you assure we cannot."

Regret filled the duke's features and he strode to his wife's side, pulling her close to him and tucking her head beneath his chin. "You are correct—I am sorry."

There were few men, let alone dukes, who would apologize to their wives—much less in front of an audience. If anything, Philippe's respect for the man increased. Yet the moment was clearly a private one.

Philippe stood in awkward silence. He glanced at Bea, questioning, and she lifted one shoulder in a shrug, as though to say she wasn't privy to whatever withholding of information had once come between Elizabeth and the duke.

"Please, Your Grace," Philippe broke the awkward pause after several moments had passed. "It pains me to see all of you—especially Lady Bainbridge and Lady Pullington—in such distress. I am compelled to offer what help I may. Miss Medford is missing, I understand. If it is trouble with some man—"

"No. I wish it were," Alex said. "I am afraid there is much greater evil at work." He looked at Bea. "Your assessment has not changed?"

"It has not," Bea vouched. "I trust Philippe with my hea . . . yes, he can be trusted."

Trusted with what? Philippe frowned. Why would

they ask such a question? But the answer became clear with the duke's next words.

"We have just returned from Viscount Castlereagh's offices. There is almost no question as to what we had suspected before—Charity has fallen into the hands of French spies."

"What?" the question exploded from Elizabeth and Philippe simultaneously.

"Bea, tell them. Quickly," the duke instructed. He strode to the door and spoke quietly with a servant who materialized as though from thin air.

Bea spoke up. "There is no time for a lengthy explanation. I am sorry. Perhaps when all is resolved . . ." She cleared her throat, and Philippe sensed the tension was getting to her. "A couple of weeks ago, Charity and I stumbled upon a pair of men who appear to be working for Napoleon Bonaparte's cause, by attempting to provide him with confidential British documents. Knowing of their plans, we could not in good conscience ignore them."

Philippe touched a hand to his jaw, to ensure he'd not left it hanging open. Who was this woman who looked like his English rose but spoke as though she'd spent years entrenched in political intrigues? Was her "respectable widow" persona all an act?

Moments later, the duke rejoined them, carrying a small case. Philippe sized it up. Weapons.

"The ladies did the right thing," the duke vouched. "They never approached the men, but brought the information to me instead. I helped them take it to Viscount Castlereagh. Unfortunately, it seems these actions came to the attention of our adversaries, for they identified Charity, Bea, and, most likely, myself. Charity knows the least of any of us, but the spies would not know that. My best guess is that they deemed her a threat, and when she presented them with an opportunity, they seized her."

Elizabeth's face had gone pale, and she pressed a hand to her heart.

"I'm afraid that explanation must suffice for now," Bea said, "unless you have pressing questions."

"Where do you think they've taken her?" Elizabeth asked.

"We have a lead," Alex said. "An empty warehouse near the Thames. They may have used it as a base for their operations, or a meeting place."

Bea nodded, her manner brisk. She and the duke were all business now. She turned to Philippe. "Monsieur Durand?"

"I have a great many questions, in fact," Philippe retorted, his accent growing thick. He looked directly at Bea, and saw her shudder at the force of his gaze. Well, she should. Anger, betrayal, confusion— they were all justified. But not right now. He forced those seething emotions beneath a veneer of calm. "However," he continued, "my questions can wait. Miss Medford's plight is of far greater import. As I stated before, I am at your service."

"What assistance have you to offer?" the duke asked.

"I do not profess to know these evil men, nor where they might have taken Miss Medford. I *can* offer an able body and a quick mind. You say these men are French, no? I can offer translation, perhaps some insight into their thoughts and motivations— though my father, not I, is the politician.

"Most of all," Philippe added, "I would not have

Lady Pullington walk into danger without offering myself in her place." His muse was a lady with infinite facets, uncharted depths. She frustrated the hell out of him. But she was still a lady.

"Very chivalrous," the duke said.

Philippe thought he saw the barest hint of a smile touch Bea's face.

"I will accept your offer—but not in place of Beatrice," the Englishman continued. "I need you both. We leave immediately."

"Shouldn't you take more men?" Elizabeth Bainbridge worried.

Her husband opened the case he held, made a cursory check of the contents—pistols, as Philippe had suspected—and stood. "No. I fear that would only place Charity in greater danger. In this case, stealth, as opposed to posing an obvious threat, is our best bet." He looked at Philippe and Bea. "Ready?"

"Yes," they both answered. Philippe made the conscious effort to avoid his native language. Though most educated Englishmen, and women, spoke French passably, he did not care to remind his friends that he shared the nationality of the men who'd done their relative and friend harm.

"Dearest," the duke told his wife, "you'll be safest here. Just try to think positively. Pray for the best possible outcome."

The duchess looked miserable at being left behind once again. Philippe knew exactly how she felt. He also knew that, in the duke's place, he'd have done the same thing. One missing family member was awful enough—there was no way any man would choose to also put his pregnant wife in danger.

"Could Bea not stay as well?" Elizabeth asked. "Bea, aren't you afraid?"

"Bea knows more of this situation, of these men and their intentions, than either Monsieur Durand or I," Alex answered. "I need her with us. But do not worry—should we encounter danger, she shall be kept from harm's way."

Philippe nodded vigorously, confirming the duke's instinct to protect.

But as they left, Bea looked back and answered Elizabeth's last question. "Yes, E., I am afraid."

Bea, Philippe, and Alex sat in strained silence as the carriage approached their destination. Before they'd departed, Bea had noticed that the driver and footman carried weapons, in addition to those in the duke's case.

Alex had asked her a few brief questions, but since they'd already shared the ride from Montgrave to London, there was little more to cover.

"If these men are at the warehouse, holding Charity, how shall we approach them?" Philippe asked.

"It depends," Alex said. "If it were possible to sneak up on them, a pistol, trained on each man . . . but I doubt they would be so careless."

"If you have the opportunity, perhaps we might negotiate her release," Bea suggested.

"I'm listening," the duke said. "How? We must offer something that would be more valuable to them than Charity."

"They already stole the plans they were after, no?" Philippe put in. "What else could there be?"

Bea thought. "I knew more of their operations than Charity," she said slowly. "I would offer myself—"

"No," the two men emphatically interjected.

"Besides," Alex said, "you may have known more two days ago, but by now Charity will have learned enough—names, faces, habits—to pose a greater threat." Assuming she was still alive.

The duke didn't say this last, but Bea heard it nonetheless. "All right, then, a better idea," she offered. "Think like the spies. They need to deliver those plans to Bonaparte, or his men. So what they need most now is safe passage from England, correct? We offer that to them, in exchange for Charity. We would be lying, of course."

"An interesting idea," Philippe said.

"Indeed, it has merit," Alex agreed. "Should the opportunity arise, we shall try that tactic." Accustomed to decision making, he spoke with authority—though his brows drew together as he finished. "My fear is that they may already have left."

No one brought up the questions Bea knew loomed in their minds: what would they do next, if the kidnappers had left, and the warehouse was empty? Or, worse—if Charity's fate had already been decided?

The group fell silent again. Philippe leaned forward, elbows propped on his knees, his sensual lips pressed together in a pensive expression. It was a side of him she'd never seen before.

Outside, the carriage approached the river, the seamy aroma of river life filtering through the vehicle's windows. Bea peered out. A gray box of a

building, the storehouse blended well with its
surroundings. The Woolwich Dockyard, home to
numerous shipbuilding facilities and storehouses
like the one they approached, was a site of constant activity—that is, except for the particular
building they'd identified. Nearby, two men loaded
a crane with large crates, but the warehouse behind
them was still.

They passed by the building once, twice, then
drew down the street a way and stopped. The driver
appeared at the window. "Your Grace?"

"No sign of anyone from your viewpoint?" the
duke asked.

"No," the driver confirmed.

"We'll search the building. First, I intend to ask
the laborers over yonder if they've noticed any unusual comings and goings."

"Certainly," Philippe said. "My father always used
to say, 'Information is ammunition.' But may I
make a suggestion? Let me approach them. Your
clothing marks you as a nobleman, and your driver
is wearing livery. You are sure to put them on
guard." Philippe, in contrast, still wore the trousers
and shirt he normally painted in. Though of high
quality, the garments bore little embellishment.

Alex hesitated, then nodded.

Bea clenched her hands in her skirts as Philippe
left the carriage, his look serious, his stride brisk.
She wondered again at the change in him. This
chivalrous, protective side that made her heart
swell. And he was here because of her. To protect
her, and come to the aid of a young woman he
barely knew. He hadn't known the seriousness of
the situation when he'd made the decision to

come; he'd only known Bea was upset. Surely his presence now showed he cared for her as more than just a passing fancy.

Unfortunately, Philippe reappeared minutes later with nothing to report.

Alex's grim expression grew even darker. "Then we stick with the plan. We search the building ourselves, top to bottom, inside and out."

Finally. The waiting had been driving her mad. The creeping anxiety . . . she needed to *do* something. Bea shifted forward, preparing to stand.

"Bea, I am sorry," Alex said. "I cannot in good conscience allow you to come any further than this. I cannot say if those men are inside, if they have Charity. But I can tell you they are unquestionably dangerous."

"But—"

"Chérie," Philippe said, "you have admirably led us this far. If you were to come, both the duke and I would feel compelled to protect you at every turn—which may slow us in searching for your friend."

Bea squeezed her eyes shut, the frustration overwhelming, though she knew it was useless to argue. "All right," she conceded, drooping back into her seat. She knew not how to wield a weapon. The duke and Philippe were right—she would be an encumbrance, and what mattered most now was Charity.

"The driver will retreat a safe distance—a vehicle such as mine is too noticeable here," Alex told her. "Remain in the carriage. The moment we find Charity, we will return. She will need you then."

She nodded, her throat tight with fear. She suspected this—offering solace, woman to woman—

was the true reason Alex had insisted she come. If
they were lucky enough to find Charity, there was
no telling what might have befallen her in the
past twenty-some hours. If she'd been beaten, or
raped . . . dear God. Charity was an innocent. And
though Bea had always considered herself a loyal
friend to Elizabeth and her sister, she felt wretchedly
ill-equipped to provide the sort of help that would
allow Charity to cope with an enormity Bea herself barely understood.

Alex grabbed his case from beneath the carriage
seat, and both men exited into the alley next to the
warehouse.

Bea bent her head in prayer.

The duke extracted two pistols from the felt-
lined container. He tested the weight of one, then
extended the other to Philippe. "Do you know how
to use one of these?"

This was not the time to feel slighted. "I do,"
Philippe answered simply.

The duke regarded him steadily. "I am going to
trust you are the honest man that Beatrice believes
you to be. But do me one favor. If you are not, at
least refrain from shooting me in the back."

He didn't give Philippe a chance to respond
before using his boot to nudge open the door and
gesturing forward with his pistol. "Let's go. Quiet."

The duke went first. Philippe followed, gun at
the ready. The life of an artist did not include frequent gun battles, but Philippe was no stranger to
the acrid taste of fear that stung the back of his
throat now. He was old enough to remember the

Revolution—the days of hiding, travel to strange places, stern-faced officials questioning his step-father, who changed his answers depending on who was doing the asking. He'd learned to handle a weapon at an early age—about the same time he'd sworn off politics as a possible career. He was no expert, but by God, he could hit his target—if it came to that.

Sunlight filtered through the warehouse door and windows to weakly illuminate a vast empty shell of a building. A layer of dust and grit covered the floor, and the few remaining empty crates and timbers were stacked along the walls.

A rat scurried across one corner, startled by their presence. But for it, the dank warehouse appeared deserted.

Philippe pointed to the ground, drawing the duke's attention to a series of footprints made visible by the dust. Whether made by multiple men or the multiple comings and goings of one man, it was difficult to say, but they clearly led toward the east wall, where several doors marked the presence of offices for the storehouse manager and accountants.

The two men met each other's gaze, then moved forward, weapons aloft.

Farther from the entryway, the grit on the floor lessened and the prints disappeared. The duke paused, looking down, then shrugged. He quietly pushed open the first door. He peered in and shook his head.

Philippe tried the second. He knew immediately: the air here had been disturbed. Though dark and quiet now, the room smelled of human activity. He motioned Alex over.

A table and chairs, a crust of bread . . . had this place been used by the French agents, or others among London's underworld of vagrants and smugglers?

"There." Philippe kept his voice low and pointed to a woman's reticule at the table's edge. "Does that belong to Miss Medford?"

The duke quickly sifted through the contents. "Bloody hell. I *think* so. I can't be sure. I have never had cause to pay close attention—Charity must have any number of handbags. And Bea mentioned there is a woman involved in the French operations. This could belong to her."

"Safe to assume we've found their meeting place, at least."

A sliver of pink beneath the table caught Philippe's attention. He bent down and fished out an embroidered handkerchief. "C. M. Charity *has* been here." Given the strange intimacy of the situation, it seemed natural to use her first name, in spite of having met her only twice.

"Good." The duke's dark brows drew together. "But where is she now?"

Even in the dim light, Philippe could sense the waves of tension emanating from the other man as though they were visible. Understandable, but right now they needed logic more than emotion. He forced himself to think through the situation. "You said these papers were stolen only last night?"

Alex nodded.

"And your sister-in-law was taken only a few hours before that," he reasoned, speaking at a normal volume now that it was clear they weren't going to surprise a group of dangerous men. "As Lady

Pullington suggested, the informants have what they came for, and are probably now trying to leave your country. The question is, would they risk taking Charity with them?"

"I cannot fathom she'd go willingly . . . and keeping her unconscious would attract too much attention."

Philippe shifted the weight of his pistol and moved back toward the door to the small room, looking out on the seemingly empty warehouse. "If they did not keep her with them, then—"

"Do not even suggest to me that they killed her." The duke voiced the fear no one had been willing to mention when the ladies, Elizabeth and Beatrice, had been present.

"Actually," Philippe said, "I was going to suggest there would not have been time to take her far. Where else around here could a lone woman be hidden?"

"A ship's hold," the duke said dully. "Bloody Christ, we're at the *docks*. There are any number of boats, alleys, crates, cellars . . ."

Philippe swallowed hard at the unpleasant imagery. "Is there any more to this building?" He checked the door to the third office as he asked the question, but, as expected, found it empty.

"In the alley. Outside." Urgency filled the duke's tone. "Did you see a second entry—a set of stairs, leading down?"

"A cellar, this near to the water?" Philippe asked dubiously. But he and Alex were already moving in that direction.

Sure enough, outside the building at one end, adjacent to the next warehouse over, a narrow set of concrete stairs led to the building's underground level.

The duke took the steps two at a time, but the narrow space was dark and cramped. He turned to Philippe, behind him. "I can't see a thing down here. We need light."

Philippe dashed back to the room inside the warehouse, acquired a candle and match, then rejoined the duke.

At the bottom of the stairs, a low tunnel led to a single door, held closed by a thick iron bar.

Philippe's heart pounded, and he knew from Alex's harsh breath the other man felt it, too: hope, suspense, and the breath-stealing fear that on the other side of the door the search would end with evidence of an innocent life cut short.

The duke reached for the bar.

"Let me," Philippe said. He was no relation to Charity. He knew the horrible things that had been done in the quest for power in France. Though if that were the case now, he could not shield his friend from it for long. He handed the candle to the duke and set the pistol aside. Easing the bar from its slot, he propped it against the wall, then reclaimed his weapon as Alex pushed the door open to reveal a space that was more accurately described as a pit than a room.

A female figure huddled on the earthen floor. Her head was down, but her blond ringlets were unmistakable.

"Thank God." Alex breathed the prayer in unison with Philippe's utterance of its French translation. *"Remercier Dieu."*

Her head jerked up at the intrusion and she scuttled back across the ground, terror in her eyes.

Philippe and the duke looked at each other and simultaneously lowered the weapons they'd both still been holding at the ready.

"Charity," the duke spoke softly. "It's me, Alex. And Philippe Durand. We've come to help. You need not fear us."

Slowly the terror in her eyes was replaced by recognition. "Alex?" she croaked. Her chest gave a great heaving sob, and she held out her hands to him.

Even in the candlelight, Philippe could see her fingertips were scraped and bloody nubbins. His gaze flew to the door. She must have clawed at it for hours.

He fought a rising wave of rage. They might not have killed her outright, but they'd left her here to die. What kind of people could do this to a woman? To any human?

He stood back as the duke scooped his sister-in-law up into his arms, cradling her head against his shoulder as gently as though she were a baby. Her clothes, once the envy of other London misses, were torn and soiled. God only knew what they'd done to her. Whether they'd *touched* her, defiled her. His own countrymen. Philippe fought another wave of anger, this one mixed with nausea. No wonder the duke had asked whether he was to be trusted.

Alex met Philippe's eye, his gaze burning with fierce protectiveness as he cradled his sister-in-law. "No one—*no one*—is *ever* going to know what we saw here."

Philippe understood. Completely. Innocent victim or not, Charity would be ruined if word of her captivity to three men got out, let alone the conditions under which she'd been found. She would be the subject of pity and scorn—so very wrong for the once-sparkling miss who held all of London in the palm of her hand.

"I would kill myself," Philippe promised fervently, "before I would see further harm come to her."

Alex gave a terse nod, then returned his focus to Charity. "Come on, baby," he whispered. "We're going home."

Chapter 16

Elizabeth clung tearfully to her little sister, while the duke called for a doctor and sent word to Lord Castlereagh.

Charity had spoken little in the carriage as she, Bea, Philippe, and Alex had returned from the empty warehouse. She had merely clutched Bea's hand, disoriented and chilled.

"I want to go home," she'd pled upon arriving at her sister's house instead.

"Charity, you'll have to stay with us for a while," Elizabeth had gently explained, after overcoming the emotions that clogged her throat upon first seeing her sister. "Alex can ensure you receive the best care, and protection."

She'd nodded dully. Servants rushed to bring her a quilt and honey-laced tea. As the warmth seeped in, she began to perk up. "I suppose you all have a great many questions," she said, taking in the cluster of anxious faces watching her.

"They can wait until you've seen the physician," the duke told her. "And until Lord Castlereagh

arrives. I am certain he will wish to speak with you
as well. I do not expect him before morning, however, as he indicated urgent business was afoot."

Charity nodded her understanding, leaving the
group little to do but wait. Elizabeth sat next to her
sister on a sofa, patting her repeatedly and murmuring, "Don't you worry any longer. You'll be all
right now." The duke sat on Elizabeth's other side,
holding his wife's hand.

Soon, both Bea and Philippe felt like intruders to
the intimate family reunion.

Philippe shifted awkwardly. He shared their great
relief at finding Charity alive and, as far as the eye
could see, well. Indeed, he'd expected worse. But
the relief on Charity's behalf did not erase the undercurrent of tension between him and the other
nonfamilial member present in the room. He and
Bea had some things to sort out—and this time,
he wasn't going to settle for half answers and vague
explanations.

Meanwhile, Charity had covered Elizabeth's patting hand with her own. "Dear E., I am terribly
sorry to have worried you so. I shall recover,
though. You don't have to pat me as though I
might disappear in a puff of smoke if you fail to
keep a hand on me."

"Oh, yes, I do," her sister argued with a watery
smile.

Charity returned her sister's smile, but then
gazed mournfully at her injured fingertips. "I suppose," she said, "that for some time I shall be forced
to avoid outings which might require me to remove
my gloves."

Fresh tears sprang to Elizabeth's eyes, and even

Philippe felt a swell of relief and pride at the young lady's uncrushed spirit. Beside him, Bea dabbed her eyes with a handkerchief.

A tap at the door indicated the doctor's arrival, making Philippe even more uncomfortable. Miss Medford's privacy had been violated enough. He, an outsider, did not belong here. He rose to leave.

The duke went to speak in hushed tones with the professional man.

Bea stood as well. "I hope you will understand, but I really should be going. I am so very tired— though my day has not, undoubtedly, been as trying as some, it has been long."

"Of course. But Bea, we can easily put you up here," Elizabeth offered. "You're safe here."

"I believe I'd prefer the comfort of my own home, though I thank you." She flicked a glance at Philippe. Was she nervous?

"Please, E., let me know if there is anything else—the least thing, truly—I can do. I shall call on you tomorrow, and I will gladly answer any questions the Foreign Secretary has for me."

"I must also depart. I shall see Lady Pullington home safely," Philippe said.

Alex and Elizabeth looked at one another, but neither uttered a word of objection.

And so as Charity was borne upstairs by her family and the kindly doctor, Philippe escorted Bea back to a waiting carriage.

Good thing he had maintained his hotel lodgings, he thought wryly, as the interlude at Montgrave had proven shorter than he'd anticipated. Not that he was headed back to the hotel quite yet. He needed to be alone with Beatrice. Needed to shake some sense into her. Needed to issue a few choice words to her.

Needed to make love to her.

Oh, but first they would have words. He knew, finally, what sort of "business" she was involved in. He'd *seen* it in that underground room. And while he would keep the promise he'd made to Alex—no detail of what he'd observed there would ever cross his lips—his English rose had one hell of a lot of explaining to do.

Bea settled into the seat across from him, sinking into the plush velvet without any pretense at maintaining a ladylike posture. Though exhaustion and strain were written in the paleness of her face, though he was angry at the secretive, dismissive manner in which she'd treated him, he could not help but think her beautiful. And noble, in the truest sense of the word. She'd been willing to risk herself in place of her friend.

Why either one of them had been at risk in the first place, however, remained a mystery. One he needed to unravel, before he could pull his vexing beauty back into his arms, where he could both ravish and protect her.

Bea sensed Philippe's tension in the carriage, as she had in Alex and Elizabeth's home, but he did not speak until they arrived at Bea's town house.

"You are inviting me in."

It was a statement, perhaps a command, but definitely *not* a question. There was an awkward moment of silence as Bea considered denying him, then realized that would only delay the inevitable—and likely keep her tossing and turning all night.

Still, she didn't have to like it. "As you wish," she acquiesced.

The butler saw them in, and Bea informed him they would like a light repast.

"I shall see to it, my lady. The rest of the staff has retired for the evening, as we did not anticipate your return from the country. I apologize, and will see that everything is readied at once."

"No need to wake the others," Bea said tiredly. "Just a cold platter will suffice. And then you may retire as well. I have business tomorrow morning for which I shall require your alert and excellent service." Thank goodness he was the sort of servant who'd sooner die than betray the fact that his female employer was entertaining a man, alone, at such an hour. She'd been raised to understand that the lady of the house need not explain herself to a servant, yet she hoped the mention of business in the morning would stifle any misgivings her long-time employee might have.

In truth, Bea had nearly lost track of the hours since Alex arrived in Montgrave. It seemed days ago. She did know she hadn't sat down to a meal since the previous evening. As light-headed as she was feeling, she didn't relish the idea of immediate confrontation.

Philippe, unfortunately, was not of like mind.

"You are a *spy*. How could you have kept something like this from me?" he demanded as soon as the servant disappeared.

"An informant," Bea corrected stiffly. "And it did not concern you." A lie, but less hurtful than the truth: she had not confided in Philippe because *he* was one of the suspects she'd been charged with watching.

"What do you mean? Of course, it concerns me. *You* concern me."

"Because I agreed to sit for you, I must also have agreed to share all other aspects of my life as well?" The question wasn't fair. But with the emotions of the past twenty-four hours riding high, for once she didn't care about being rational.

"You know that isn't so. I believe we *willingly* shared a great deal."

"Maybe so." Bea dropped her gaze. The hurt in his eyes was matched only by the heat of his anger. She ran a fingernail across the back of the sofa, studying the pattern she traced. "Trust me, it is only by accident I came into this role. It is not one I would have chosen for myself."

Philippe paced. "That may be. But it does not change the fact that what we shared . . . or rather, what I *thought* we shared . . . it does not change the fact that I do not *know* you. I do not know, when you speak, what is truth, what is half truth, or mere deception. And yet you ask me to trust you?"

"I promise, I am telling you the truth now. If you would but try to listen, to understand—"

"Ah." Philippe interrupted. "That night at the theater—when you disappeared in such a hurry. *That* is what you were doing. You knew, even then, the Wilbournes' footman was involved in this terrible plot."

"Yes," Bea admitted. "I did not know he was the Wilbournes' footman until you identified him later, but . . . yes. Everything I did, I was doing only out of loyalty to my country, and in the hope that whatever small information I could provide might somehow spare lives and end our nation's conflict sooner."

He put a hand to his forehead. "I am a fool."

"No," Bea countered. "You are a good man. Of which, I have learned of late, the world contains too few."

"You think me insignificant," he accused her. "A mere artiste. A simpleton who plays with paints, while greater men—and, apparently, women—handle the more important matters of nations." His lips twisted as though the words tasted bitter. "I know. You are hardly the first to think such thoughts." He paced the room. "I was ever a disappointment to my father."

"No, Philippe," she protested. "I do not think you a fool. Indeed, if more men like you existed, the world would hold more beauty and less strife."

She could see the disbelief in his eyes. Had she treated him so shabbily, so dismissively, then? A creeping guilt told her she had. She prayed the damage could be undone.

A tap on the door signaled the butler's entry. Bea used the interruption to carefully consider her next words. She made no move for the food, though—her stomach was too tied in knots to consider eating.

Alone once more, she told Philippe, "You have honor, which you showed today, along with an abundance of bravery. Beyond that, every day you seek that which is good, which is beautiful and wondrous, in the people you know and the world you live in. And *that* is a rare gift."

He blew out a breath and passed a hand through his hair, but he stopped pacing. "That was my belief for a long time," he admitted. "But I have come to understand this 'gift' is not respected or shared by many, nor can it sufficiently safeguard those I love from the ills of the world.

"Beatrice, don't you realize?" He gestured toward her, passion giving force to the motion. "That could have been *you* in that room—captured, dragged through town, and left to die." His anger could not mask the fear behind his words.

"It *should* have been me," Bea said fiercely. "I am the one who got us into this mess, and I would give anything to have spared Charity from such . . ." she gulped, "such terror."

"I would never wish such a thing upon you," he replied seriously. "I can barely stand imagining it. I do, though, admire the strength, the loyalty of your friendship, for I believe you truly mean that. And I cannot help but wonder . . . what would happen, if you were to give that same devotion to a man—to a lover? He would be lucky indeed."

How did one reply to such a thing? His words wound her in circles. Did he refer to himself? Did *he* want that kind of devotion from her? But he'd never promised any lasting devotion of his own. "If I met a man who showed me devotion of that same kind, I should willingly give him mine," she whispered.

"Have you not met such a man?" he asked softly.

She turned away. "I have met a man who is gallant and courteous, sensual and captivating. But devotion? We do not speak of that. More the fool am I, for losing my heart to an artiste whose popularity with the ladies is legendary. I had no more sense, no more discretion, than any of them."

"*Have* you lost your heart to me, Beatrice?" Some of the anger in his tone had dissipated, yet Bea did not answer. She couldn't. She turned her head, just enough to see that he stood with head bowed. Her body ached to go to him, let him take her in his arms and make her forget everything—but if she did, she would be left to face the same demons the moment he let go.

"If you had," he said, his voice hoarse, "lost your heart to me, that is, I would not trample on it. Though, if indeed that is true, you have a most unusual way of showing it. Your heart, perhaps, but not your soul, the hidden secrets that make you who you are."

Shame seeped through her defenses, filling her conscience, for his words were even truer than he knew. Intentionally or not, she'd hurt him. Hurt the man she admired, respected, and even loved. How could she expect devotion from a man she'd deliberately held at arm's length?

"I am so very sorry," she whispered. "Please understand. I could not share this with *anyone*. Not my dearest friend, or even my parents. Charity knew only because she was with me when we discovered the lovers we'd mischievously thought to eavesdrop on were engaged in something quite different from romance.

"We were in far over our heads, so we turned to the duke—he was the only one we told. Once he got us to the officials, our instructions were to speak of it to no one. That is why even Elizabeth, my close friend, was unable to tell you much when

Charity went missing. She has been my confidante for years—if I could not go to her, please do not feel slighted I could not confide in you either, though I wished desperately to become closer to you."

"And you did. Or so I thought. I know you do not take lovers lightly, Bea. What you may not understand is that I do not either." He cleared his throat. "I admit to enjoying a good flirtation—I would be ashamed to call myself a man, let alone a Frenchman, if I did not." When she cracked a smile, he continued, "But you, Beatrice, ceased being a mere flirtation nearly from the moment I met you."

Her breath caught. He'd never directly spoken of feelings for her—at least not feelings beyond desire. Desire to paint her, to make love to her. But beyond that? She willed her heart to calm its noisy thudding, for she desperately needed to hear his next words.

He unfolded his long frame from where he leaned against the wall and came to her, taking both her hands in his, then sliding down the length of her forearm until he held her lightly at the elbows. Close, but not too close. Or not close enough. Which was it?

"You, *chérie*, are far more than I bargained for in coming to England."

"How so?" He was back to calling her *chérie*. That had to be a good sign.

"I have been captivated since I first laid eyes on you. We have spent hour upon hour together, and yet I have only begun to scratch the surface, to truly know you. I wake each morning anticipating the moment I will see you, wondering if I can do you justice, convey your contemplative yet passionate spirit through art in a way that pleases you. No other woman has ever held my attention so utterly.

"Beatrice, the rest of the world drops away when I am with you." His searing gaze made her throat go dry. Behind her elbows, his hands exerted gentle pressure until she stepped forward. Scant inches remained between them. "And then," he told her, "there is this."

His lips dropped to hers, tasting. A sensual haze stole over Bea, as it always did when she touched this man. Instinctively she moved closer, her hips and breasts pressing against his lean muscle as she opened her mouth to his kiss.

He made a sound in his throat that resembled a growl as he took advantage of her offering, his tongue driving in to stroke hers. The kiss took on a wild edge, thrusting and stroking until Bea's knees buckled and she clung to him for balance, desperate that he never let go. Finally she had to pause to draw a breath. As she pulled back, she knew the fierce need she saw in his eyes was matched in her own.

"Yes," she murmured, after retrieving her voice from the dark jungle of passion into which it had disappeared, "there is *that*."

Philippe expelled a choked laugh, staring at the flushed and beautiful woman before him.

He could think of no more words—in French or English—that could even begin to convey his need to love and touch her, possess her, *know* her. To be as close as two people could be. He only hoped that where words had failed him, touch would not.

He claimed her mouth again with a kiss both powerful and hungry. Her response was immediate, and he tightened his arms, hauling her against his length as the fear that had driven them earlier that day gave way to a desire, a *need* for intimacy that could not be restrained.

His gaze dropped to her bosom, displayed to mouthwatering advantage by a gown cut in the French style—not as flimsy as the rose silk in which he'd begun to paint her, but still no match for his determined fingers. He tugged the bodice down, cupping her breast, lifting it as he bent his lips to her tightly peaked nipple. She moaned, her body molding to his. His trousers had grown uncomfortably tight. She exacerbated the problem, rubbing her hips against his hardness. This time, he wasn't sure who moaned.

He raised his head to take her mouth again, his tongue delving into the welcoming warmth, tangling with hers, promising more.

Mon Dieu. He had to have her.

Bea understood, and apparently shared, his need, for she tore her mouth from his long enough to get out the word "upstairs."

A few hurried adjustments of clothing and a peek out the door to check for servants, and Bea grabbed his hand and tugged him toward the stairs. He followed willingly. When he dared to smooth a hand over the enticing backside just ahead of him on the stairs, she stumbled and he laughed softly.

Then they were in her room, and there was no more laughter—only a frenzy of fingers undoing hooks and buttons as they shed their clothing. Then a hushed "oh" as he came back to her, pulled her into his arms and felt the softness of her breasts against his chest, her body warm and welcoming in all the places he needed it.

His erection pressed against her stomach. He was harder than he could ever remember—and on the verge of losing control. There would be time to linger later. Not now.

He hooked one of her legs around his hips, cradling her head as it fell back, giving him access to her neck, her breasts. He drew a nipple into his mouth.

"More," she begged, and the knowledge that she wanted him as badly as he did her sent him over the edge.

He found her entrance, wet and ready. He lifted her to the edge of the bed. She wrapped her other leg around him and he drove into her, filling her in one deep thrust.

She was so warm, so tight. He wasn't going to last long.

Neither, he hoped, was she. Her spine arched as she fell backward, and her breath came in short gasps that matched the timing of his thrusts.

He pinched her nipples lightly, eliciting another moan of pleasure before switching the attention of his fingers to the sensitive nub at the opening to her sex. He thrust deeper, faster, stroking the nub all the while. Her head tossed back and forth on the bedding. Need for release hammered at him and he tried desperately to hold back, increasing the pressure of his fingers, the tempo, until she shrieked and convulsed around him.

Not a moment too soon, for his own orgasm ripped through him, his cock throbbing with release, pulsing into her, until he collapsed. He rolled to the side, pulling her with him. They couldn't stay like this all night. But he'd be damned if he was going to let her go now.

He couldn't stay. To do so would mean certain ruin.

Bea knew this as surely as she knew her life would never be the same for having met Jean Philippe Durand. But they'd already risked enough. If he remained in her home—let alone in her bed—until morning, and the full staff began stirring, the damage would be irreparable. As much as she trusted her servants, gossip like that was bound to get out.

She was hardly the first widow in the ton to take a lover, but discretion was paramount in such matters.

Beside her, Philippe raised his head. "*Chérie*, it is my fondest dream to hold you as you drift into slumber. Instead, I fear I must sneak away, like a thief in the night."

"I fear you must," she agreed, disappointed and yet relieved to know he understood the capricious nature of societal standards as well as she.

Bea slid from the bed and drew on a robe as Philippe dressed. She directed him to a side entrance, where he could leave unobserved. She hated this. The need to hide him, the way his slipping into the dark made her feel.

"I will call on you in the morning, *ma belle*," he promised, kissing her good-bye.

Bea returned to her room and drew the covers over her head. She'd expected the turmoil of the last day—had it only been a day?—to leave her exhausted, but instead she tossed in bed, unable to sleep. She'd never spent the night with Philippe, yet she felt bereft at his sudden absence. The sheet was still warm where he'd lain next to her.

Lord, she loved that man. His passion for finding beauty in the world and replicating it, his easy charm, and, more than that, the ingrained honor that made him set all else aside to assist a friend in need.

It wasn't the love she'd planned. She'd thought to find a man for whom she held a simple affection, a courtship that led to marriage and family, perhaps growing someday into a steady sort of love. Instead she'd found Philippe, and a greater passion than she'd ever imagined, tempered by uncertainty about their future.

Was there any hope this could last, and even expand to include those things she'd dreamed of? Or was she being greedy, hoping for too much?

One thing she knew. There was no hope for them at all if their relationship was not built on honesty.

Last night he'd accused her of not being open with him—an accusation in which he'd been fully justified. No longer, Bea decided. Her love demanded she open herself to him. He already knew her as a widow, a lady, a lover, and a spy. When he called upon her tomorrow morning, she would come to him as a poet.

Chapter 17

When Philippe returned to his hotel lodgings in the wee hours of the morning, he was infinitely grateful that the social practices of London's ton routinely involved late-night partying during the Season. The manager didn't blink an eye; he simply handed Philippe the mail that had accumulated during his absence.

Philippe glanced through it absentmindedly on his way upstairs, registering another letter from Lord Owen. He set that one aside. He'd respond in the morning. First, he needed sleep.

But as it turned out, responding to Lord Owen's letter was unnecessary, because the man himself called on Philippe at the earliest decent hour the following day.

He showed his father into the sitting area of his suite, each man eyeing the other awkwardly. After all, Philippe realized, their only previous meeting had been, for lack of a better term, intense.

But Lord Owen cleared his throat and straightened his spine. "Though I cannot atone for the mistakes of my past, I can, at least, stop perpetuating them. Philippe, you are my family, however unconventional. There is a home for you here in London. My home."

Though he might be uncomfortable, the older man was clearly sincere. A warm smile accompanied Philippe's reply. "I did receive your kind letter of invitation. I apologize for my lack of response. I have only just returned to London, and the past days have been . . . busy."

Lord Owen chuckled. "Ah, yes. The woman who has captured your interest."

That, and a good deal more. "Indeed. I have promised to call on her today." Already he was anxious to see Bea again. He also suspected the aftermath of yesterday's events was not yet over. There would be questions to answer.

"I shan't keep you long, my boy," Lord Owen said. "It seemed foolish to continue to write when you are so close—and I admit, my heart desired to confirm that my aging eyes had not deceived me, nor my aging mind invented you. And I am satisfied." He smiled. "You are my son."

Philippe swallowed, an unfamiliar ache in his throat.

"I have taken the liberty of having a suite readied for you," Henry Owen continued. "And of having a studio installed. I believe you will find the space, and the light, far superior to what you have here."

Philippe swallowed again. This man who barely knew him had accepted him as family, had gone to great lengths to accommodate his artistic needs, while the man who'd actually raised him had merely tolerated those needs. He'd already planned to accept Owen's written offer. Now it was clear he was being offered so much more than space and light.

His father must have mistaken Philippe's silence for dissent, for he said, "But perhaps I presume too much?" He rubbed a thumb across the knuckles of his opposite hand as though they ached. "You could be angry with me for the way I treated your mother."

The emotion clogging Philippe's throat broke free. "No, I am not angry. To dwell on the past would only rob us of the future, and I do not believe that is what my *maman* hoped to accomplish in sending me to you. I would be honored to stay in your home."

Bea blew dry the ink on the line of script she'd just written, then set the quill down, fingers trembling. It was some of her best work. She could feel that. But she was terrified to share it. Spying for her government might have placed her in physical danger, but that was nothing compared to the danger of the possibility that her creative work, her very soul, might face rejection.

These past weeks she'd discovered passion—first through Philippe's art, and later in his arms. Living with anything less was no longer an option.

He'd described her as his muse—flattering, to be sure—but Bea needed him to see her for what she was, to see that she held a creative spirit of her own, even if her work was not renowned across the Continent the way his was.

But she'd never before written a poem for a man, nor felt such intense trepidation, such *need*, for that man to approve.

She folded the paper and sealed it neatly. She had to find just the right way to give it to him.

Unfortunately, instructions from Lord Castlereagh arrived shortly before Philippe.

"I would invite you to sit, but I am afraid we must proceed immediately to Lord Bainbridge's home," she told her lover when the butler ushered him in. "The British Foreign Secretary has been apprised of yesterday's events, and he desires each of us to provide our own accounting. He awaits us at Alex and Elizabeth's house."

"*Naturellement.* That is to be expected. Though," Philippe grinned, "I hope this official of yours does not wish an accounting of *all* of yesterday's events."

She laughed at his suggestive tone and swatted him. "Only the relevant ones."

He swept her a gallant bow. "In that case, my lady, may I have the honor of escorting you to the duke's residence?"

He was back to being the high-spirited showman who'd so dazzled her in the beginning. Courageous and loyal, gallant and charming . . . how could she not love this man?

Bea tucked her poem into her reticule and offered Philippe her arm, eagerly anticipating the moment Lord Castlereigh's business was finished and she could present the poem that would show Philippe not only that she shared his creative passion, but also how much he meant to her.

Upon arrival, Bea and Philippe were shown to the formal salon of the Bainbridges' home, where they found Elizabeth sitting alone. She looked more exhausted than usual, even, Bea thought, considering that her friend's expectant state often left her tired.

Elizabeth greeted them both, clasping Bea in a quick hug. "I'm so glad you and Charity are both safe. She's resting now. Poor dear. She seems so strong, but it took her a good while to settle into a peaceful sleep."

Ah. That explained it. "I thought Lord Castlereagh wished to speak with us?" Bea asked.

"He does. He had just finished with Charity when one of his men arrived. They are cloistered, along with Alex, in the study."

"You should be resting, too," Bea suggested to her friend.

"I will. I'll feel better knowing this ordeal is over."

The door opened, and the duke and the Foreign Secretary entered.

"Lady Pullington. Monsieur Durand," Lord Castlereagh acknowledged them. "Thank you for your prompt appearance." He paused, glanced at Alex, and then at Philippe. "I hope you will not take offence, Monsieur Durand, but as your role in this is, as yet, unclear to me, I must ask you to step out of the room a moment until I can speak with you one-on-one and, ideally, clear up the matter."

Philippe frowned.

"Monsieur Durand has proven he deserves—" Bea began indignantly, but a raised hand from Lord Castlereagh silenced her.

"It is merely a precaution. I understand he helped rescue Miss Medford, for which we are most grateful. However, in my work we make a practice always to separate the participants in an event. By listening to their separate accountings, we not only ensure the stories match, but we often identify details one party may have forgotten, or misinterpreted. And by piecing together the separate threads, we form a more complete understanding of what happened."

"A reasonable explanation," Philippe acknowledged. He gave a bow and stepped out.

"Lady Pullington," the Secretary continued, "I have already heard from each of the Bainbridges, and Miss Medford, and would like next to speak with you. Before we do, though, I can tell you ladies what the duke already knows: we have received good news on two fronts. First, your friends, Lord and Lady Wilbourne, have been—for the time being, at least—cleared of any misdoings. There is no evidence that anyone outside of the one servant was involved in feeding information to our enemies."

"Well, of course, Alicia Wilbourne wouldn't do such a thing," Elizabeth said. "And the other news?"

"We have captured the servant who did, and one of his companions."

Bea clasped her hands together. "That *is* good news. But there were more than two. The others?"

"Unfortunately, they remain at large, though we hope interrogations of the two in custody will lead to their whereabouts." He glanced from Alex to Elizabeth. "Lady Bainbridge, when your sister has rested, I will need her to identify one of the detainees. The servant. The second is Rose Kettridge, the actress. As a publicly known figure, there is no need to confirm her identity, only the extent of her role in this plot."

"I will act as Miss Medford's escort to wherever these people are being held," Alex said.

"Very good. For now, we have them at a private residence—actually, semiprivate. It is used by my agents for a number of purposes, and is well equipped and less apt to draw attention than an actual prison. Of course, should they stand trial, they will have to be moved." Lord Castlereagh gave them the address. "And now, Lady Pullington, if you'd be so kind as to come with me to the study? Oh, and Your Grace, if you wish to invite Monsieur Durand back in, please do. Just keep the discussion focused on other topics."

Bea followed the government official into the duke's study. She felt her role in Charity's disappearance and rescue had been limited at best, but Lord Castlereagh made her go over each action, beginning with the arrival of his own messenger to Montgrave, multiple times. Finally he seemed satisfied.

Bea still had a question of her own—one that had been bothering her since yesterday. "About the loss of the plans . . . Britain is not terribly endangered?" she asked. If she'd paid more attention to spying and less to falling in love, perhaps things would never have gotten so out of hand.

Lord Castlereagh smiled gently. "No, my dear. Our armies have adjusted accordingly. And, to be honest, even if they had not, I truly believe the outcome of this war is already decided. Napoleon Bonaparte *cannot* win. He is outnumbered, and the will of many nations is against him. France's troops have rallied to his cause, it is true, but trained soldiers are in limited supply in that country—as are young men of an age to fight."

"Thank you, my lord."

"I think we are done here." He stood, and the two returned to the salon. "Do not fear, Lady Pullington. This is the last gasp of an overzealous ruler who cannot admit he is already defeated. Britain, and the coalition, will triumph, and peace will come once again to the Continent."

Across the room, the duke nodded his agreement. A sense of calm stole over Bea—the first in many days. "I pray it is so," she said. "We could all use some peace."

When Philippe had also been questioned to Lord Castlereagh's satisfaction, he and Bea took their leave of the Bainbridges once more. Bea relaxed in the vehicle, nearly giddy with relief. Now that Castlereagh knew Philippe's only role in the French plot had been to help find Charity, the guilt that had torn her over her feelings toward him had been lifted.

"Shall we try this again?" Philippe teased as the coach deposited them in front of Bea's home. "I had hoped to call on you for social purposes this morning, and while I enjoy your company in any situation, being interrogated by government officials was not entirely what I'd envisioned."

"Oh, my." Bea matched his flirtatious tone and fluttered her lashes. "I am destitute at the thought of having disappointed you. Please, do come in and I shall make amends."

Inside, Bea signaled a footman for refreshments,

then closed the drapes of the formal salon, shutting out the view of the black carriage that had followed them from the duke's home. Protection. A reminder that, although everyone in their little party was home safe now, the danger had not entirely passed. The feeling of giddiness faded.

Philippe stood behind and to her side. "It is only a precaution."

"I know." Lord Castlereagh, Alex, and Philippe had agreed unanimously that none of the women were going anywhere for the foreseeable future without guards—especially since, as she'd learned while Philippe was closeted with the British Foreign Secretary, at least one person had already been killed as a result of this plot. The duke's staff at Montgrave had found the body of Reilly, the first messenger she'd entrusted, deep within the woods.

The guards were a necessity. And knowing that made her uncomfortable.

Philippe touched a hand to the small of her back.

"I want to believe it is over," Bea told him.

"But?"

She could only shake her head. The papers were gone, and two spies caught. But their leader, and the rogue French ruler they supported, were still at large.

"Pray tell me your government has not asked more of you."

"They have not."

"And you, *ma belle*?" The gentle pressure of his hand on her back turned her toward him. "You are not going to go looking for trouble?"

Bea shivered at the echo of the warning she'd issued to Charity. Could she heed her own advice?

Philippe looked at her a long moment, then his lips quirked in a smile. He indicated the closed drapes. "Enough. When shall we return to more pleasurable pursuits?"

She looked up, mouth open in surprise, and he laughed. "No, *chérie*, I meant only," he nodded to the drapes again, "let us put them from our minds. I am eager to return to painting, or at the very least, a pleasant and witty conversation. Though," he mused, his voice dropping to a husky murmur as he used one finger to trace the line of her cheek, her throat, "if there were other pleasures my lady wished to return to, I am, as always, utterly at her service."

It was an offer she couldn't resist. She leaned in and his lips brushed hers. The kiss lingered, and she sank willingly into the sensual warmth.

"Mmm," she breathed.

He kissed her temple, then bit gently at her earlobe. "We probably shouldn't make a habit of this," he whispered.

"Hmm?" Bea was having a hard time thinking straight. "Of kissing?"

The corners of his blue eyes crinkled in amusement. "I was thinking of what happened the last time we began kissing in this room."

A discrete tap on the door spared Bea from having to respond. They sprang apart as a footman entered, and Bea turned away to hide her flaming cheeks. The servant placed a tray of refreshments on the side table and, just as discretely, left.

In the interruption, Bea remembered the poem she'd written for Philippe.

She moved toward the tray and poured his coffee—

the French kind she'd ordered specially for him. She recalled the feeling of worldliness when she'd placed the order earlier that morning, a confident woman making plans for her lover. If only she could summon that confidence now.

"I have something for you."

He was already eyeing the tray. "Sandwiches, and coffee, it appears."

"No, silly. Well, yes. And something else."

She tried to still her trembling fingers as she set the cup on a saucer. Next to it, she placed the folded paper containing her poem.

The scent of the coffee, dark and intense, filled her nostrils as she offered the beverage to him.

He picked up the paper, a bemused smile on his face. "What is this?"

"It's for you," she said softly, her heart hammering so loudly she could barely hear her own words.

He slit open the seal and unfolded it. Bea knew the moment he recognized it as a poem, for his gaze took on that contemplative intensity she'd come to know so well. He leaned against the mantel as he read—a casual pose. The morning sunlight slanted through the windows, highlighting his chiseled features. Dear Lord, he was handsome.

Bea forced herself to breathe as she waited. He didn't rush through the poem—she liked that. But his face gave away no other expression than absorption.

Finally he looked up. "This is incredible. Thank you for sharing it with me. Where did you find it?"

Disappointment pierced her heart. He hadn't recognized it as inherently *hers*. But why would he? She'd never given him reason to think of her that way.

She shook her head slightly, wet her lips. "It's mine. I wrote it this morning, though the idea has been tumbling about my brain for somewhat longer. I wrote it for you." Her heart's hammering grew wilder.

His blue eyes grew dark. "Yours?" He returned his gaze to the paper.

Seconds ticked by endlessly. Bea twisted her hands in her skirt, not caring that it would cause wrinkles.

Slowly he nodded. "*Oui.* Of course, this is yours." The hand holding the paper fell to his side and he gazed at her as though seeing her for the first time. "You did not tell me you are a poet."

"I . . . it's not something I share often," she said, her worry growing. He'd called her poem "incredible." But something was still wrong. Why was it her poems were only well-received when no one knew it was she who'd written them?

"Well, Beatrice, I thank you for sharing it with me. You're very talented." He refolded the paper. "I've an appointment this morning, I only just remembered. Lord Henry Owen has graciously opened his home to me, including a studio in which to paint. We are to meet today, and so I must be on my way."

He stepped forward, cupped her shoulders lightly, and pressed a quick kiss to her forehead.

He never kissed her like that.

Bea's chest hurt. What had she done wrong? His withdrawal was so obvious it was nearly palpable.

She was frozen, speechless, as he stepped back

and gave her the lavish showman's bow and grin that usually made her giggle. "I shall be in touch."

Seconds later, he was gone. With him went the folded paper, its creases a match for the fissures forming and cracking apart her heart.

Chapter 18

"Beatrice, think of your family, your sisters."

Bea had been dreading this conversation from the moment she'd picked up the morning gossip sheet and discovered:

"Lady P was observed alighting from a coach in front of her home with a certain monsieur— normally not an event worthy of report, except in this instance, the hour was shortly before noon. One wonders from whence the couple was returning at such an unusual hour? Intriguingly, a second coach followed them, from which no one at all emerged. This author is no expert on matters of the heart, but our monsieur is of a known amorous nature, and it appears that the lovely Lady P has captured his attention, even beyond the confines of the studio."

Well, she'd thought irreverently, thank heaven they'd only been observed in *public* conversation. Bea could recall nothing particularly scandalous about the few moments they'd been outside, long enough only to climb the stairs and wait for the butler to open the door. Had she somehow given herself away—stood too close, or gazed too directly? Whoever reported for this morning's column must have thought so.

Amazingly, a full hour had passed before Beatrice's mother, Lady Margaret Russell, had arrived on Bea's doorstep in high dudgeon.

They'd barely made it to the family salon before her mother rounded on her, eyes blazing.

"Please, have a seat, Mama," Bea said, mustering both stamina and patience for what was to come.

Lady Russell waved a sheet of paper in her direction. Bea recognized it immediately as that morning's gossip sheet. "I'm far too agitated to sit just yet. Why, Sarah is yet unmarried. How can we hope to make her a respectable match when the talk of the ton is your scandalous behavior?"

"Mother, surely you are overreacting. You know how the gossips are. Truly, there is nothing so harmful in that paper."

It was the wrong thing to say.

"Overreacting?" Lady Russell's chest puffed with indignation.

Bea sighed and tried a different tack. "So what if I have attracted Monsieur Durand's attention? It is of little consequence."

"I beg to differ. Half of London is speculating as to how far that attraction has gone. They *know* you are sitting for him, but what else might you be doing?"

"Half of London is jealous," Bea countered. Thank God her mother hadn't the slightest comprehension of what else Bea had been doing. Lady

Russell would not have cared in the least that the British Foreign Secretary himself had requested Bea's help—or that her extraordinarily unladylike behavior may actually have helped ensure the downfall of a rogue Emperor, and saved the life of her good friend.

Bea sighed and stuck to what her mother *would* comprehend. "I've been asked to sit for a famous painter. Most of the women who speak so scathingly do so because they were not extended the same invitation."

"And why is that, do you think?"

"I cannot say, Mother, but surely you would not have had me turn him down."

Lady Russell pursed her lips. "Do not try to deflect me, Beatrice. I know you too well to believe you've done no more than pose innocently to be painted. What I don't understand is why? You've always been a good girl, respectable. I should have known the tide was turning when you insisted upon living alone. Who ever heard of such a thing?"

The familiar twinges of guilt pricked her, but Bea pushed them away. That was the old Bea—and the old Bea had never had any fun. "As I said, Mother, there is no cause for such concern. Just consider. A year ago no one would even speak to Elizabeth Medford. Yet all that has long since been forgotten, and she is at the pinnacle of society."

"Exactly." Her mother leaned forward. "Elizabeth *Bainbridge's* scandalous behavior earned her a marriage proposal from a duke. A risk, to be sure, but not an unwise one. But *you,* daughter, are having an affair with a *commoner.* 'Tis hardly comparable."

Bea's hands fisted in her skirts, but she raised her head and looked her mother straight in the eye. "Philippe is hardly common. In fact, he is the *least* common man I have ever met. He's incredibly talented and intelligent. His work is revered throughout Europe. Is nobility all that matters to you? Titles and stuffy responsibility? Well, I've done all that for you once, Mother. It never brought me happiness."

Lady Russell was silent for a moment. Then slowly, she seemed to deflate. "It was never my intent to cause you unhappiness, Bea."

Some of Bea's ire dissipated as well. "I know, Mama."

"Still, I can hardly condone you flaunting your indiscretions before all of Society."

Bea sighed. "Mother, I refuse to promise you I won't speak with Philippe, or meet him. After all, there is his painting to complete. But I shall endeavor not to, as you say, 'flaunt my indiscretions.'"

"Well. That is something, I suppose. I'd best take my leave. I promised Sarah a trip to the milliner's today."

Bea saw her mother to the door with an awkward embrace. Relief settled over her. They would never see eye to eye on this matter, but she'd stood her ground. And she'd made it clear she *would* see Philippe again. Given his abrupt departure the previous day, she hoped that was true. Her heart couldn't bear it if it wasn't.

Philippe settled into Lord Owen's London home, going through the motions of arranging the studio: setting up canvasses and laying out brushes.

The sunny breakfast nook-turned-studio offered excellent light. But he did not invite Bea over for a sitting.

He knew she hadn't actually betrayed him. Yet logic had nothing to do with the betrayal in his heart. How could Bea have kept such a secret from him?

He could understand—to a point—why she'd felt unable to tell him about her work for the British government. But why would she hide the fact that she wrote poetry?

Little things made sense now . . . the Wordsworth poem she'd quoted that captured the exact sentiment of finding the abandoned rose garden . . . or, for that matter, the way she'd known, intuitively, how to guide him to exactly the perfect place in which to set her portrait. Had she been secretly laughing at him as he called her a muse, knowing that in truth, she was a fellow creator?

Once again, he'd been left out. She'd told him now, but how could he trust himself to love a woman when every time he turned around, she'd assumed a new identity?

And he did love her. Unlike the reserved English, the French did not hesitate to put a name to their passions. They were also aware that love often brought as much sorrow as joy. Love could be unrequited, love could be torn apart by wars and death . . . or by distrust. Oh, he'd fallen in love with Beatrice Pullington, but that didn't mean he was happy about it. He wasn't even really sure who she was.

As for what she'd written, that was no mere dabbling of a poem. She wasn't the first woman to present him with a poem, but usually such gifts were copied from another author, or at best, amateur attempts that bordered between trite and foolish. Bea's poem was night to their day. She had talent, deep and pure.

How had he failed, so utterly, to recognize that in her? He, who prided himself on seeing beneath the surface, then rendering what he saw in his art? Yet he'd failed the two most important women in his life.

And if Beatrice Pullington could keep that from him, what else might she be hiding?

The trouble with living with family, Philippe soon discovered, was that they were nosy. Or at least Henry Owen was.

On the surface, the living arrangements proved less awkward than Philippe had anticipated. The house was roomy enough for two men accustomed to their own space, though Philippe's use of the breakfast room left the formal dining room the only available place for actually serving breakfast. One stilted morning of that, and both men had taken to simply having trays in their rooms.

It was one thing to move in with a father you'd never known, but quite another to figure out what to say to him before one's first cup of coffee—or tea, in the Englishman's case.

No, the problem was not lack of space. It was the obvious lack of progress on Philippe's painting.

And unlike most men, his father did not avoid discussing such topics. Philippe could enjoy a game of cards with Robert Wilbourne, or a fencing match with Alex Bainbridge, without fear of either friend prying too deeply into his thoughts. But Henry Owen, in his efforts to make up for lost time, had abandoned the rules that normally governed the interactions of men.

On the third day of his stay, Philippe was puttering aimlessly in the studio when his father tapped lightly on the door and joined him, coming to stand in front of the easel where he'd propped the beginnings of Bea's painting.

The older man studied the canvas. "You have made little progress of late."

"I have made no progress at all," Philippe admitted. "I haven't been working on it."

"Ah." Henry Owen rocked back on his heels, using his cane for balance. "Where is Lady Pullington? Not ill, I hope."

"I canceled our session."

"I see," Lord Owen said, and Philippe had the feeling he did.

Henry took a seat in the one padded chair remaining in the room, set off in a corner. There would be no escape from this conversation. Philippe tried to summon irritation at the man's continued presence, but found it wasn't in him.

Instead, he went back to puttering—polishing palette knives, organizing stacks of sketches that didn't need organizing.

"She has disappointed you in some way," his father speculated.

"Not disappointed, exactly," Philippe answered, uncannily aware that his father's choice of the seat in the corner allowed them to speak without actually looking at one another. The old man was a smart devil. Philippe set down a tiny jar of pigment. "She's a poet," he announced, as though that explained everything.

"A poet," his father repeated.

"Exactly." He shoved the jar of pigment an inch to the right, then decided that didn't please him either, and moved it two inches to the left. He dared a glance at his father, who leaned back in the chair, seeming perfectly relaxed.

"I didn't know she was a poet," Philippe admitted.

"Ah." Now there was a note of understanding in the older man's response.

"An extraordinary one, no less. And I don't think anyone else knows."

"A Gaudet among poets, as it were?" his father asked.

Philippe renewed his appreciation for the old man's superior perceptiveness, for now he knew exactly why Bea's revelation bothered him so.

"She wrote this." He handed the poem, which he'd kept on his person for the past three days, to his father.

Henry read in silence for a few minutes, then looked up. Philippe waited. "Talent, yes," his father said softly, "as well as an incredible tribute. She loves you."

"She keeps secrets from me," Philippe argued. "How can one love and not trust?"

"You walked away, didn't you."

It was more statement than question. As such, Philippe didn't bother to confirm the fact.

Lord Owen shook his head. "The young are ever blind. She came to you, did she not? Tried to share with you, something that obviously meant a great deal to her, and what did you do? Rejected her for attempting to do the very thing you say you wanted her to do."

Philippe frowned and busied himself once more with the many jars and artist's tools spread on the table. "When you put it that way . . ."

Both men grew quiet. Having run out of things to organize, Philippe selected a sketchbook and charcoal. His father didn't appear to be going anywhere, so Philippe began sketching him.

The older man raised a brow, then shrugged. As Philippe sketched, he began talking again. "I walked away from the woman I loved. It is the curse of the old, to vainly hope the young will learn from the mistakes of past generations rather than making their own. I know that. But I cannot sit idly by and watch it done without at least commenting on the folly. The price of loneliness is terribly high."

Philippe continued sketching.

"Did you ever think she might be scared?"

"Who?"

"Your lady friend. Or, for that matter, your mother."

"Scared?" Philippe frowned.

"Not everyone is like you."

"What do you mean?"

His father smiled. "You live, and thrive, in the public eye. Many do not. Just as nature has many forms, so do people—as an artiste you already know this, and celebrate it. But as a man?" He paused. "Permit me to be frank."

"You already are," Philippe grunted.

Lord Owen chuckled. "True. I am too old for polite trivialities. So I will simply say this: It is time you forgive your mother."

"Pardon?"

"Solange hurt you by keeping secrets, but I

sincerely doubt that was ever her intention. She did everything in her life out of love for you. Her marriage, giving up art—I see now she did those things in order to offer her child a stable home." At Philippe's look of skepticism, he added, "Or as stable as possible, given the turmoil of the past few decades in your country. She gave you that."

Philippe waited, unable to deny his mother had done much to cater to his childhood and later, his budding career.

"Even if you were shaken to discover your roots," Lord Owen indicated himself with a rueful smile, "were not what you thought, you must know that it was her love that gave you a strong enough foundation not to be destroyed by that."

"Why was she so determined to hide her past?" Philippe protested. "Surely it was nothing to be ashamed of. Her work was brilliant. She *knew* how much I admired Gaudet, how much art meant to me, and yet she held back."

Lord Owen smiled gently. "Perhaps she wished to put the past behind her. She was an artiste, with child and alone. Her work carried a small following, but not one as great as that her son would one day enjoy. I believe she saw Richard Durand's marriage offer as a rescue, an escape, and that she did not understand the sacrifice he asked her to make until much later."

"I could never make such a choice—to turn my back on the very core of my soul?"

"Could you not, in her position?"

Philippe was silent.

Lord Owen sighed. "You may not understand her choices, but you must never doubt her love for you."

"How can I not?" His life had been built on lies.

"Painting was, undoubtedly, difficult for your mother to abandon. In fact, Solange did complete one last painting, though not under the name of Gaudet."

Philippe raised his head, curiosity piqued. "Under her own?"

"No. In fact, she chose not to share the work with the world at all."

"How do you know this? I thought you never saw her after her marriage." And why had he never mentioned it before? Philippe refrained from asking the last question aloud—he'd learned Henry Owen was a man apt to reveal more in his own time than if pressed for information before he was ready.

"I did not see her. But a mention of the painting was in her last letter to me—a missive whose significance I did not comprehend until *you* arrived on my doorstep thirty years later. I did not respond to that letter."

"Why?"

"It was painful to think she had moved on. She had not, of course. She had entered willingly, but blindly, into a trap—but her soul remained the same. That I did not respond when she last reached out to me—it is yet another regret to add to an old man's list."

"The painting. Where is it now?"

He shook his head. "I know not."

"The subject matter? Have you any idea?"

"Yes." He gave a rueful chuckle. "It was you. She could not give up art without at least once painting her son."

Philippe swallowed. It was, perhaps, evidence of

his mother's love. But love and trust did not always go hand in hand. As an artist he might appreciate the mystery of the fairer sex, but when that mystery crossed the bounds into his personal life, the matter was different. If he hadn't *known* his mother, had he truly loved her?

And then there was Beatrice. She meant more to him than he'd ever anticipated; he'd been on the brink of declaring his love just before discovering he hadn't known her, either.

Or had he? His temple throbbed.

"I'd rather not discuss this any longer."

"Huh." Lord Owen grunted. Slowly he stood, gripping his cane. "I'll respect your wishes, for now. I realize I've no right to give fatherly lectures. But I trust you'll think about what I've said."

Philippe thought about it. Though by nightfall, as he dressed for an evening at White's, he had found no answers—except on one point. Actually, two. The first was simple. He needed a drink. Several of them, preferably. The second was a bit more complicated. He needed to return to France, to sort through his mother's belongings and claim her last painting. He prayed he would find it.

As far as forgiveness, there was nothing to be gained in holding grudges against the dead. Whatever her faults, his mother had done her best by him.

Beatrice Pullington, quietly respectable widow, passionate lover, intrepid spy, and brilliant poet, was another matter entirely. About her, he remained as confused as ever.

Hence the need for a drink. He'd agreed to meet

Lords Stockton and Garrett at White's for an evening of cards. In need of a third, they'd invited him, in spite of his admitted lack of skill at gaming. And since Philippe fully intended to get drunk, he didn't think the question of skill mattered anyway.

Philippe was about halfway to drunk, and two thirds of the way to losing a fortune, when their table was approached by a uniformed constable— *not* a common occurrence at the respectable gentlemen's club. The three men shot each other questioning glances.

The constable cleared his throat. "Monsieur Durand. Might I have a word with you?"

Philippe excused himself from the table, a sense of foreboding mixing unpleasantly with the liquor he'd consumed.

"Monsieur Durand, you are wanted for questioning by the British Foreign Office."

"Pardon?" He'd already been questioned. The Foreign Secretary himself had been satisfied with Philippe's accounting of rescuing Charity, and outside of that single incident, neither France nor England's government had ever shown the slightest interest in him.

"You are wanted for questioning," the constable repeated. "You are a French citizen with known political associations that are of concern to my country's officials."

Philippe grew warier. He had no political associations—only his stepfather did. "I don't understand."

"We have evidence that someone in London has been attempting to pass information to certain French parties. I cannot divulge details here, but your stay in England, as well as your extensive connections, have not gone unnoticed."

"Ha! *Certes,* you jest. I am an artiste," Philippe declared, one hand to his heart. He could hear his accent grow thick, but his indignation was too great for proper English. "I have no interest in government affairs. I have already spoken of this matter with your Foreign Secretary."

"Ah. You know of what I speak. You are involved," the constable said.

Philippe stopped short. It was true. He was. But for entirely different reasons—he'd been drawn in by the mysterious Englishwoman who'd captured his imagination and passion, and chivalry compelled him to aid her missing friend.

He pulled the constable farther into the corner, speaking in a lower tone now, though anger simmered in each word. "Do you think me a fool? My only involvement was to help rescue one of Britain's own. A lady, no less. If I were a spy, as you suggest, why would I do such a thing?"

The man gave an apologetic shrug. "It is not for me to say. If you will come with me, you will be taken before the magistrate, who I am sure will explain matters more fully. You will have the opportunity to make your case to him."

"And if I choose not to go with you?"

The constable looked him dead in the eye. "Monsieur, I would advise against that. It is not really an option."

Chapter 19

"Lord Owen?" Bea greeted her unexpected visitor.

The older man rose as she entered the salon. "A pleasure to make your acquaintance, my lady. You are every bit as lovely as Philippe described you."

She hadn't heard from Philippe in three days. She tried not to let the desperation show as she asked, "And how fares Monsieur Durand?"

Lord Owen shifted his cane. Bea gestured for him to sit, but he shook his head. "That is why I am here. Unfortunately, I do not bear good news. Philippe has been arrested."

"What?" Bea's legs wobbled and she quickly sat on the nearest chair, a stiff, hard-backed piece that matched her décor but which no one ever actually sat in. "What happened?"

Lord Owen followed her lead, easing back down to his seat. "As I understand, he was playing cards with Lords Stockton and Garrett, when a constable arrived with a warrant. Mindful of causing a scene, Philippe went with him to the magistrate's office, believing this was a misunderstanding about some, ah, adventure he shared with you, and which could be cleared up with a word from Lord Castlereagh."

Henry Owen's raised eyebrows plainly indicated his curiosity, but Bea offered no answers.

"At any rate, Lord Stockton knew Philippe was my guest, and hastened to inform me of the incident. I made immediate inquiries, though it took some hours to find him. Philippe's initial hope, that the misunderstanding could be easily rectified, did not come to fruition. In fact, the situation is quite worrisome. The papers have not yet gotten hold of this tidbit, but I fear the reprieve is temporary, Lady Pullington, and I wanted you to hear the news from me first."

He passed a hand across his forehead as though weary. No doubt he was, if all that had happened overnight. Bea wrapped her arms around her waist, struggling to take it in. Just days ago Philippe had been questioned and cleared by the British Foreign Secretary. What could have changed?

"What has he been charged with?"

"Formal charges have not yet been filed. But from what I gather . . . there is no easy way to say this. Espionage."

Bea nodded. It was what she'd expected.

The old man observed her reaction with keen eyes. "You do not act surprised," he mused, "which leads me to wonder what sort of adventures the two of you have been having outside the studio."

"Philippe Durand is not a spy."

"I did not think so either."

"I *know* so," Bea declared.

"Really?" Lord Owen leaned back, finding a more comfortable position. "And how is that?"

"Because," Bea told him, sensing she could trust him with her secret, "I am the spy who was assigned to determine whether or not *he* was a spy."

"I see." A smile touched her guest's lips. "Beautiful and fascinating. No wonder he is captivated."

Whether or not Philippe was still captivated was a tricky subject—one Bea preferred not to address at the moment. "Where is he being held?"

"At my house. That is the one thing I have been able to do for him. He is under house arrest, with guards."

"Surely that is uncomfortable for you."

Lord Owen shrugged, then gave her a smile that hinted at the mischief of youth. "Why, I haven't had such excitement in years."

"Can he receive visitors?"

"For a short duration, and with guards present. No items, particularly weapons or anything bearing writing that might constitute a message, may be exchanged."

Bea pressed her lips together. "Do you have any idea why they suspect him?"

"No, Lady Pullington. I am sorry. No one I spoke with would divulge that information—they would advise me only that they believed I was making an unwise choice in offering up my home to hold him."

Bea stood. "Lord Owen, I am infinitely grateful to you for coming to me with these tidings. Now I am afraid I must excuse myself. I need to pay a visit to our Foreign Secretary."

Bea sensed a change before she even saw Viscount Castlereagh. He was an understandably busy man, but in the past, she'd been treated as a priority—

he'd cut meetings short in order to confer with her and Alex Bainbridge.

This time, she waited for hours.

Her inquiries to his assistant were met with thinly-veiled impatience. The Foreign Secretary was a busy man. Many urgent meetings. And she, after all, had not scheduled an appointment in advance. Well, how could she have? Bea tapped her foot in frustration.

Finally, she was ushered into the Foreign Secretary's office. As she entered, Castlereagh looked up from the document he'd been reviewing, and announced, "I know why you have come, Lady Pullington, but I am afraid I cannot help you."

The breath whooshed from Bea's chest and the speech she'd had hours to perfect vanished from her mind. "Why?"

"You wish me to release Jean Philippe Durand. I cannot. New evidence has come to light that throws into doubt our earlier assessment that Monsieur Durand is uninvolved in the plot to steal British military plans to aid the cause of Napoleon Bonaparte."

Bea frowned. "What new evidence?"

He folded his arms. "It is odd, isn't it, that Monsieur Durand's decision to travel to England coincided so neatly with Napoleon's return?"

"Perhaps." Bea wasn't giving an inch. "*What* new evidence?" she repeated.

"And it is known that Monsieur Durand's father, Msr. Richard Durand, served with Bonaparte in the French army, and later worked as an advisor to him."

He was evading her. That wasn't new evidence. Nor was it relevant. "Philippe does not share the political ambition of his father."

Viscount Castlereagh raised a brow. "How do you know this? Did you, in the course of sitting for a portrait, learn his character so thoroughly as to testify to it with certainty?"

Bea swallowed hard at his biting tone.

"Lady Pullington, I am sorry. But I cannot trust you," Castlereagh told her. "Your plea speaks of emotion, not of reason. I am not deaf to the gossip of the ton, particularly when that gossip includes speculation about one of my informants and the subject I asked her to observe. Though," he admitted, "it is not uncommon to employ seduction in this line of work—indeed, an intimate acquaintance will often prove a fruitful source of information."

"I didn't—" Bea protested.

He held up a hand, cutting off her reply. "And that is what troubles me. The lines of professional and personal interest have been blurred. Did you seduce him for the purposes of learning his secrets? Or did you fall prey to *his* charms, perhaps risking not only your heart, but our nation's secrets?"

At her stunned silence, he continued. "You see? I cannot say with absolute certainty where your loyalties lie. And therefore, I cannot help you. The matter is too grave to take further risks."

Somehow, Bea managed to stay upright, to keep her voice steady, when she felt more like collapsing into a shaky, sobbing heap. "Wait. If it is known that the elder Durand acted as an advisor to Bonaparte, why do you suspect Philippe, and not him?"

"An astute question, but our inquiries show that with the Emperor's downfall, Monsieur Durand denounced Bonaparte. He had ambitions of election to the French Chamber of Deputies under Louis

XVIII's new constitution. Supporting Bonaparte's mad attempt to return would surely not serve those interests, and would paint Durand as fickle, if not traitorous."

"But—"

"Lady Pullington, I realize you showed an unusual prescience in deciphering the original message you came across, and in bringing this situation to the British government's attention, but matters are out of your hands now. I no longer require, or request, your services."

It took all her effort to keep her spine straight. "Viscount Castlereagh. I see that, circumstances as they are, my word alone is of no value. If, however, I can bring you proof, or evidence more convincing than my own pleas, will you reconsider?"

He regarded her gravely. "Have you such proof?"

"No—not yet," Bea admitted. "But if you would tell me what evidence has come to light against him, I will better understand how to counter it. Or," she swallowed but met his eyes with her chin up, "if the evidence is such that any effort on my part is but a fool's errand, I will understand that as well."

He pressed his lips together. "I will tell you this. The two spies we captured the night your Miss Medford was recovered? We have had ample time to interrogate them, and have learned little, but for one thing: when asked for whom they worked, both provided the same name. Monsieur Jean Philippe Durand."

Her government had let her down. Bea prayed her friends would not do the same.

Only Elizabeth was home when Bea arrived at the Bainbridge town house—a place she'd once considered almost a second home but she was now beginning to associate with dire situations.

"They've taken Philippe," Bea wailed, as the composure she'd maintained with the Foreign Secretary deserted her.

"What?" Her friend's green eyes registered alarm. "Kidnapped?"

"No. Worse. Arrested."

Elizabeth stood and came to Bea, gently leading her to the sofa. "All right, let's try to make sense of this. Arrested is bad, but surely not worse than kidnapping. It is most likely a mistake."

Bea shook her head in misery. "It's not a mistake." She explained what had happened at the Foreign Secretary's office. "And," she finished, "he's angry with me. Until Lord Owen showed up this morning, I hadn't heard from Philippe in three days."

"Oh, dear." Elizabeth pressed the tips of her fingers to her lips. "Why?"

Why *was* he so upset? "He, uh, thinks I've been holding back, hiding things from him. Which, I suppose, is true. I thought we'd settled the matter, but . . ." The Frenchman's behavior defied explanation.

Elizabeth considered this in silence a long while before saying gently, "Perhaps it's best to simply let him go. You confided to me, not so very long ago, that you hoped to remarry. There's still hope for that, I think, if you put this behind you and look to gentlemen who are, ah, a bit more settled."

Bea took a deep, gulping breath. "E., I can't let

him go. I love him." It came out as a tortured whisper rather than the strong declaration she'd intended, but it was out.

Elizabeth paused, watching her with a searching gaze, and then her face softened. "Oh. Oh, I see." She clasped Bea's hand with one of hers, her fingers warm against Bea's icy ones. She leaned back against the sofa, eyes raised to the ceiling as she absentmindedly rubbed the growing mound of her belly. "You and I, we chose rather difficult paths in finding love, didn't we?"

"What am I to do?"

Elizabeth squeezed her hand. "You're my dearest friend, and I'll never forget that you were there for me when no one else was. Bea, I trust you. If Philippe Durand is the man you love, then he must be worthy of that love. I take back my earlier words. You cannot let him go. You must do everything in your power to clear his name."

Bea gave a shaky laugh. "Now you sound more like my matchmaking friend."

Elizabeth clapped a hand to her forehead. "Oh, dear. I'd quite forgotten." She peered anxiously at Bea. "I very nearly thrust the two of you together, didn't I? Have I made a terrible mess of things, then?"

"Don't you blame yourself for a minute. Thrusting two people together does not guarantee they will fall in love. I did that entirely on my own."

"True enough." Elizabeth gave her an encouraging smile.

Bea swallowed hard, struggling to summon some of Elizabeth's plucky attitude for herself. If she fought for Philippe's release, it would be akin to publicly admitting her affair with a suspected spy—rendering her unmarriageable to anyone *but* Philippe. She'd be sacrificing her reputation, the very foundation which had given her comfort these past few years. And for what? In their last conversation, when she'd offered him the poem that declared her love, his withdrawal had been so obvious, she'd felt it like a physical tug.

Even if she could fathom a way to help him from this quagmire, there was every chance that, given his freedom, Jean Philippe Durand would return to France and forget she'd ever existed.

Elizabeth waited, wearing a hopeful expression.

Bea sighed. She wasn't opposed to the occasional gamble—she even enjoyed a good game of cards. But never had she played for stakes so high.

"You see?" Lady Russell wailed. "I predicted no good could come of this, and look what has happened. Bea, how could you?"

Alex shot her a quelling look, for which Bea was infinitely grateful. Thankfully, the rest of the room's occupants seemed unfazed by Bea's mother's hysterics. Or perhaps they were simply used to them, Bea thought as she watched her father take a swallow of brandy and pat the pocket where she knew he kept his pipe.

With Elizabeth offering staunch moral support, as well as the use of her home, Bea had summoned the small circle of people closest to Philippe for an emergency council. The Wilbournes had departed for the country after the scandal of discovering a spy amongst their servants, and Charity was off at a picnic with a group of companions, limiting Philippe's supporters to herself, Alex and Elizabeth, and Lord Owen. As an afterthought, Bea had included her parents, knowing they were likely to hear of this anyway. Better to get the story straight from her than after it had passed through eight iterations of the gossip mill. Though, given her mother's tendency to overreact, Bea reflected, perhaps she should have limited the invitation to her father.

To be fair, Bea's parents had the least understanding of anyone in the room as to the serious nature of the situation. Alex had offered a brief summary of events, downplaying Bea and Charity's roles. Bea had a feeling he would have left them out entirely, had it not been relevant to point out Philippe's role in finding Charity and getting her home safe.

"I don't see why this must concern you any longer, though, Beatrice," Lady Russell argued. "Of course, it's a shame your portrait won't be completed, but if you wash your hands of the matter now, tell everyone you'd grown suspicious, that you'd decided to cancel the painting yourself. Yes, that would work—it would explain your earlier-than-expected return from Montgrave, and help dispel the rumors about your, ah"—her glance flitted about the room—"well, rumors that Monsieur Durand might have grown overly affectionate."

"Mother, I cannot do that. It is untrue, and what is more, I believe Philippe innocent of these accusations. How could I live with myself, knowing I consigned him to such a fate when he, in contrast, came striding in to offer help—in the face of danger, I might add—when Charity Medford needed it."

Lord Owen cleared his throat. "I realize I am a near stranger in this room, but if I may speak?" When no one objected, he continued, "I cannot claim to have known Philippe for long, but I did know his mother—and the man she married. Richard Durand's political ambition knows no bounds. But to my knowledge, neither Solange nor her son were ever involved in such matters. Solange's soul was driven by her art, and my brief acquaintance with Philippe gives me every reason to think he is the same."

"Yes, exactly," Bea concurred. "Political matters hold no interest for him—unless they bring danger to his friends."

"The fact remains, he stands accused," Lord Russell pointed out. "And, my daughter, while I commend your desire to see justice served, I've no wish to see your name dragged through the mud any longer."

"Accused, but what proof is there of his guilt?" Bea argued, ignoring the last part of her father's speech.

"That remains to be seen," Alex said.

"Consider the situation fully," Bea begged of them. "The spies stole the plans Wednesday night, correct? From their perspective, they'd succeeded in their goal. If Philippe were involved, if they worked for him, then why would he stay around all the following day, helping *us*?

"When the duke and I left Montgrave to go after Charity, we left Philippe behind, completely free. If he were a spy, he'd just been handed the perfect opportunity to rejoin his network and flee the country—exactly as the others were attempting to do. But instead, he followed us, offered his help to rescue Charity from the very enemies he is supposedly in league with—aware he'd be on display, his whereabouts known to our government? It simply makes no sense."

"It does seem odd," Alex agreed. "But why would the others give his name?"

"Philippe is a very public figure. *Everyone* knew of his stay in London. How very convenient—by naming *him,* they distract us, draw our attention away from the *real* culprit."

"Bea, you are an oddly rational female."

Bea cocked her head. "Thank you, I think." Was she winning him over?

The duke chuckled. "Indeed, I meant it as a compliment. Many women would resort to emotional pleas, but your reliance on logic is far more convincing. If I help you, it is not merely to soothe an overwrought friend of my wife's, but because I am utterly convinced it is the right thing to do—and that if I do not act, a dangerous man may slip away undetected."

Bea felt a swell of pride. The duke believed her. What's more, he respected her thoughts.

"And," Alex continued, his tone darkening, "if that dangerous man had anything to do with what happened to my sister-in-law, I would be personally remiss if I did not seek out any opportunity to hunt him down and kill him like the vermin he is."

"And you'll be helping an innocent man, a man whose only desire is to make the world more beautiful through art, regain his deserved freedom,"

Bea reminded him, lest his thoughts dwell too long on what he'd like to do to those responsible for Charity's mishap.

Alex regarded her and the corners of his eyes crinkled in a hint of a smile. "I would not say that is Philippe Durand's *only* desire, my lady."

Bea's cheeks grew warm.

"But on the whole, you have the right of it."

Around the room, heads were nodding. Bea closed her eyes and took a deep breath. She wasn't alone in this. Thank heaven, because the task before them would not be an easy one.

"Men who engage in intrigue are not often fools," Lord Owen cautioned. "If someone has set up Philippe to take the blame, it is likely they have also considered the need for evidence."

Bea shrank back in her seat, wrapping her arms around her middle as though to literally hold herself together. She'd anticipated difficulty, but she hadn't thought of *that*. How elaborate was this scheme? How badly did someone want Philippe in jail? The odds of clearing his name were not yet insurmountable, but they were certainly stacking up.

"You make a good point," the duke told Lord Owen. "But I must ask, and hope you forgive my rudeness: what is it that makes you, given your limited acquaintance with Monsieur Durand, believe so strongly in his innocence?"

The older man paused as though weighing his answer. "I may not have known him long, but I know the heart of Philippe Durand. He is my son." Lord Owen nodded, acknowledging the shocked expressions around the room, then added, "Though I cannot claim to have been a good father."

Bea closed her eyes as a weight seemed to pull her down. Philippe had never told her his "old family friend" was anything more than that. Not that she'd expect him to announce it publicly, but . . . how well *did* she know him? Lord Owen's announcement complicated things.

But Bea, ever loyal, refused to reel for long. She opened her eyes. If Philippe came to England to learn of his English roots, it was even less likely he'd been working *against* England.

"He was raised as the acknowledged son of Richard and Solange Durand," Lord Owen explained. "Only on her deathbed, it seems, did Solange tell Philippe the truth and encourage him to seek me out."

Lady Russell paled. "Are you informing us that Monsieur Durand is illegitimate?"

"Oh, heavens." Bea expelled an exasperated breath. "Truly, mother, does that matter at this moment? Philippe, a good man whatever his birth, has been unjustly *imprisoned*."

Lady Russell glanced around the room. When no one acted to confirm her concern, she lowered her gaze. "No, I suppose not."

"All right, then," Alex said, breaking the tension between mother and daughter. "Even if Lord Owen and Beatrice are correct, and another entity is to blame for this quagmire, it will be the devil to prove it. We've nothing but a gut feeling to go on."

Bea felt as though someone had closed a fist around her heart. She *couldn't* sit idly by while Philippe was left to rot in prison, which is where he would surely end up if *someone* didn't come to his defense. "Alex, surely you have some resources."

The duke gave her a reassuring smile. "Bea, of course, I will do everything in my power to aid you—that is, to aid Monsieur Durand. But I do not wish to make you false promises. At this point, I do not know enough to predict any outcome. Nor would we be wise to forget that, on this point at least, Viscount Castlereagh's opinion stands in opposition to our own."

Bea nodded. "I understand, and thank you." She could only pray that whatever they came up with, it would be enough.

His studio had become a prison. The well-appointed suite in Lord Owen's house, a cell. Just when he'd begun to embrace the heritage that made him half British, the country had turned against him. More than ever, he felt like an outsider.

The men who came and went from his father's home treated him with suspicion. For years he'd relied on his easy, congenial ways to win people over, but these men were impervious.

He suspected it was only Lord Owen's influence that kept them from hauling him off to a true prison and torturing him for information he could not provide.

Before Philippe's arrest, Lord Owen and he had agreed not to announce the familiar nature of their relationship to the rest of London. *Dieu merci*. Were it known, Owen's support would be discounted as biased, and the buffer between Philippe and the wrath of the British government would vanish.

Anger and indignation battled against despair. Alone in this house, he had no avenue to defend himself. As a Frenchman he was no stranger to injustice, but for the first time in his adult life, his choice to eschew politics in favor of focusing solely on art seemed ill-fated. If he could somehow get a note to his father—not Lord Owen, but the man under whose roof he'd been raised—perhaps he could be of help. But as yet, Philippe was not allowed to send anything written through the post. He could only hope news of his arrest reached Paris, and Richard Durand was not too embroiled in his own interests to come to his aid. They might not see eye to eye, might not have spoken in months, but surely he'd take *some* action—though what sway, if any, he would have with the British, Philippe could not guess.

To make matters worse, the barely-begun painting of Beatrice stood on its easel and mocked him. The curve of an arm, a wash of dark where her hair was meant to be. A leaf, the tip still curled.

In theory, there was nothing to prevent him from working on it. He had more time on his hands than ever before. He just couldn't concentrate, couldn't pour his heart and soul into the work as he usually did. Not under these conditions.

And not without Bea.

She'd visited once, accompanied by her friends, the Duke of Beaufort and his wife. Sharp-eyed guards monitored the little meeting, always looking and listening for anything they might use against him. The conversation had been stilted at best. Hardly a time to sort out the misunderstandings between he and his English rose. She had, at least, assured him she believed him innocent and hoped to see his name cleared. But she hadn't visited since.

Finally, he turned the painting to face the wall.

Free of its mocking stare, he turned his mind to prayer. For every one prayer that he did not meet his end in a dark British prison, paying for a crime he hadn't committed, Philippe said three asking that Beatrice Pullington did not get herself killed in some foolhardy scheme to find the person who *had* committed that crime.

Days ticked by. Bea read the news more avidly than ever before. The armies of the coalition were closing in on Bonaparte's troops. Britain was confident of victory. Monsieur Jean Philippe Durand was still under arrest. And, if the gossip sheets were to be believed, Bea's previously immaculate reputation had, all along, been a mere cover for secret communication with the Frenchman.

Speculation ran rampant. The ton, never known to let a good tale go unembellished, scrutinized Bea everywhere she went, hoping for even the scrappiest morsel on which to hang a new tale. The fact that, wherever Bea did go, she was followed by an unmarked carriage or suited men who stood at a respectful distance did not help.

"Well, it makes more sense now," one hawk-nosed matron opined to a friend as they stood drinking lemonade after a musicale. Bea had attended in desperate hope of taking her mind off her troubles, and she *knew* the other woman was aware of her presence as she said, "I admit, I was baffled at first. Why would such a talented artiste choose to paint *her*? She's pretty enough, but, well, you know what I mean. Of course, none of us knew they'd known each other all along. They certainly had us fooled."

Disgusted, Bea stopped attending such events. Alex and Elizabeth did, too. Only Charity continued going, her social schedule increasing to a relentless pace as though she were trying to compensate for the others' absence.

In fact, Charity was the very purpose behind Bea's visit to Alex and Elizabeth this morning. A week had passed since Philippe's arrest, and in spite of Alex's efforts to help, they'd made little progress. Viscount Castlereagh had made it clear that, while he respected the duke and Lady Pullington's loyalty to their friend, the British government wanted no interference that could hamper the investigation.

Thus, Bea was grasping at straws. Both Alex and Philippe had been maddeningly tight-lipped when it came to discussing their rescue of Elizabeth's sister. All they would say was that they'd found her in sound condition, which Bea took to mean she hadn't been sexually violated. Thank God for small things. As for Charity, she too had said little. Not that she'd been around much to chat. Her social schedule ensured that she was putting the incident far behind her as fast as possible.

Bea still worried about her—though at the moment, more of her worries centered on Philippe, who had lost his freedom not long after helping Charity gain hers.

If she were going to come to his aid, she needed Alex Bainbridge on her side. She knew if she could just make the duke see reason, he would put the full weight of his position behind her—unless he knew something she didn't.

Bea entered the Bainbridges' salon to find Alex sitting on the sofa beside Elizabeth, one hand resting lightly on her shoulder. Her chest constricted at the obvious love and concern between them. She'd thought she'd found that with Philippe, but clearly she'd been wrong. Even now she couldn't understand what had gone wrong.

"Please, sit," the duke invited when Bea hesitated to interrupt them. "Elizabeth has been lonely of late, and she will scold me incessantly if I deprive her of your company," Alex declared, earning himself a poke in the ribs, along with a mischievous grin, from Elizabeth.

Bea took a seat, but remained at its edge, nervous. It was *her* fault Elizabeth was lonely. "Your Grace, I know how trying this has been for your family, and I want you to know how much I appreciate your continued friendship."

"Oh, don't take Alex seriously, Bea. I am not lonely. And, of course, our friendship remains true. You stood by me through worse. And in your case, you've done nothing but try to help our rulers keep Britain safe for the very people who turn their backs on you now. Try not to let it upset you so."

"I was trying to help Britain," Bea acknowledged, "but it is Philippe I most want to help now."

The duke frowned. "As to that, I'm afraid I have only bad news."

Bea's gaze flew to him and she clenched her fists in her skirts. "How bad?"

He pressed his lips together. "Bad enough."

"Alex, I think both Bea and I are of sound enough mind and strong enough constitution that you may speak freely to us," Elizabeth said.

"They found maps in his room. At the hotel where he'd been staying before moving over to

Lord Owen's home. Terrain maps of the sort the military might use, complete with arrows marking what could only be troop movements. They were wedged behind an armoire."

Bea slowly shook her head side to side, but the fog seeping into her mind would not clear. "I don't understand."

"When questioned, Philippe claimed they weren't his. Said he had no idea where they'd come from."

Could it be? But, no. Bea forced the disloyal thought from her mind. She mustn't waiver in her faith, for if she were wrong about Philippe, how could she ever trust her own judgment again?

"It could be as Lord Owen thought," Bea suggested, "and someone planted the maps in his room, knowing it would be searched. It makes sense, doesn't it? If they were his, why would he leave them there?"

"It could be," the duke replied. "But until we have a way of proving that is the case, things look grim for your artiste friend."

The pressure to come up with something, anything—anything valid, that is—was suddenly even greater than before. Bea took a steadying breath. "Alex, I need to know what happened when you and Philippe went into that warehouse—when you rescued Charity," she said.

"No, you don't." His tone wasn't mean, but it was firm enough to imply the topic was *not* open for negotiation.

Bea persisted anyway. "Yes, I do. Or at least Philippe's part of it. When you two went in there, no one confronted you, did they? No one was killed? No one to negotiate with?"

He gave a shrug of assent, indicating she was correct so far.

"Was there anything Philippe did—anything at all—that made you think he already knew where to find Charity? Or that perhaps the reason the place was emptied out was because he'd tipped them off?"

Alex paused long enough to consider her question. "No, nothing."

Bea moistened her lips. "Then the discovery of the maps is nothing more than we expected. The problem is, the one person who knows the most, has seen and heard the most, has been left out of our efforts."

Elizabeth opened her mouth, but Bea didn't let her get a word in. "Alex, E., I know the doctor recommended we do our best to help Charity forget, and I know she's been made to recount the experience by Lord Castlereagh already, but I cannot let this matter drop. If there is *anything* she heard, anything she saw that could exonerate Philippe . . ." Her throat grew thick.

The married couple hesitated, but finally Alex answered, "All right. But be as quick and gentle as you can. E., darling, go ahead and summon your sister."

Charity flounced into the room moments later, questioning, "Will this take long? Really, all of you, I am happy to oblige, but we've been through this already—and I was just on my way to a lovely picnic to which Baron Callow invited me."

Indeed, she was dressed to the height of fashion, her gown appropriately pale for a debutante, but cut daringly low for the same, and . . . Bea narrowed her eyes. Had Charity actually darkened her lashes with kohl? That would certainly flout decorum. Bea flicked a glance at Elizabeth, and her friend's cocked head made her think she was not the only one wondering. But perhaps it was just the shadows around Charity's eyes. Elizabeth had quietly confided, earlier that week, that her younger sister had had difficulty sleeping since what everyone was now referring to as "the incident."

Bea forced herself to focus on the most pressing problem. "I promise not to take too long, Charity. But there are a few things I must ask, and I beg of you to strain your mind . . . even the tiniest detail which seemed insignificant could help now."

"Help with Philippe, you mean?"

"Yes. If we could learn the identities of the ones who were not captured, or an idea of who they were working for . . ."

Charity took a seat on the same couch as Elizabeth and Alex, who then moved closer as though to protect her. The younger woman fiddled with her gloves. "I do not really see where I can be of help. Just look at the mess I made the last time I thought I was 'helping.'"

"Please try," Bea urged. "You saw, and heard, more than any of us."

Charity bent her head. Without meeting Bea's eye, she answered, "And that is why I cannot help."

Bea waited, trying to breathe normally in spite of the sudden constriction in her chest. She couldn't even blame the tight feeling on her corset, as she wasn't wearing one.

"It could mean nothing," Charity muttered.

"What could mean nothing?" her sister gently prompted.

Charity sighed. "I thought, when he helped to rescue me, maybe I had been mistaken . . . I don't understand, still, why he would . . ." She trailed off, then started again, struggling slowly through the words. "When those men took me, I was in a corner. They thought I was asleep—they'd made me drink something, but then I awoke and began listening to their conversation. One of them spoke his name. Monsieur Durand."

The invisible bands around Bea's chest tightened until she could no longer breathe. A long, uncomfortable silence permeated the room.

"What did they say about him?" the duke finally asked.

Charity shook her head. "Nothing. I gasped, and they realized I was awake."

Alex and Elizabeth shared a glance, but Bea couldn't tell what her friends were thinking. "Well, then what were they talking about *before* his name was spoken?"

"I told you before, my French is poor, fit only for discussing trivial matters, weather and fashion and such. They were speaking so rapidly . . . something about the time, and they were waiting on someone, or someone was coming, I'm not sure which, and they mentioned papers—the plans, perhaps—and then I fell behind, I couldn't translate fast enough. And then one said 'Monsieur Durand.'"

The gazes of Alex and Elizabeth turned toward Bea, and this time, Bea read pity in them.

"I'm sorry, Bea," Charity whispered miserably. "They weren't talking about attending an art salon."

Chapter 20

Bea slunk from Alex and Elizabeth's home feeling smaller, friendless, and more lost than ever.

"But Charity doesn't know *why* they mentioned him," Bea had argued fiercely after the younger woman had departed the room. "They could have been discussing their plan to set him up. How perfect. Everyone will be so fascinated by the news their favorite artiste is actually a spy, they'll never think to question such a sensational story, let alone hunt for the real culprits. Alex, Charity admitted her French is miserable. Surely you cannot base a judgment of guilt on a mere mention of Philippe's name."

She'd seen the pity in his reply. "I cannot. But I also cannot continue to place my family's safety and reputation at risk for a cause that grows ever more hopeless."

She understood. She couldn't even fault him. But that didn't ease the crushing loneliness of having staked her reputation, her faith, and her heart on a chance at real love, only to have everything torn apart, leaving her with even less than she'd had before.

Aside from the spies' naming of Philippe, Bea had gleaned one other interesting piece of information from Charity.

"They were questioning me, and then there was a knock on the door. The man outside hummed something, then the man asking the questions hummed in return and stepped out," she'd told them. "But I never saw who it was he spoke with."

Bea knew the mysterious visitor hadn't been Philippe. He'd been with her at Montgrave at the time. And without a face, or clear understanding of what had transpired, Charity's revelation, while interesting, gave her little else to go on.

Bea dragged her feet, weary as though she'd walked all day, into her home, collapsed into the seat at her writing desk, and put her head down on the desk's surface.

Could she have been so very wrong?

Philippe had said he'd never cared for politics, that such matters had been his stepfather's forte, and she'd believed him.

Wait. Could it be? Could the French spies have been referring to a *different* "Monsieur Durand"? Hope flared in her chest and she raised her head. Could they have meant Philippe's father? Or, rather, his stepfather?

But the hope faded as quickly as it had come. Only one Monsieur Durand had frequented London of late, and that was Philippe.

The operatives who'd been captured had named Philippe specifically. And the Foreign Secretary, with all the resources of the British government at hand, had already investigated and dismissed Philippe's stepfather as a possibility.

Bea lifted her head from the desk, then set it back down. Why bother? She had nowhere to go. Society scorned her, and even her friends and family had been sorely strained by this crazy relationship of hers.

Hah. Who did she think she was fooling? "Relationship" implied the feelings went both ways. But she'd been so starry-eyed, she'd willingly done anything and everything for the charming Frenchman, and the only thing he'd promised in return was a painting.

Oh, she'd *felt* the promise of more in his touch, in his gaze, the way when they were together, the whole world fell away. But it was only too clear now that her infatuation had been one-sided.

She'd placed her faith in Philippe. But why? How could she have been so stupid? She'd been warned, more than once, that the artist was a known charmer, but never once had she thought to guard herself against the effects of those charms.

He'd made her no promises of love or loyalty. And if, dear God, the accusations were true and Philippe was a spy, he was also the vilest snake to slither through London, for he'd had the gall to act hurt when he accused *her* of keeping secrets. She already knew, from Lord Owen's revelation that he was Philippe's father, that Philippe had kept secrets of his own. What else had he been hiding?

The inexplicable thing was, Philippe's rejection of her poem, the one aspect of her he *ought* to have understood, stung even worse than the mounting evidence that Monsieur Jean Philippe Durand was, indeed, a spy.

Bea had one strand of hope left to cling to: the fact that Philippe hadn't disappeared when he'd had the opportunity. Surely someone intelligent enough to direct a ring of French operatives would have recognized his chance to leave. So either he wasn't their leader, or, if he was, he'd cared enough about *her* to risk being caught.

Or—Bea banged her head on the desk—the charming French artist was simply too arrogant to believe he'd be held accountable. During the single awkward visit she'd paid him since the arrest, it had been impossible to say which case held true.

The next week passed more slowly than Bea would have ever thought possible. More than anything she wished she could escape somewhere far away, where no one knew anything about her, and no one had ever heard of—let alone admired—the work of Jean Philippe Durand. She now understood with perfect clarity why her former companion and spinster cousin, Ernesta, had willingly abandoned her life here for the chance to start anew in America. If Philippe was found guilty, Bea promised herself, that was exactly what she would do. Until then, she consigned herself to an endless stretch of lonely hours spent reading or stitching. Because she just couldn't leave until she knew for certain there was no hope left.

"Lady Pullington, I am giving you a second chance."

Bea eyed the Foreign Secretary warily, remembering all too well her last meeting with him. His arrival this morning had been, to say the least, unexpected. "Whatever can you mean?"

"You have a good mind, and a way with words. I'd like your take on something one of the spies said— or, to be more precise, *sang*—during questioning."

He had her attention. "Sang?"

"Indeed. Until recently, the only piece of information we got out of either Peters or the actress was Monsieur Durand's name. We are keeping them separated, as is policy. When our interrogators suggested—not untruthfully, I might add—that the ease with which she'd been caught made us suspicious, Miss Rose Kettridge grew very contemplative. A short while later, she began humming, then singing, the following tune:

> *Ô Bonaparte! Ô mon roi!*
> *L'univers t'abandonne;*
> *Sur la terre il n'est donc que moi*
> *Qui m'intéresse à ta personne!*
> *Moi seul dans l'univers,*
> *Voudrais briser tes fers,*
> *Et tout le reste t'abandonne!*

The British Foreign Secretary sang in a mild tenor. Not bad, Bea thought, though what a strange tale he unfolded.

"Since then," he finished, "Miss Kettridge has said nothing. Whenever she is questioned, or even spoken to, her only response is this song."

"It does seem very odd," Bea said. "Though I'm not quite certain why you have sought me out. What is it you would have me do?"

"I want you to figure out why she is singing it."

Bea raised her eyebrows.

"I've got the Deciphering Branch studying it already. We know the song was a favorite of royalists during the French Revolution, an adaptation from an aria in Gretry's opera, *Richard the Lionheart.* I suppose, in a way, the supporters of Napoleon Bonaparte today are also royalists, so the adaptation makes sense. But as far as we can tell, the song contains no mathematical ciphers, no hidden codes, that would indicate any further message."

"Hmm."

He grimaced. "I think there is more to Miss Kettridge's singing than political fervor. Her guards believe she is simply beginning to crack—some people do, under intense pressure. But I think there is something she wants us to know."

"You think she wants *us* to know something? Something we might find hidden in her song?"

"Possibly. Like the hidden message in the description of a garden, which you deciphered weeks ago—leading us, I might add, to the discovery of this plot in the first place. Not a mathematical cipher, such as I used to communicate with you, but a message hidden in the words themselves."

Now that he needed her, Lord Castlereagh seemed far more apt to credit her intelligence than he had upon Philippe's arrest, Bea observed wryly. Then again, this could be her only chance to save him.

Still, she reasoned, "That garden note was communication from one spy to another, or should have been. The intended recipient of that note would have already known how to read the message. Why would Miss Kettridge try to speak to us in code?"

"Fear, perhaps. Whoever she's working for, I doubt she would want him—or her—to know she'd given information to the Brits."

"Whoever she's working for?" Did this mean Lord Castlereagh no longer assumed the spies had been working for Philippe? The buzz of excitement, of hope, filled her.

His expression was impassive as he told her, "Monsieur Durand has not yet been cleared. That said, aside from the maps found in his room, which I presume you already know about, we have uncovered nothing else in his history that confirms his involvement. Either he is very, very good, or very, very unfortunate. But, Lady Pullington," he cautioned, "in asking your help with this song, I am asking you to help Britain. If what you uncover helps your French friend, all the better. But if it points us back to him, I want your word you will not fail to report back to me."

It was a risk she had to take. "You have my word." A gentlemen's contract. But then, this was hardly a lady's business she'd gotten into.

Bea's mind already whirred with possibilities. There was something about that song . . . "Sing the words for me one more time, would you, my lord?"

This time, she copied them down in translation as he sang:

O Bonaparte! O my king!
The Universe abandons you!
On earth, it is only me
Who is interested in you!
Alone in the universe

I would break the chains
when everyone else deserted you!

"Can you think of anything?" the Secretary asked
when he'd finished.

Bea pressed her lips together. "Let me study on
it. And there are a few people of whom I need to
ask a question or two." Including, if the song came
from where she thought it did, Philippe Durand.
Not that she was going to mention that to Lord
Castlereagh just yet.

First on her list was Charity Medford, who was
not at all pleased when Bea showed up, uninvited,
at the Sutherby's garden party, and nearly dragged
her from the lavishly-decorated white tent. Min-
gling guests paused mid-sentence to stare as the
ton's reigning darling was none-too-gently grabbed
by the ton's reigning queen of scandal and tugged
toward the street.

"You're causing a scene," Charity hissed in protest.

"Charity Medford, I do not care a fig if I am causing a scene. You are coming with me if I have to
pull you by your hair. Now."

That got her cooperation. "If you put it that way,
fine." She flounced forward, shaking off Bea's grip.
"Whatever has *you* in such a high state must make
for better gossip than anything at this little soiree.
So spill."

"Actually, you're the one who needs to spill."

"Pardon?"

"I must ask you a question. In your report to

Lord Castlereagh, you told him you heard the French spies—"

"This again?" Charity interrupted, heaving a sigh. "I am heartily sick of all things French."

Bea grasped the younger woman's wrist, pulling her to a halt in front of the waiting carriage. What had happened to the cheery spirit she'd always admired in Charity? The new version of her friend seemed brittle, a person who laughed more but with less joy.

"I will make this fast," Bea promised. "Charity. The song you heard the French informants hum . . . did it go like this?" She hummed the opening bars of the aria from Gretry's *Richard the Lionheart*.

"Yes, yes, that's it exactly." Charity's eyes lit up, her rigid stance eased. "I think they used it as a password of some kind. Is it important?"

"Quite possibly."

"Why? What have you found out?"

"I'm not sure what it means just yet," Bea admitted. "One of the spies they detained has been singing the tune repeatedly. Charity, when you heard it used, did anyone else say anything about the song?"

"No . . . as soon as the visitor outside hummed it, and the one questioning me hummed in return, the others grew silent. They all seemed to recognize its importance, but no one spoke until their leader returned—and even then they did not speak of anything that had transpired outside the room, only of the need to depart immediately."

"All right. Thank you, Charity. Even your confirmation that it's the same song may prove useful." Bea turned toward her carriage.

"That's it?" Charity plunked her hands on her

hips, and Bea turned back. "You're letting me go? What do you expect me to tell everyone else about why I was dragged from their midst and have suddenly returned?"

"I didn't care about causing a scene when I interrupted your little party, and I care even less about what you tell them when you return. The good news is, you will not lack for attention, for everyone is sure to ask."

"I never lack for attention," Charity huffed with a hint of her old self.

Bea laughed. "Then you'd best tell them I accosted you against your will, and you returned because you gave me the cut direct. I am a pariah to most of them after all."

"I couldn't do that to you."

"Then at least pretend. My efforts to clear Philippe's name are as good as a public declaration that we are lovers."

Charity perked up, eyes wide. "*Are* you lovers?"

Bea rolled her eyes. "As if I'm going to answer that. It doesn't matter. I've been judged and found guilty. You could tell your friends I've discovered I'm carrying the child of my illicit spy-lover, and most of them would sniff and say it's what I deserved."

"*Are* you carrying his child?" Now Charity was grinning.

"I was only making a point! You are incorrigible. And no, I am not. Now, be off with you."

She'd learned what she needed to know. The Gretry aria served as a password of sorts, indicating to one spy the arrival of another. Gut instinct told her whoever had arrived during that mysterious

visit was the man she sought. Someone who'd
been very careful not to be seen. She just needed
one more piece of information to confirm her
suspicions. She prayed Philippe would be able
to provide it.

Chapter 21

This time, Bea came alone. That is, except for the ever-present guards.

Philippe's chest constricted at the sight of her. She stood tall, shoulders squared, but there were shadows beneath her eyes. Between updates from Lord Owen and reading the gossip sheets, Philippe knew the once-respectable widow was in a living hell.

"You shouldn't be here," he told her, though he desperately wanted her to stay. His voice turned hoarse as he continued, "You should denounce me, as publicly as possible. Then you can have your life back."

She stepped closer and he saw that, in spite of the shadows beneath them, there was fire burning in her eyes. "I'm not here to denounce you," she said. "I'm here to save you."

While Philippe digested that incredible proclamation, Bea picked her way across the cluttered studio, coming to a halt in front of the canvas bearing the beginnings of her portrait. The canvas which now faced the wall.

He could tell by the way her lips pressed together she didn't like its new position. "*Je m'explique:* It bothered me to stare at it every day," he tried to explain, "unable to continue."

She gave a shrug as though it didn't matter, but the gesture didn't hide the hurt in her eyes when she turned to face him fully. "I'm going to need your help."

"I am ever at your service, *ma belle*. Though," he gestured toward the walls he now knew too well, "in a somewhat limited capacity these days." As much as he longed to simply pull her into his arms and kiss her until she forgot the capricious world outside, the strain was too great.

"Your imprisonment will not matter for what I have in mind." To Philippe's utter amazement, she burst into song.

Ô Bonaparte! Ô mon roi!
L'univers t'abandonne . . .

He recognized the tune immediately. An odd choice, but her French was flawless, her voice clear as she finished the verse.

"*Très bien, ma biche.*" He applauded. "But you have altered the words. It should begin 'Ô Richard!' rather than 'Ô Bonaparte!'"

Finally he noticed the odd gleam in her eye as she observed his reaction.

"Philippe," she asked carefully, "how did you come to know this song?"

He answered truthfully. "It is a favorite of my

father's. He has ever been enchanted by the plight of one who follows an admired leader faithfully, even when that leader has fallen from favor with the rest of the world. It is a sentiment Frenchmen have had many opportunities to practice in my lifetime . . . if the faithful follower is willing to accept the same fate as the deposed ruler. Understandably, very few are."

Her expression cleared. But then she frowned again.

"I presume you did not come here simply to perform for me," Philippe said. "What is it about that tune that troubles you?"

"What troubles me," she answered slowly, "is that the ring of French spies that you are accused of directing, the ring that kidnapped Charity, uses this very song to identify its members. Charity heard them hum it as a password of sorts, and now one of the imprisoned spies sings it repeatedly, as though it holds great meaning."

"Ah." He closed his eyes, used his thumb and middle finger to pinch the bridge of his nose, but the pressure building there did not ease. "You think that because I knew the song so easily, it confirms my involvement."

"No. I think as I always have—that someone set you up. I do not make accusations lightly, but Philippe, I think that person may be closer to home than either of us would like."

The answer was painfully clear. He met her gaze. "My father."

"Yes. Stepfather, that is," Bea amended.

"Ah. You know who Lord Owen is to me, then?"

"Yes. And that your stepfather acted as an advisor to Bonaparte."

Philippe nodded. "*Oui*. They served in the army together, and later my father—stepfather—worked for him." That was public knowledge. It still felt strange to refer to the man he'd grown up with as someone besides his father.

"Does he serve him still?"

Philippe frowned. "To my knowledge, no. At least not openly. A Frenchman who is too vocal, too forthcoming with allegiance to one ruler, is a Frenchman who does not live to old age. Though with Bonaparte's return . . . I can only speculate. I left Paris for England shortly after he reclaimed the empire. As to my father's actions since then, I cannot say."

"Some reports suggest he hoped to rise to the Chamber of Deputies under Louis XVIII."

"Perhaps I should have paid closer attention to my father's—to Richard's, that is—dealings. I confess I never took an interest in politics."

"If I may be so bold, it is time that you did."

Philippe accepted the chastisement with a wry chuckle. His English rose had a point, and bristling over it would get them nowhere. "Undoubtedly."

He paused. "Though I greatly desire my freedom, I've no wish to become a traitor to my country."

Bea nodded, oddly businesslike. "I can respect that, but your position is precarious. You must ask yourself—where do your loyalties truly lie?"

"Though I have recently gained certain familial ties to Britain, and an admiration for certain of its ladies, I remain a citizen of France. It is where I was raised."

His flattery earned him a small smile, but Bea pressed on. "But to which French leader does your allegiance belong?"

Ah. A question not so simple. "One that will bring peace to my country."

"Napoleon Bonaparte will never do that."

"You are likely correct," Philippe admitted.

"The Congress of Vienna has declared Bonaparte an outlaw. Though he may call himself Emperor, he rules illegally. If you are able to provide information that aids in his defeat, you will not be a traitor to France. If anything, you may help bring the peace you so desire."

"Are you here to save me, beautiful one, or England?"

"England does not need saving," she replied proudly. "I am here to see that the right man is brought to justice for crimes against my country and against my dear friend Charity, and I pray— I *know*—that man is not you."

Her faith in him was humbling. "I could not understand why those spies would direct you to me," he said, "unless they were merely trying to throw you off the trail by naming a Frenchman of some standing who was known to be in your country. Now, I fear their intent was not to lead to the wrong conclusion—only to the wrong Durand. That song was a favorite of my stepfather's not only because of its sentiment, but because the King, Richard the Lionheart, shared the same given name with him. It is, I believe, of *Richard* Durand that the French spy sings." Each word felt like the stab of a knife in his back. They hadn't been close, but he'd believed the man was his father for most of his life. Now it appeared Richard's ambition outweighed that family tie.

The studio fell quiet as they both thought this over.

Finally Bea crossed the distance to him and took his hand. The light touch wasn't enough—it served as a reminder of so much more—but it was more than he deserved. He stroked the inside of her palm, tracing a slow circle with his thumb, and watched her take a shuddery breath. As confused and complicated as matters were, that breath told him what he needed to know. She still held feelings for him. He held that thought like a candle in the dark.

How could a man be so ruthless?

"Philippe," Bea requested softly, "tell me how to find him."

Philippe's gaze tracked the swish of Bea's skirts as she turned the corner and disappeared. He'd given her all the information she'd asked for, and a good deal more. Addresses, acquaintances, detailed sketches, all produced while the bitter taste of betrayal stung his throat.

The coalition could take down Napoleon Bonaparte. It was up to Philippe to take down his stepfather. For justice. For love. For the good of France.

As for the lovely Lady Pullington, he could only speculate as to what she would do next. Amazing. Her selfless desire to help others, he admired. But her utter disregard for her own reputation and safety was going to drive him crazy.

Not that he wasn't grateful—her efforts on his behalf gave him more hope than he'd felt in days. He just feared that, once his name was cleared, whatever worthy cause Bea took up next would be the one that got her killed.

And so Philippe came to a conclusion he suspected had been inevitable from the first moment he'd laid eyes on Beatrice Pullington. There was only one way to protect that woman from herself. He was going to have to marry her.

She'd done all she could. Every scrap of information was now in the capable hands of the British government, who would, God willing, use it for the greater good. And for the freedom, in particular, of one Monsieur Jean Philippe Durand.

"Don't judge him too harshly," Lord Owen had begged of her when she departed his home on her last visit with Philippe. "In the past months, he has learned his father is not the man he always thought he was, and that was the lesser of the secrets his mother kept from him. Did Philippe tell you he spent his whole life trying to emulate an elusive French artiste by the name of Henri Gaudet? Not even on her deathbed did Solange tell him *she* was Gaudet—she left that revelation to me. And now, after years of popularity in most cultural circles of Europe, Philippe has traded popularity and admiration for notoriety and suspicion. His foundations have been shaken. How can he know in what, or in whom, to trust?"

"He can trust me," she'd told Lord Owen simply. Though the older man had assured her Philippe was in no way being mistreated, he'd looked different. Older, as though each day of captivity had added a year to his age. And although he'd still been impeccably dressed, his usual confident charm had been subdued. How dare they take that from him?

Philippe might not love her, but Bea knew with a clear conscience she'd done her best by him—without compromise. She'd been loyal to her country, and to the man she loved.

But that loyalty had come with a cost, and all Bea wanted now was to get out of London before she suffocated in the thick fog of disapproving, mistrustful glances that surrounded her everywhere she went.

When Lord Pullington had died, he'd left Bea a wealthy widow, but the title and estates had passed to a son born of an earlier marriage. With no country home of her own to retreat to, she turned to her closest friend.

Elizabeth had come to call almost daily. Though she and her husband had withdrawn from the situation with Philippe, Elizabeth had not, as Bea had first feared, abandoned her as a friend. Yet the trips to Gunther's, or the milliner's, rarely cheered Bea up. Nor did helping to embroider tiny blankets and caps, since happiness for Elizabeth was dampened by pangs of regret for all she could not have.

So when Elizabeth arrived two mornings after Bea had turned her report over to Viscount Castlereagh, Bea shook her head at the suggestion they walk in the park.

"E.," she asked instead, "I once provided sanctuary for you when you were in need. Might I ask the favor be returned? I want to go back to Montgrave."

Elizabeth hugged her, and Bea could feel the slight swell where her friend's child grew. "Montgrave is open to you for as long as you wish. Are you sure, though, that is where you wish to be?"

"Yes." If Bea's assessment of the spies' song was correct, Philippe would soon be freed. Richard Durand—if he could be found—was the man the British government would call to account. The question was, though, when the arrest was lifted, what would Philippe do?

And that was a question Bea couldn't answer. If he packed his bags and sailed immediately for France—a decision she half-expected, and for which she could hardly blame him, she didn't want to be around to observe the ton's reaction to his rejection of her.

If he did hope to mend things, if he thought there was a chance their love could survive the shattered trust of the past few weeks, he would call on her. Bea's butler had already been instructed, should Monsieur Durand call, to hand him a note that said simply:

Meet me in the garden.

"I do hope you've saved at least *some* of the brandy," Bea announced upon finding Lily Moffett still in residence at Montgrave.

Lily's mouth fell open at this highly unconventional greeting, but she hastily closed it and nodded, eyes wide.

"Good. Because I have every intention of drinking. Too."

Lily choked back an appalled laugh. "Montgrave

is such a lovely place to escape the pressures of the city, my lady."

From this, Bea assumed Lily had read enough of the papers to know exactly what "pressures" had led Bea to flee. That was perfectly fine with her—it saved the trouble of hashing through it once again. Though, after a few brandy-soaked evenings, bits and pieces of her woes spilled out. Lily might not meet societal standards for a prim lady's companion, but these days, Bea didn't meet societal standards for a lady—and never once did Lily judge her for it.

Talking to Lily kept the loneliness at bay, especially in the evenings, when there was little to take Bea's mind off her troubles. Since Bea refused to read the papers there was even less to do. She scanned them for the first few days, until she saw confirmation that Philippe's name had been cleared. After that, she didn't want to know.

Did he still care for her at all? Or had too much passed—too much time, and too much misunderstanding? The unanswered questions could drive a person to madness.

During the daylight hours, Bea went faithfully to the rose garden. It was different now. Though her last visit had been mere weeks ago, time left nothing unchanged. The vines had long overgrown their trellises to tangle about the feet of the bench or wrap around the stone basin, colorful blooms popping up where the eye least expected them.

Bea brought pen and paper, and every day she wrote. She wrote until her hand ached, until her whole body ached, and yet the poetry flowed forth. In the past few months, her world had expanded tenfold, and when she shrank that world back down, confined it to the space of the little garden, the new thoughts and complex emotions and reflections on life came rushing forward, demanding she set them to paper.

So she did, and tried not to wonder if she'd lost her only chance at love.

Even on the morning her gaze fell accidentally upon the gossip sheet—hastily snatched away by a sad-eyed Lily—that reported one Monsieur Jean Philippe Durand had sailed for France, Bea went to the garden to write.

Chapter 22

That was how Philippe found her. Pen in hand, head bent over a notebook, biting her bottom lip in intense concentration. Dear God, he loved her.

Not that he deserved her. He'd rejected her poem, her written declaration of love. When he'd been cast as a spy, she should have been the first to reject him in return. Yet she'd stood in the face of all Society and fought to prove his innocence, because no matter how he'd treated her, her integrity demanded it. Society had scorned her for doing so, perhaps even more than they'd scorned him. And yet, she'd given him one last chance. *Meet me in the garden.*

She hadn't seen, or heard, him yet. He admired the soft curve of her cheek, the endearing way she'd tucked her feet up beside her on the bench, and he ached to yank her into his arms and forget the past. Before he could, he *had* to convince her that her faith in him had not been misplaced.

In all the world, no one else, man or woman, had loved him as truly, as selflessly as Bea. He would happily spend the rest of his life proving himself worthy of that love.

"Beatrice."

She gasped, scattering papers as her mouth formed a perfect O of surprise.

"Philippe." She blinked, then blinked again, as though she thought him a hallucination. "You sailed for France."

He entered the clearing, stopping only when he was near enough to see the wild beat of her pulse at her throat. "*Non.* I have unfinished business here."

"I feared I would never see you again," she whispered.

He gave her a rueful smile, hating every moment of doubt he'd caused her. "I could not allow that to happen."

She smiled up at him, but her eyes still held questions.

"Beatrice." He gathered her hands in his, his chest aching as he felt her tremble. "I have been tried and found wanting."

She frowned. "No, all that is over. Your name is clear."

He shook his head slowly, his gaze never leaving hers. "No, I mean to say I have been unworthy of your devotion."

"Oh." Good manners dictated she deny this truth, but Bea said nothing else.

Well, he'd take silent candor over anger, Philippe reflected. "You trusted me with something precious. I know better than anyone how a poem, any work of art, is a part of one's self, yet I rejected you because of it."

"I know why you did."

He tipped his head. "Pardon?"

"Your father. He explained how your mother hid from you the truth of her birth, and her art. You thought I was doing the same."

He nodded. "I shall have to thank him. Though the explanation does not fully excuse my behavior. Especially when I have you to thank for clearing my name. How brave you have become, Beatrice."

And, he realized, in spite of her faults, he had his mother to thank as well. If she hadn't elicited from him the promise to visit England, he'd never have met the woman with whom he planned to spend the rest of his life. He smiled apologetically. "Every woman has her secrets. I should have been honored by the opportunity to discover yours."

He squeezed her hands lightly, his thumbs rubbing, stroking until Bea closed her eyes, a soft catch in her breath.

"*S'il vous plait,* Beatrice," he murmured, his accent thickening. "Allow this foolish Frenchman another chance, and I promise I shall prove worthy. I cannot bear to lose you again."

Bea opened her eyes, determined to guard her heart with more care this time. Philippe had always had a way with words, but it was the sincerity in his gaze, the desperation she heard beneath the charming phrases that determined her answer. "Yes."

He took a seat beside her on the bench, slid his hands up her arms and into the hair at her nape, cradling her head. *"Je t'aime."*

She needed no translation. Bea's throat grew thick and her heart filled at the words she'd waited so long to hear. "I love you, too." She swallowed. "And I am sorry for doubting you."

He pressed a finger against her lips. *"N'en parlons plus."* Let us speak of this no more.

Removing his finger, he lowered his lips to hers, kissing her slowly, lingering with each brush of his lips, until her body melted into his on a choked sob. His arms came around her, supporting, embracing her as he tucked her head beneath his chin and simply held her.

Long moments later, the flood of emotion retreated enough for her to lift her head. "Where do we go now?"

"My studio," he said, as though the answer were obvious. "If I am lucky, by way of my bed."

She laughed and batted him, knowing he teased only to lighten the moment. "Wicked man, you are as outrageous as ever. But you are to return to France."

His lips quirked and he shook his head. "Not yet. And you, *ma chérie,* are sorely mistaken if you think I am going anywhere without you. I have a painting to finish."

She smiled, the full warmth of the summer sun a mere fraction of the glow that filled her inside. And that was *before* he added, "And, if you will have me, a wedding to plan."

She cupped his face, made blurry by her tears of joy, and nodded.

There was one other reason to remain in England, but Philippe neglected to mention it: his release had been conditional on his agreement to testify against the man who'd raised him. *If* Richard Durand could be found.

At the moment, that was the furthest thing from Philippe's mind. The closest was the intoxicating taste of Bea's lips, and the soft press of her body to his—a sensation to which his own body's response was decidedly *not* soft.

He dipped his head for another kiss, reveling in her response, the abandon with which her head fell back, offering him the creamy length of her neck, and a view of the enticing hollow between her breasts.

He stroked her back, slid his hands up her sides, cupping her breasts, and felt his body harden further.

"Please," he begged her, "tell me you do not expect company in the garden today."

She shook her head.

He pulled her into his lap, deepening the kiss. The soft curve of her hip against his groin was torture. If this went any further . . .

He forced himself to still. "I would do no further harm to you, or to your reputation, *ma chérie*. If you are uncomfortable . . ."

Her only response was a whimper of need. His control broke.

He pushed her skirts aside, her woman's center pressed against his hardness. She rocked against him and he groaned. Her lips were parted, her breath coming in short pants. He bent his head to her breast, tugging at the filmy fabric of her gown until he bared a nipple.

Her fingers dug into his back as his mouth closed over her breast. His erection throbbed, straining at the layers of fabric between them. He couldn't take it anymore.

He lifted her from him. Understanding, Bea shrugged out of her drawers as he unfastened his trousers. He sat back on the bench and crooked a finger at her.

She raised her eyebrows.

He smiled, realizing that although they'd made love in this garden before, they'd lain upon the grass. "*Oui,* just like this," he confirmed, pulling her to straddle him again, holding her hips above him. His erection nudged her moist entrance.

"Oh," she breathed, and slid down to take him inside her fully. "Oh," she said again.

Philippe's head fell back at the sheer bliss of being inside her again. Using his hands, he guided her into a gentle rocking motion. Need hammered at him. He wasn't going to be able to last.

But then, it seemed, neither was Bea. She rocked harder, faster, grinding against his thrusts. *Mon Dieu.* Any moment now . . . He flicked her nipple with his tongue, pinched the other between his thumb and forefinger.

She shrieked and came in a shower of convulsions, squeezing him as he too gave in to the raging need for release, spilling himself inside her as they collapsed against one another, spent.

Philippe closed his eyes. Suddenly, England felt like home.

June 22, 1815

London's church bells pealed joyfully, celebrating the coalition's victory, but across the English Channel,

Richard Durand allowed his head to sink into his hands. It was over.

Napoleon Bonaparte had lost. The defeat at Waterloo four days ago had decimated the French army and crushed the spirit of those who'd celebrated the Emperor's return. A brief visit to the battlefield had sickened Richard in body and heart. The once-rolling farmland of Belgium was strewn with the bodies of dead and dying men.

Napoleon had failed. Richard had failed. The British war plans he'd personally delivered had come too late. Though from the battle reports, he wasn't sure any amount of military intelligence could have salvaged the campaign.

Word was, Bonaparte had abdicated for the second time. Richard knew there would not be a third.

Already there were rumors of another White Terror. During the first, the Jacobins who'd supported the Revolution had been systematically routed, attacked and murdered in the night, or forced to stand trial. The trials had all been shams, the end result the same. Death. He shuddered. This time, it would be supporters of Napoleon who faced such a fate. How many people knew Richard was one of them?

He glanced around at the familiar furnishings of his Parisian home, to which he'd retreated. He'd hidden his actions well. The best recourse now was to disavow any association with the fallen Emperor. No one would know how much he'd staked on Napoleon—that Richard's coffers were now empty, his son estranged. Richard could survive. He always survived. He'd simply keep his head down until the storm blew over.

Right now, though, he needed a drink. A visit to his club would garner him the latest news, and would further the impression he had nothing to hide, Richard reasoned as he donned his hat.

The Paris streets were busy enough that the plain black carriage that followed him went unnoticed. Only when Richard emerged several hours later onto a darkened street, having consumed enough liquor to dull the bitterness of defeat, and heard the words, *"Monsieur Durand, vous êtes en état d'arrestation,"* spoken with a clipped British accent, did he realize he was in trouble.

"You have no authority over me," he hissed at the officer who hustled him toward an unfamiliar carriage.

"Au contraire. You are charged with committing a crime on British soil."

"Absurd. I have not set foot in England in years."

The evening shadows masked any expression on the Brit's face as he replied, "I believe otherwise."

"Check the ships' rosters," Richard snarled.

"Oh, I've no doubt we'd find them all in proper order. You are intelligent enough to have seen to that. Now get in."

A glance at the driver revealed a pistol aimed directly at him. Richard climbed inside. The Brit settled across from him, tapped twice on the window, and the vehicle moved off.

"What crime?" Richard asked.

"Theft. In particular, theft of a set of military

plans, stolen with intent to provide information to British adversaries. In short, you are accused of spying."

"I have no idea what you refer to."

"Hmm." That didn't seem to bother the man.

"Where are you taking me?"

"Back to England, to stand trial. Rather inefficient, in my opinion, but my superiors insisted." His tone darkened. "My usual method of dealing with spies is far more expeditious."

Richard swallowed. Fear, combined with the copious amounts of liquor he'd consumed, set his stomach to churning. "I am a well connected man," he blustered. "You'll hang for this."

The Brit's lips twisted in a semblance of a smile. "How would anyone know I was here? I never set foot in France."

Richard Durand remained confident—right up until he saw the court document listing the lineup of those prepared to testify against him. Kettridge. Peters. He'd expected as much. Miss Charity Medford. He'd never heard of her. Monsieur Jean Philippe Durand, and his newly wedded wife, Beatrice. Well. His son had married the lady spy.

He had two options left: play innocent and act hurt by Philippe's betrayal, or offer up secrets of his own in exchange for his life.

He paced the small room where he waited for the proceedings to begin.

The kings counsellors, prosecuting him on the charge of high treason, had wasted no time securing a court date. Most certainly his home and offices had been searched, but even then Richard had not despaired. He rarely committed to writing anything that could link him to unsavory matters. It was why he insisted on face-to-face meetings—he'd seen too many men brought down by mere slips of paper. Indeed, had that idiot Peters not misplaced his note in Beatrice Pullington's coat so many weeks ago, Richard might be free and far from here.

Someone knocked on the door. A guard poked his head in and informed him that the younger Monsieur Durand had requested an audience with him prior to the proceedings.

Ah. Option one, then: act hurt. Richard followed the guard into the courtroom, as yet sparsely populated, though court officials were beginning to file in. Philippe stood toward the front.

"My dear son, it has been so long." Richard moved to embrace Philippe, but a warning shake of the younger man's head stopped him. Richard looked down at his hands. "I saw—but it cannot be—a mistake, of course. This foolish British court has listed you as a witness for the prosecution."

Philippe shook his head again, his jaw clenched. "It is not a mistake."

"Not a mistake?" Suddenly Richard felt very old, and it occurred to him for the first time, how very few men in his profession lived to enjoy old age. Would he?

Richard gestured to their courtroom surroundings. "How can you do this to your father?"

Philippe's blue eyes pierced him. "You are not my father."

Richard felt the sting of truth in that verbal blow. Wearily, he took a seat on a nearby wooden bench.

Indeed, he'd long known the implications of his son's early arrival into the world. When he'd married Solange, he'd been the one to suggest a quick wedding, citing the need to return to military duty, but Solange had immediately agreed. Later, he'd suspected. But since he and Solange never had other children, and she accommodated his every request in other matters, he'd pushed it from his mind.

"For that matter," Philippe continued, his features hard, "what sort of father would frame his son for espionage?"

"I don't know what you're talking about." He was losing ground.

"Richard, I am not the fool you seem to think me."

Time to switch tactics, regain the offensive. He folded his arms. "Fine. You were in bed with a British spy. I had every reason to believe you'd turned against your own country."

"Against Bonaparte, perhaps. All of Europe has turned against him. But I would never turn against France."

Richard looked hard at Philippe and felt, for the first time, a grudging respect for the son he'd never understood. The man who stood before him was confident, articulate in matters well outside the studio. He'd never seen that before—and now it was too late.

"They're going to convict me, aren't they?" He'd been a fool to believe Napoleon could win. Faced with his own trial, he had no desire to remain a fool.

"Yes." Philippe stated the truth without malice.

"I could provide information. The names of all the others."

"They already have those names. Though I doubt the men they belong to still use them."

A buzzing filled Richard's ears. Somewhere far away, André Denis and his one remaining henchman were beginning new lives. Perhaps they would be caught. Perhaps not. Richard would never know. Everyone in the courtroom seemed to be moving as though underwater.

So this was what it felt like when your world collapsed. He'd caused this for so many others, and spent his whole career trying to avoid experiencing it himself.

"Philippe," Richard said finally, slowly, "I see now I was wrong about you, and I am sorry it has come to this. I do not deserve your mercy, but I will beg it of you anyway. If I am found guilty, they will sentence me to hang." He lowered his voice. "Spare me only the humiliation of that public death. Give me money to bribe my guards tonight. Not for escape—only that they will allow me the means to make my end privately." He swallowed. "I have always been a private man."

Philippe stared at him for a long, long moment, then reached into his satchel.

Epilogue

There was just one secret Bea had left. And though she and Philippe had both promised to be open with each other, she'd waited to find just the right way of telling him this one.

Tonight seemed perfect.

They'd held a salon, the first since Philippe's arrest, to celebrate his return to the artistic community, and the completion of the first painting he'd ever done on English soil.

When the portrait of Beatrice had been unveiled, the room had filled with cheers. Bea's eyes had filled with tears.

It wasn't quite what they'd originally planned. By the time she and Philippe had reunited, the blush of spring, the seasonal essence he'd hoped to capture, had given way into the full flush of summer. No matter, he'd told her, for he'd chosen to paint her not as a muse, but as a goddess, and a goddess deserved nature in all its glory for her backdrop.

Though she'd posed for many an afternoon,

he'd kept the finished product from her view until tonight's unveiling.

In the portrait, the abandoned rose garden bloomed in wild profusion, and Philippe had spoken true. No amount of blooms could detract from the painting's centerpiece: a woman whose allure, whose sensuality, drew more from her confidence than from the filmy fabric that draped and clung to her curves in ways the Greek sculptors of old would have yearned to imitate.

Bea was simultaneously proud of the woman she'd become, and grateful for the love of a man who recognized and valued her so. She truly had it all.

As the last of the guests bid their farewells, Bea came to stand at her husband's side. "You are a success, my love. A resounding one."

"*Non.* It is you they admire."

"Only because of your talent. Had anyone else painted me, the work would soon be relegated to the attic. For *your* work, admirers turn out in droves."

He winked. "Perhaps. What better way to get a close-up look at the artiste who was almost a spy?"

"Who knew your notoriety on that account would turn into such a boon?" Bea acknowledged the truth behind Philippe's teasing tone. Her new husband had more followers than ever before, if tonight's event was any indication. Basic human curiosity, coupled with an open invitation, was too much to resist for London's gossip-hungry upper class.

Thank heaven the extent of her own activities had stayed out of the papers, Bea reflected. She guessed the public would not be as forgiving of her—nor had she been as innocent.

But that was all past. Next week she and Philippe sailed for France, where her portrait would be displayed to patrons of art in Paris. Bea smiled at the giddy rush that always overtook her when she thought of this unbelievable fact. Come spring, they would return to England. They planned to live in London most of the year, for Philippe acknowledged Bea's close ties to family and friends there, and hoped to strengthen his own bond with Lord Owen.

But first he needed to put his own past to rest. His stepfather's betrayal and death had hurt, she knew, but it was Solange who haunted him. He'd confided a desire to sort through his mother's estate, in hopes of coming to peace with the questions about her life first as an artist, then as wife to a ruthlessly ambitious man. And in hopes of finding the portrait she'd allegedly painted of him as a young child.

Which brought Bea back to the secret she ached to tell. She slipped an arm about Philippe's waist and tilted up her face to his. "I have a request to make."

"Anything, *mon coeur.*"

He brushed his lips to hers, and she savored the touch before leaning back to finish her plea. Her heart beat faster, spurred by both desire for Philippe and anticipation of his reaction.

"I know you always chose your own subjects," she said, a smile playing at her lips, "and you do not accept requests or commissions. But I hope you'll make an exception."

"You wish I should do another of you? Is one not enough?" he teased.

She batted him playfully. "Not me."

He frowned. "Who is it you desire I should paint?"

Her smile burst forth in full. "Our child."

His eyes widened, lit by a fiercely proud gleam as he lifted her in the air and spun her in circles. "When?"

"April, I think." She laughed.

He set her down with a sound kiss.

Moments later, Philippe lifted his head long enough to say, "That, *ma chérie*, is an exception I shall be overjoyed to make." He lowered his head once more, and Bea promptly forgot the rest of her surroundings as they fell away—as they always did—before the man who'd introduced her first to passion, then offered her his love.

Books by Bestselling Author
Fern Michaels

___The Jury	0-8217-7878-1	$6.99US/$9.99CAN
___Sweet Revenge	0-8217-7879-X	$6.99US/$9.99CAN
___Lethal Justice	0-8217-7880-3	$6.99US/$9.99CAN
___Free Fall	0-8217-7881-1	$6.99US/$9.99CAN
___Fool Me Once	0-8217-8071-9	$7.99US/$10.99CAN
___Vegas Rich	0-8217-8112-X	$7.99US/$10.99CAN
___Hide and Seek	1-4201-0184-6	$6.99US/$9.99CAN
___Hokus Pokus	1-4201-0185-4	$6.99US/$9.99CAN
___Fast Track	1-4201-0186-2	$6.99US/$9.99CAN
___Collateral Damage	1-4201-0187-0	$6.99US/$9.99CAN
___Final Justice	1-4201-0188-9	$6.99US/$9.99CAN
___Up Close and Personal	0-8217-7956-7	$7.99US/$9.99CAN
___Under the Radar	1-4201-0683-X	$6.99US/$9.99CAN
___Razor Sharp	1-4201-0684-8	$7.99US/$10.99CAN
___Yesterday	1-4201-1494-8	$5.99US/$6.99CAN
___Vanishing Act	1-4201-0685-6	$7.99US/$10.99CAN
___Sara's Song	1-4201-1493-X	$5.99US/$6.99CAN
___Deadly Deals	1-4201-0686-4	$7.99US/$10.99CAN
___Game Over	1-4201-0687-2	$7.99US/$10.99CAN
___Sins of Omission	1-4201-1153-1	$7.99US/$10.99CAN
___Sins of the Flesh	1-4201-1154-X	$7.99US/$10.99CAN
___Cross Roads	1-4201-1192-2	$7.99US/$10.99CAN

Available Wherever Books Are Sold!
Check out our website at **www.kensingtonbooks.com**